An orphaned American boy wounded by Mossad and the CIA…

'They will try to turn you into a machine. Don't let them do that!'

If he were a machine, could he be switched off? For the first time in his war-torn life, he doubted it. He felt as though life had gripped him in a vice and would not let go. Any hope of recasting himself as a peaceful, compassionate person had been erased.

The chilling biographical novel based on the life, loyalties, loves and hates of KENT LINES – one-time wartime sniper and trained assassin!

COVER IMAGE

Golda Meir, the prime minister of Israel 1969-1974. She showed strong leadership when Syrian and Egyptian military forces launched a surprise attack on the unprepared Israeli forces, on the holiest day of the Jewish year, Yom Kippur, 6 October 1973.
With Israel's survival as a nation at stake, Golda Meir tried desperately to expedite American military aid. At the same time, she authorized Israel Defense Forces to go on alert with nuclear-armed Jericho missiles – the ultimate option.

Kent Lines was their link...

ABOUT THE AUTHORS

In early 2012, Kent Lines sought help through the South Australian Writers Centre for the writing of his novel. We worked together for about a year while Kent's health deteriorated, stemming from injuries he had received in the Vietnam War. We wrote this largely biographical novel based on his experiences in the USA, Vietnam and Israel.

In March 2013, he passed away in Adelaide, and I felt obliged to finish the story. I have taken some liberties but feel they are in keeping with what he would have wished.

Since retirement I do part-time work in editing scientific papers written in English for the Harbin University of Engineering, North-East China, and write in my spare time.

Thomas Mann

Kent Keefer Lines was born in Idaho in 1952, and he grew up in an orphanage. Graduating from Idaho Falls High School in 1970, he continued his education at Yale University and Idaho State University, majoring in biochemistry and microbiology. He served in the US Army in Vietnam War and in Israel on special assignment for the CIA.

From 1983, he lived in the Netherlands, New Zealand and Australia. His brain condition, similar to a form of epilepsy, resulted from an injury received during service in Vietnam, and worsened over the years.

Vale

KENT KEEFER LINES

1952-2013

At his request, his ashes were spread over the ocean from a helicopter.

Published by

CUSTOM BOOK PUBLICATIONS

First Edition

JERICHO MAN

A chillingly gruesome life of war and killing…

by

Kent Lines & Tom Mann

Orphans always make the best recruits…

Judy Dench as M in the James Bond film Skyfall

CHAPTER ONE

Cameron Campbell flopped down on the bunk bed of a cell in a Wyoming courthouse and contemplated his fate. A steel toilet bowl gleamed in the stark shadows cast by a single fluorescent light. A musty, dank odor reeked of past residents. Like the room he had lived in most of his childhood the cell gave him no comfort.

A tough upbringing in a boy's home, a disposition to violence and a growing sense of injustice had led to his arrest.

A fat cop walked up to the bars. 'On your feet,' he snapped.

'What for?'

'The circuit judge wants to talk to you.'

'What about?'

'You little bastard! Stand… you do what I tell you when I tell you.'

He was right. Cameron, or Cam as everyone called him, was a bastard. At least in the sense of being illegitimate. He had plenty of reminders during his childhood and early youth. He was not small. He stood five feet nine in his socks and showed muscle. Not body building muscle but the kind that pit bulls have – knots of it, unleashed in a second if need be. He stood up.

'Back away into the far corner,' the cop said.

The cop swayed on his feet causing his fat belly to jiggle. His eyes lit up as he pulled his revolver and pointed it at Cam. He saw the glint and knew the cop was eager to shoot. Instead he kept his eyes on Cam.

'All right, Judge, I have him bailed up. You can come to the bars.'

Judge Fleary had been on the circuit court bench for eighteen years. In Wyoming County he was not known for leniency. He had seen every type of criminal, from petty thief to killers, and had put them away in the state prison or had kept them in county jails. Tall and rangy, wearing a tan-colored uniform, and with an easy smile creasing his face, he looked at Cam with flinty eyes that tolerated no nonsense.

The judge carried no weapon, not that he needed to. No criminal would challenge him, and no cop would dare contradict him.

Cam had heard of the judge's reputation and wondered if he was in deep trouble. He had seriously injured a public employee – a pedophile.

The judge eyed the cop. 'Fred, what the hell are you doing? Put that pea shooter away and open the door. I'm going to speak to this young man and I don't need you hanging around listening.'

'But, Judge, this here is one of them little bastard hooligans from over the Rest. You can't trust any one of them any more than you can a diamond rattlesnake. I can't leave you without protection.'

The judge turned to Cam. 'Boy, you going to jump me and make the great escape?'

'No sir, I'm not.'

'All right, thought not. Fred, go away. If you hear me getting a whopping, stroll back this way.'

Fred cursed under his breath and left.

'Sorry about that, son. He's not too bright sometimes.'

'That's all right, Judge. We're all used to being called names, some worse than bastard,' Cam replied.

'And I'm sorry about that too, son. Some folks don't have the education they need to distinguish between bad people and those who have had a raw deal. Let's see now, you're locked up for beating the tar out of that Jem Nettles over at the Rest. He's going to spend a while at the county hospital getting his face fixed up. Want to tell me why you messed him up?'

'Well, I couldn't take it anymore, how he's pawing at the little kids who are scared of him. He tried it on me when I was little, and I bit his hand hard, drew blood. He never touched me again, but he made my life even more like hell since then. He's been doing it for as long as I remember, and shouldn't get away with it, just because the kids have no family. About time somebody put a stop to it.'

'Couldn't agree more, son. You have finally shined a light on this thing, and I will be dealing with old Jem shortly. Nobody is going to see him anymore around here. They don't like child molesters over at Rawlins, and I expect what he'll get there will be a lot worse than what you gave him. We may have to isolate him.'

'Now, I understand you are called Cam. Is that right?' the judge said, switching his focus.

'Yes sir.'

'I know your history,' said the judge. 'You are top of your junior class at St Anthony High and a sportsman, football and track; right?'

'Yes sir. I am.'

'I don't reckon I will be charging you with anything, given the circumstances. But you better watch your back around town. Old Jem has some friends, believe it or not.'

'Been watching my back all my life, sir. There better be more than two coming after me. Thank you kindly for letting me out.'

'Cam, at seventeen years of age, you're a bit young to be left on your own, but if I find somebody for you to live with, would you like to get out of the Rest?'

'Damn right. When can I get my stuff? Not that it's much.'

'Few days likely. Can you stomach the Rest for that long?'

'Yes sir. Judge, I didn't know I was seventeen. Nobody ever told me anything. Thought I was about that, being in junior year at high school, but never knew. You know when my birthday is?'

'Yes son. I have the record right here. It's June 11, 1951.'

'Fred, get on in here and let this boy out,' the judge shouted.

'Ah, Judge, you ain't letting this little bastard out, are ya? He'll just go back to thieving and beating people up. You know none of them Rest kids is good for anything.'

'Enough of that. This boy is doing better than any kid his age in this town. Open the door and let him out. I'll be seeing you soon, Cam.'

Fred shook his head in dismay. 'All right, boy, you get out of here. In my opinion the judge is making a big mistake. Just lock your kind up and throw away the key, is what I say. I'll be watching you close, boy.'

'Well, you'll have to lose some of that blubber, because I move pretty quick.'

'Turn around, boy; hands behind your back. I'm putting on the cuffs until I get you outside. Don't trust you one damn bit.'

Cam felt the cuffs go on tight and knew the cop meant to hurt him as much as possible before letting him go. He just hoped the cop didn't hit him with his nightstick on the way to the door. Cam doubted he had the nerve to do it, the judge being decent to him. Standing at the top of the court house steps, he waited for the cuffs to come off. The cop jammed his arms up high behind his back, causing more pain as he unlocked them. 'Git your ass outa here, boy.' The cop kicked him in the butt as a goodbye gesture.

Cam walked down the four worn granite steps to the street and crossed over to a nearby park. He sat down on a bench to enjoy the bright freshness of a Wyoming spring morning and to reflect on his situation.

He had been in a kind of prison all his life – ridiculously named, he thought, as the Children's Rest. Everything was basic. Even small comforts were denied as though they might unduly raise the hope and expectation of a better life. Above all, the boys lacked the most basic needs for emotional development, being shown love and affection, to be nurtured and wanted. Cam had grown up in the Rest as it was commonly known, from a very young age. He never saw or knew anything about his parents. No one let him know who they were. If they existed they never visited him.

Adults, it seemed, blamed the children for being without parents, be they orphans or illegitimate. None would turn out to be a respectable citizen. How could it be possible to wash away the stain, the terrible blight on their souls? They were forever damned. The nastiest threat any parent could give to a misbehaving child was to threaten to send the child to the Rest. The home was located on the outskirts of St Anthony in the state of Wyoming. A dirt track leading in turned to mud in the rainy season and could be thigh deep in snow in winter. Sagging steps led up to the porch of a long, flat-roofed building. Inside, bare, pock-marked gray walls reflected the somber living conditions of institutional life. In open space dormitories crammed with beds, the boys slept on thin, uncomfortable mattresses with only single woolen blankets.

The blocks at the end of the dormitories smelled of mold and harsh cleanser; they each housed bare toilets and three showers. The boys took turns to scrub the floor, toilets, and walls as high as they could reach. In the evening they studied in an open hall – a large, bare room, apart from the badly scarred desks and wooden chairs.

Food was less than basic, consisting of a gruel of oatmeal cooked in water for breakfast, no lunch, and a basic dinner of overcooked vegetables and greasy meat – mostly mutton. Maggots appeared from time to time as extras. No thought was given to nutrients or the quantities required for growing kids.

Each day at the Rest was the same except for the fights that broke out periodically. Cam had learned to take care of himself by the age of ten. Broken noses, lost teeth, cracked ribs, bruises and cuts all received little attention; a gauze dressing would be wrapped around a deep cut. From the age of twelve, Cam defended smaller boys from bullies and child molesters. Cam recognized those that would not fit in – the frightened, the suspicious, and the potential criminal. The system allowed them to become sociopaths. And there were those with dull, lifeless eyes. He knew he was emotionally closed and distrusting, never showing sympathy, and rarely compassion. He acted on his own version of truth for survival, which he knew would cause problems in his life.

Cam would never be fooled by religion, something, in his opinion, had caused most problems in the world. He had read widely about atrocities in wars and could not understand how a benevolent being would allow such acts of evil. It seemed to him that the whole human race was wired for violence. Emperors, tyrants, leaders and politicians all exploited violence for their own ends.

And why should homeless children be treated so badly? Jem Nettles, the caretaker, had addressed them in his usual manner that morning.

'All right, you little bastards, get ready to face another day in your miserable, good-for-nothing lives.'

A big man with a protruding belly, Nettles stank of sweat, bourbon and tobacco. Cam jumped out of bed and grabbed his washing and shaving gear. As he walked to the toilet block he passed Nettles, who was sitting on the bed of a boy of about six. The boy cringed with fear. Nettles had been targeting the boy for a week and had his hand under the bedclothes. Cam knew of his intent from previous times. Something in Cam snapped. 'Nettles, get away from that boy and do it now.'

Nettles looked at Cam with a greasy smile and continued with what he was doing. 'Boy, you aiming for a beatin' if you talk that way to me.'

Cam dropped his gear, stepped over to Nettles and knocked him off with a right hand straight to the middle of his face. Nettles sat stunned for a few seconds. Fury then took over. 'Boy, I'm going beat you to death or as near as I can get you to it.'

Cam stood his ground as Nettles plowed a wild right. Cam ducked and came back with three quick lefts that snapped Nettles' head back each time. He followed with a right to the face. Nettles rushed in, trying to get his arms around Cam to immobilize him. Cam flattened his hands and brought them smashing onto Nettles' ears. Nettles yelped, let go and brought his hands up to cover the ringing pain. With Nettles' face unprotected, Cam put all he had into a right fist to his nose. Cartilage gave way and blood sprayed out. Cam spun Nettles around and delivered four brutal punches to the kidneys, bringing him to his knees. Stepping back, Cam brought his knee up into Nettles' face twice. Nettles sank to the floor unconscious.

The entire fight was over in less than a minute. At first the boys who had watched were awestruck but, in a matter of seconds after Nettles had gone down, they cheered and whistled. Their tormentor lay bleeding on the floor.

'Boys, I've got to call the police,' Cam said. 'Everybody think of what story to tell the cops. Get together if you want. This asshole is not going to hurt you anymore and the cops need to know what he is.'

The police came and took Cam to the courthouse.

After Judge Fleary released Cam, he thought to contact his friend Ralph Pines. Ralph was a lifelong resident of St Anthony with the exception of three years he spent in the Pacific during World War II. He would not talk about those years and neither did he join the Veterans of Foreign Wars. His wife had passed away two years before, leaving Ralph to lead a solitary life for the most part, although he did enjoy his poker with Judge Fleary and a few other men with whom he could stand to be around for more than a few minutes. Beers went down well at these events, and a bottle of Scotch whisky came out on a special occasion.

He also enjoyed his fly fishing and wild game hunting.

The judge phoned him.

'Ralph, I've just let a boy out of jail and I think you may want to meet him. He's been in the Rest all his seventeen years, and yesterday he beat the crap out of that skunk Jem Nettles. About time, too. His name is Cameron Campbell. He calls himself Cam and I'd like to get him out of the Rest and into more convivial surroundings.'

'What you mean, Judge, is that you want to foist him on me because I've got that little apartment that nobody ever uses. Why in the hell would I want to take on that kind of responsibility?'

'At least take a look at the kid. Meet us at Annie's Nickel for lunch at 12.30 tomorrow.'

'Jesus, Judge, twist my arm 'til it hurts. All right, I'll meet you there, but don't waste my time with some juvenile delinquent.' The judge rang off and arranged to get a message to Cam about the lunch.

Annie's Nickel was a café two blocks from the courthouse where the courthouse population, including the cops, ate lunch and drank coffee. They came especially for the blueberry cobbler.

Inside the café, eight chrome stools with round seats, upholstered in blood-red leather, stood next to a white, red-veined marble counter. Booths, upholstered in the same blood-red, looked out on to the street. A jukebox in a corner pulsed with the colors of the rainbow from neon arteries on its front and played the latest hits.

In a space behind the counter the fry cook, in his peaked white cap and stained linen apron, sweated over his kingdom of steam table and greasy griddle. Orange heat lamps glowed over the serving table like cat's eyes, keeping the plates of food warm until they made their way to hungry customers.

You could get a beer at the Nickel, but if you wanted anything stronger you had to walk down the street to a bar. The Nickel offered a little in the way of solace to solitary figures hunched over their glasses.

'Ralph, I'd like you to meet Cameron Campbell who has resided at the Rest for seventeen years but is looking to broaden his horizons. You can call him Cam,' the judge said.

Cam extended his hand and Pines took it strongly, but not in the way men do to assert their dominance. Stocky, but not fat beneath his plaid shirt, and with silver hair moulded against his skull, he looked capable, Cam thought. 'Nice to meet you, sir.'

'Likewise, but you can drop the sir business. Call me Ralph.'

The judge and Cam sat side by side in the booth. They exchanged small talk about Cam's junior years at high school. Pines tucked away the information about the top grades and the sports. Just to get a reaction, Pines asked Cam if he was one for chasing the girls.

'I like to chase them, but they don't seem to want to get caught. They all know I live at the Rest, and their parents have told them to stay away from me, or at least I think somebody has.'

Pines took this in, realizing that there was probably much in the boy's life that would need guidance. He liked the way Cam spoke about himself, no teenage bragging or whining about how hard it had been. The kid had an appetite, too, having demolished one bacon, lettuce and tomato sandwich and accepting another when it was offered. Pines would learn about the usual diet at the Rest later; he would see to it that this boy would eat properly.

'Cam, come by my place later this afternoon and see if the room suits you. Nothing fancy, believe me.'

*****

CHAPTER TWO

Cam arrived at Pines' house and climbed a flight of stairs to the front door. Pines welcomed him in. Inside, two small rooms – a bedroom and a lounge – seemed luxurious to Cam. A kitchen, with a tiny fridge, two-coil hotplate and a small bathroom completed the space.

'I doubt I can afford to live here,' Cam said.

'I'm not asking for any rent. The place has been empty for years so I won't be missing any income. You can move in when you like. Here's the key. Don't lose it and don't lend it. I won't be keeping track of your comings and goings, just don't make a racket. You're on your own.'

The day after Cam moved in, Pines knocked on the door.

'I doubt you've done any fishing with artificial flies,' Pines said, as soon as the door opened. 'The season has started, and I generally wet a line every couple of days. If you want to learn about the best way to contemplate nature, come with me tomorrow. I've got gear for you.'

Cam's affair with fly fishing began. He learned how to select a suitable fly, and when to use a wet fly that would sink, or a dry fly that would float. Pines taught him how to tie a fly on the line, to cast, and to read the water. They fished for trout often that summer.

Occasionally moose stepped delicately into the river to graze on water plants. Deer came to drink. Beavers paddled past with neatly cut branches for food or shelter; they slapped the water with their flat tails like kayak paddles, warning fishermen to keep their distance. Coyotes crept through the brush and peered at them with yellowish eyes.

The summer passed quickly and, three days after helping to muster the cattle, Cam was back at school for the senior year. Studying had always been a pleasure; he liked learning about the world and how things worked. He read all kinds of books from the school library.

At the end of October, Pines, carrying a six-pack, knocked on the door. 'Fancy a beer,' he said.

'I won't say no, Ralph. Come on in.'

After a beer and a second well underway, Pines asked, 'What are your plans for next year?'

'I'm going to try to get to a university. I figure that's the only way to get out of this town and out into the world. Don't know how I'm going to pay for it, though.'

'I'm glad you want to get a real education. Just to let you know, I talked to the school guidance counselor, and she thinks you have a good chance for a scholarship. You'll still have to work, but that never hurt anybody.'

Cam met with the counselor, and she suggested that he apply to Yale and Harvard. Up to that point only one man from Wyoming had made it to Yale, and she wanted him to be the next. She went to a good deal of trouble to help fill out the forms and compose letters. The applications went out in mid-November. It would be five months before he received a reply.

At the beginning of November bird hunting season started and Pines was keen to teach Cam how to shoot. Pines arrived at the apartment.

'Cam, I've come to give you a second lesson in how to feed yourself.'

'And how is that then?'

'Come down to the house and I'll show you.'

In the front room of Pines' house were two shotguns, their two tubes of blued steel locked into polished walnut stocks. Cam liked the elegant look of the guns.

'Cam, the bird hunting season is open and I can guarantee you that you will never have a finer meal than pheasant and grouse. We're going to get some. This shotgun is for you.'

It was a clean twenty-gauge. Cam took it and held a weapon for the first time – an epiphany.

'This other one is mine. I've been shooting with it since I was younger than you. It is a sixteen-gauge, a little unusual these days. Most of these Sunday shooters get off with a twelve-gauge, but I tell you, that is just too much testosterone talking. It takes skill to bring down a bird with a smaller gauge. Less wounding of birds, too. Now, the first thing you do is not shoot an animal you won't eat. We are in the business of providing game here, not some asshole's idea of being wild with a deadly weapon. We shoot for the table.'

'When do we get to teaching me?' Cam asked, intrigued by the whole concept.

'Right now. Grab a box of shells and let's go.'

They climbed into Pines' International Harvester and, after driving a few miles into the countryside, they stopped.

'All right, I just need to set up the clay bird machine.'

When that was done, Pines said, 'Time to load up. You always keep the barrel of the weapon pointed at the ground or in a direction away from other people. Keep it broken until you are ready to use it.'

Cam broke the gun and chambered two shells.

'Cam, there is no way to teach someone how to shoot. It is a matter of intrinsic talent, a matter of eye and hand coordination. You should be a natural at this. I'm going to put this clay bird in the air, in an easy way, so you can get used to the idea.'

Cam closed the breach and stood ready.

'Don't bring the gun up until you see the bird fly. Don't close your eyes. Follow the bird along the length of the barrels, just a touch in front of the flight path. That's the way it works in the field.'

Pines let the clay bird fly. Cam brought the gun up and fired. The gun was so well-balanced it felt like an extension of his arm. Pines flew twenty clay birds and Cam missed only two.

'Well, I guess you're ready for the real thing. Never seen anyone take to it the way you do. Meat on the table, I reckon.'

Cam got his game license and two days later they went hunting. Pines had some favorite fields on farms where he was on good terms with the owners. Grouse flew up before them as they walked through the tall grass. In twenty minutes Cam had two birds, the legal limit for a day. He hung them by the neck on a wire carrier attached to his belt, something that Pines had insisted on as a safety measure, because it kept the hands free to take care of the weapon.

'Well, I guess we can go home now, since you just got through a whole day's hunting in a few minutes. Damn, I hate you little experts,' Pines sighed.

Cam was exhilarated. There was no way he wanted to go home. 'Come on, we need to get your two birds, and I reckon we've scared away any other poor souls in this field. I want to see you shoot.'

'Jeez, you're really full of it. Mind I don't shoot you to shut you up.'

They drove to another field and within twenty minutes the other two birds were in the bag.

'Is it always this easy?'

'Not always.'

They went hunting three to four times a week during the season and came back with a full score every time. One day Judge Fleary showed up with his shotgun, which showed a beautiful hand-tooled stock made of teak. Cam knew the judge had come to see how he was doing as well as hunt.

'This weapon is a Purdy. They make them for royalty in England, so I guess I'm pretty elegant,' Judge Fleary said.

'Very nice balance, sir.'

'If Ralph doesn't mind not being called "sir", I suppose I can live with that, too. Just call me "Judge", everybody else does, including my wife.'

'Yes, Judge.'

'I hear you've applied to some pretty good schools for next year. Any news yet?'

'No Judge. I think I'll hear something in the spring.'

'Well, the birds are waiting to become part of our diet, so let's not disappoint them.'

By the end of the season they had stocked the freezer to capacity. Cam relished his new life better than anything he could remember at the Rest.

*****

CHAPTER THREE

Cam walked into Annie's Nickel and sat on a stool at the counter. It was named the Nickel because Annie claimed she opened the place on her last one. She was an institution at St Anthony, having been around forever, it seemed. A big woman, but no one would mention it; in fact, nobody really noticed. She was greatly liked and probably had fed most of the population, especially the men.

Cam had been visiting the Nickel since he was ten. He had wandered in like a stray cat just because the place smelled of cinnamon buns and bacon. Annie had taken a hard look at him and realized he was probably from the Rest, so she had asked him whether he was. 'Yes,' he had blurted out. Annie gave him a cookie. He was in love.

Cam came in frequently after that. Annie didn't mind at all. She watched him grow up.

Annie's eggs tasted delicious, with fresh watercress added from a nearby creek. On this particular day, Cam ordered his favorite – scrambled eggs on toast.

The door opened and a ragged-looking man walked in, not someone Cam had seen around town before. His clothes were dirty, he had not shaved for a few days, and he stank. A tangled mat of greasy-brown hair fell out of a hole in his fedora hat. Dandruff dusted his well-worn coat and a boot had popped a seam.

'Give me coffee and a piece of that apple pie,' he demanded.

Annie didn't like his tone but poured a cup, cut the pie, and set both down in front of the man. He drank some of the coffee and bit into the pie. He spat it out.

'What you call this here piece of shit? Horse apples with crust? It ain't no pie.'

Annie never took any insolence and several times had beaten ugly customers with a rolling pin. 'What did you just say to me?'

'I haven't said it yet, you ugly fat bitch.'

Annie leaned over the counter to smack the man, but he was quick and grabbed her hair. He pushed her head into the counter. That was enough for Cam. He jumped over two stools and punched the man hard in the kidneys. The man let go of Annie and tried to stand up, but Cam grabbed the back of his neck with his right hand and slammed the man's head into the edge of the counter four times as hard as he could. The man went down and stayed down.

'Jesus, Annie; you all right?'

'Yeh, yeh… the prick didn't hurt me.'

But Annie had a split bleeding lip.

'I'm calling the cops,' she said. 'You stay here to make sure this son of a bitch stays down.'

When a cop arrived, it was Fred. He scanned the room, saw Cam, the unconscious man, and Annie's bleeding lip. He pulled his revolver and, with a shaky two-hand stance, held it on Cam.

'I knew I'd get you for something, you little bastard.'

'Fred, Cam just saved my ass from this bum. Are you nuts?'

'No, this time I've got this piece of shit. He's going away for assault and anything else I can think of. Get on your knees, boy, and put your hands on your head. I'm going to call for backup. You move and you're dead.'

Cam did as he was told and kept still.

By this time Annie was on the phone to the police. 'You let me talk to Detective Glen Carson, now.'

The detective took the phone.

'Glen, it's Annie at the Nickel. Some vagrant tried to attack me just now and Cam was here. He's put the creep down, well and truly, but I've got your stupid cop Fred here holding a gun on Cam. That man is an unrepentant idiot. You get over here right now to sort this out.'

Fred kept his aim on Cam's head. Cam kept still.

Five minutes later Detective Carson arrived, took one look around the place and said, 'Fred, you are too stupid to live. Holster that weapon and let the boy up.'

'No, I ain't. He's practically killed that man and he's finally going to get put away where he belongs.'

'Fred, I swear I'll shoot you myself if you don't holster. You dimwit, this bum hit Annie, and Cam helped her. Only person going anywhere is the guy on the floor. Get out to the car and alert the ambulance. You stay with this prisoner at all times, and I mean in the ambulance and at the hospital. If he gets away from you or hurts anybody else I'll have your badge.'

Fred finally got the message and backed off, but Cam could see in his eyes that he really had wanted to shoot him.

'Annie, let me take a look at that lip,' Cam said.

'It won't need stitches but it will be painful for a few days,' Cam said after a closer look.

Annie turned to the detective. 'Damn it, Glen, if Cam hadn't been here I might have got real hurt. I'm sure as hell not raising any complaint. I'm going to give him free eggs for a week. Just tell me what I have to do to get that vagrant in the lockup.'

'Goddamn son, you sure do get into scrapes,' the detective said. 'Cam, you just get on home. I imagine Pines will have a good laugh about the whole thing. But please try to stay out of trouble.'

'Detective, I never look for trouble, it seems to look for me.'

*****

CHAPTER FOUR

Winter deepened with Cam totally ignoring Christmas day as he had done for years. No point when nothing good is going to happen, he thought. He just wished that somebody would do something for the kids at the Rest, like feed them a decent meal. It seemed like another calculated punishment, carefully crafted because the kids knew all about Christmas, but would never get one that was memorable.

And Pines hated Christmas.

He truly believed all religion was for the weak-minded. When the whole world was covered in misery who could actually believe in a supreme being? He liked to read history; he knew from the written chronicle of mankind that there had always been a war somewhere, a war fought over religion or land.

Regardless of his beliefs, Pines cooked a piece of elk tenderloin for Christmas that a poker buddy had given him after the elk season. He had marinated it for three days in whisky and HP brown sauce, and had invited Cam down to savor it. Pines brought out a bottle of red wine.

'Cam, you've never had a taste of this, I would think. Perhaps an acquired taste.'

After Cam's first glass he had acquired the taste. The New Year was also something that both Pines and Cam had paid no attention. But this year Pines thought he would invite some poker buddies over and cook a turkey. It was a success. White wine was served and Cam liked it better than the red. In a merry mood, the poker buddies and Cam stayed at Pines' place for the night.

In late April, Cam was admitted to the University of Wyoming, but that was a given as his grade point average was way above the average for his year, and he was a citizen of Wyoming, so they had to take him.

In mid-May a fat envelope arrived from Yale. Cam had been accepted, and they were going to pay for everything except his books. He would have to work but not too much.

As graduation from St Anthony neared, excitement focused on the senior prom. Cam knew he would not be going. None of the girls would date him. They liked him well enough, but when he had asked a few out during his junior years their parents chased him off. One father had threatened him with a baseball bat. Now that he was on his way out of St Anthony he did not care about the knock backs.

Cam settled into Yale. He studied hard, went to classes, worked for two hours a day at his scholarship job and exercised in the gym. Just as he was starting to enjoy university life, he received a letter from the United States Government. He had been drafted and was to report to Fort Bragg in the first week of October for basic combat training. He knew he would be going to Vietnam.

Cam sought advice from the dean.

'Cam, I am terribly disturbed by this news. What our current government is thinking, I have no idea. First Johnson and now Nixon. Both total mental retards, in my opinion. You will still have your place here and your scholarship will be waiting for you if – I do beg your pardon – when you return. My best wishes to you and I am convinced you will present yourself as a true Yale man, as so many have done before you.'

Cam called Pines for advice. 'Hey, Ralph, how's everything in St Anthony?'

'Just the same, but you're not calling to ask about that, are you?'

'I've been drafted, Ralph. In a week I have to report to Fort Bragg for basic combat training. Looks like I'm headed for Vietnam.'

There was silence at Pines' end for about thirty seconds.

'Goddamn it, Cam, I had hoped you would be spared this. The war I fought had to be done and, by God, the men and women of my generation won it, but this Vietnam business is completely different. It is totally useless and is not about saving the free world, like my war. It is just a bunch of politicians sending boys to fight and die for nothing. I wish I could get those damn politicians in a room, give them each a club, close the door and see who comes out. Then I'd shoot whoever that is. Damn, I hate this.'

'Me too, Ralph, but it's either report or go to Canada, which you know I'm not going to do. Just give me some advice about what to expect in boot camp.'

'First, you will pay a price for surviving. They will try to turn you into a machine. Don't let them do that! If you get a good drill sergeant he will teach you to survive if you pay attention. He will see what you are made of, that you are one tough son of a bitch. You will lose some things, but what you gain will sustain you in moments of great intensity. Do not be afraid of anything. Embrace the experience. It's all you can do.'

Pines then detailed to Cam what to expect from drill sergeants.

'These are sergeants, staff sergeants or sergeants first class. Drill sergeants volunteer or are selected by the US Army Resources Command School. They attend the drill sergeant school for ten weeks, with the same activities as basic training for draftees – drill and ceremony, basic rifle marksmanship, obstacle and confidence courses, field training exercises, training management and leadership. The drill sergeants usually have no combat experience. To stand out and let everyone know who they are, they wear the World War I campaign hat, nicknamed the Brown Round. It makes them look like Smokey the Bear. Respect your drill sergeant at all times, but don't be afraid of him. Drill sergeants are masters of verbal intimidation.' Pines thought that he, with all his years in a children's prison, would not have any problems. He would make one of the best recruits.

'Do what you are told and do it fast,' Pines said.

'While I am away, can you do me a favor?' asked Cam.

'Sure Cam. What is it?'

'All I know about me is what happened at the Rest. I don't know where I come from. Could you…'

'No need to explain, Cam, I'll see what I can do.'

*****

CHAPTER FIVE

After a two-day bus journey, Cam reached Fort Bragg. He asked a cab driver how to get to the intake area.

'Get in, son, I'll take you.'

'I don't have enough to pay the fare, thanks all the same.'

'No, get in. I figure it's the least I can do for you youngsters who are forced to go fight this god-awful war. It will only be a short ride.'

At the intake area he thanked the cabby and walked through the door of a rusting, corrugated-steel barn that had the appearance of a pen in an abattoir with stock waiting to be slaughtered. A man in uniform sat at a table covered with papers.

'Good morning and welcome to the United States Army. Let's see your draft notice.' Cam handed it over. The man stamped it and put it on a pile of papers.

'Mr. Campbell, you are now part of D Company, second platoon. You will train for nine weeks. Your fellow soldiers are mostly here already. Go through that door to collect your gear and get your inoculations.'

His gear consisted of two complete sets of olive drab – OD fatigues, under garments and one pair of boots with a black leather bottom, green canvas top and steel plated sole. They would be comfortable enough, he thought. After his jabs, a barber cut his hair short. He felt odd but refreshed as cool air blew over his scalp.

He was ushered into another building where his military companions had gathered. A man with sergeant's stripes on his sleeves entered. He counted the men assembled, checked off something on a clipboard, and seemed satisfied about the number of bodies he had registered. 'Listen up, maggots. I am your drill instructor, Sergeant Grimm.' The name was stenciled on his fatigue blouse.

'You are now my sole property. Your mommies and daddies are far, far away and will not be able to dry your tears. For the next nine weeks I will be your only hope of survival. Do exactly what I say and we will have no problems. If you do not do what I say, your life will resemble the very darkest hole in hell possible. There are no second chances in my platoon.'

Cam had taken a look at his companions and concluded that most were going to have a hard time. They appeared frightened. Only five or so looked like they had any sports experience.

Most were fat, but a few were painfully thin, possibly ganja smokers. Among this motley crew, he could be fairly certain of being a survivor.

'Fall in line and stand at attention.'

The men shuffled into a straggly line.

'Goddamnit, get in a straight line. Don't you know what a straight line is? Why in the hell do I always get the pick of the dickheads every time? Attention means you go rigid with your hands glued to the sides of your legs and you do not move until I release you.'

Sergeant Grimm walked slowly down the line. At every third man he got as close to a face as his head gear would allow and shouted, leaving little doubt about where the new recruit had come from. He stopped at Cam.

'Are you afraid of me, boy?'

'No, Sergeant, I'm not.' Pines had advised that this was the best way to deal with indoctrination. Calm and respectful, don't address him as 'Sir', just 'Sergeant'.

'Look here, gentlemen, we have a tough guy. All right, tough guy, drop and give me twenty pushups.'

Cam did as requested, very easily. Twenty was not enough to make him breathe hard. He got back on his feet.

'Drop and give me forty.'

He did.

'Damn you, drop and give me sixty.'

He did but the last ten took a bit of effort. The sergeant gave him the fish eye.

'Gentlemen, you should be very proud to be here for basic combat training. I will teach you self-discipline, which is a rare commodity among you spoiled brats. I am going to run your butts so hard you are going to wish you had never been born. I am going to smoke you until you are not able to stand.'

Sergeant Grimm walked in front of the line again, a line of mostly frightened young men. He called six to step forward.

'You are not fit enough to even be standing here where brave men have been trained. I am not wasting my time on you. You are immediately transferred to Fat Camp for four weeks.'

For the next nine weeks of intensive training and mock combat, Sergeant Grimm lived up to his name.

The platoon graduated to Advanced Individual Training, AIT. Cam was called before Sergeant Grimm and the company commander.

'Campbell, the Ground Fighting Technique unit has presented an invitation for you to join them for your AIT, and, if you pass, you become a member of their team. Do you accept?' the commander asked.

Cam had not expected this at all. He had done well in unarmed combat training, but that was due to his previous street fighting experience and having little fear of being injured. He had stood out in the platoon because of the lack of fighting ability of most of his compatriots. But having been trained by an elite unarmed combat team, he knew he was not at their level. They were like professional athletes, and no matter how hard he trained, he would not reach their level of skills.

'Sir, I must decline their invitation. A man has to know his limitations, and I think I would be better suited to another military specialty for my AIT. I would like to be assigned to the Infantry School at Fort Benning to be trained for sniper duty.'

The company commander and the sergeant stared at him.

'That is one of the most difficult assignments in the army,' the commander said. 'It is harder than becoming an unarmed expert. Why in the world would you want to attempt this?'

'Sir, I have been alone all of my life and think a solitary job like that of a sniper would suit me.'

What Cam would not say was that he did not want to serve with an incompetent young officer who had no idea how to fight. Training for fighting was a world apart from actual fighting. He simply thought he had a better chance of surviving in a solo job like a sniper.

'But you have shown you are a natural leader by the good work you have done for your squad and for your platoon,' Sergeant Grimm said. 'We need leaders, because many of the young officers in the field are not as proficient as we would like, due to the brevity of their training.'

Cam had heard how poorly some of the grunts were doing because of the extremely negative attitude to the war. Everybody just wanted to give up and go home, and who could blame them. He did not like his chances with a platoon of demoralized men who probably hated their officers. His chances were better on missions where a team of only two highly trained men would look out for each other.

'Sir, I would like to formally request a transfer to Fort Benning for sniper school.'

'This is most unusual. Do you realize that you need an enlisted rank of E-3 to E-7 to complete the course?'

'Yes sir, I do. Is there anything that can be done for me to achieve that rank?'

'I'll look into it with the course convening authority. Because we are in a war, I can make reasonable promotions. As of now, in view of your record in basic, I am assigning you the rank of E-4 specialist. I'll try to arrange for a rank of E-7 sergeant first class if you complete the school. We still need leaders no matter what specialty they pursue. I am confident you will succeed and have no hesitation in recommending you.'

'Sir… thank you sir.'

Grimm followed him out of the commander's office.

'Campbell, you could have just about any advanced training you want. Are you absolutely sure about sniper school?'

'Sergeant, what is the likelihood of me being sent to Vietnam in a combat unit?'

'At this point in the war, at least ninety-five percent.'

'Then I think I'm better off as a hunter without a master.' Grimm shook his head but extended his hand. Cam took it.

'In my opinion, you have every chance of surviving, simply because you are a survivor. You're not afraid of anything I've thrown at you and you think independently. I don't hold out that much hope for the majority of the young men who come through here. Best of luck.'

*****

CHAPTER SIX

In three days he was at Fort Benning, in a barrack identical to the one he had lived in at Fort Bragg.

An introduction to the sniper course began the following day. As he walked into the room he saw four rifles and eight men. The instructor was tabbed as a master sergeant.

'Gentlemen, you are here today because you have volunteered and been accepted by the United States Army Sniper School. This assignment will test you in every way about your skill in combat, your intelligence and your willingness to kill the enemy. That is what you will be trained for and, if you graduate, that is what you will do. Many times over. The majority of our washouts are those who cannot accept the fact that they will be shooting to death fellow human beings who are not aware of the presence of the man who will kill them. That will be you. You will see violent death, close up and personal, through a telescopic sight. You will live with that and still retain your ability to function normally in society outside of the military. At various times during this course you will be evaluated psychologically as to your ability to carry out your duties without having tendencies to enjoy killing for killing's sake. I cannot put it more bluntly than that. We do not train psychopaths. We train the best soldiers in the United States Army.'

The instructor introduced the weapons.

'You have seen the weapons on inspection for you. There are four weapons and eight men. At the end of the school, four of you will be sniper team leaders and the other four will be team spotters. However, both members of a sniper team will learn to be proficient in the use of the weapon.'

The instructor held up one of the rifles.

'This weapon is based on the Remington Arms model 700. It has a heavy contour barrel and a long action bolt face, and is neither automatic nor semiautomatic. You will learn to shoot with precision. You will learn to make every round from your weapon a fatal round. It fires a 7.62 by 51 millimeter 175 grain bullet, known as a NATO round, based on the point 308 Winchester, at a velocity of 786 meters per second or 2580 feet per second. It has an effective range of 1600 meters or 1750 yards in capable hands. You will note that the weapon is attached to a bipod to hold it steady under combat shooting conditions. You will also be using a small sandbag that can be employed where the bipod is not your best choice. Attached to this weapon is a Leupold Mark IV 10 by 40 millimeter telescopic sight which you will become so acquainted with that you will use it in your sleep.'

The instructor compared the scope to the mouth of a lamprey,

'The lamprey has a round, gaping hole of a mouth, lined with many razor teeth. Looking into this mouth is the stuff bad dreams are made of. The lamprey attaches itself to a larger fish and sucks the life out with its mouth. A scope sucks light in and magnifies it, allowing the sniper to drain the life from his target, just like the lamprey and its victim. Both deal in death.'

Based on their records, the men were paired up.

'I will read out the names of each pair. Take a good look at the man paired with you, as only about fifty percent will graduate from this school.'

Cam was paired with a blonde man, Jon Daniels, who did not fit Cam's concept of a sniper. Despite looking fit, he was slight, sensitive looking and too eager. He did not look as though he could pull a trigger on anyone. Cam reminded himself that everyone had been profiled and chosen for the course. He thought maybe he was one of those stone cold killers that no one suspected.

'You will now begin to familiarize yourselves with this weapon by repeated disassembling, cleaning and reassembling. You will be able to do this in total darkness.'

The teams learnt how to detect and stalk targets, and make ghillie suits.

A specialist on ghillies addressed them:

'Everyone wonders where the name comes from. It is derived from Gaelic and means 'servant', which was a working man assisting rich bastards in deer hunting and fishing in the Scottish Highlands. The first recorded military use was during the Boer War, and in 1916 it was used by the British Army's first sniper unit. A ghillie suit, for our purpose, is a type of camouflage clothing, designed to resemble heavy foliage.

'You have been given a used but freshly laundered one-piece olive drab coverall which will serve as the base for the ghillie. It has been issued in your size, and in barracks tonight you will try it on to be sure it fits comfortably. If it does not, see me as soon as you can because you are likely to be wearing this outfit for days at a time. You do not want to be chaffed or pinched, believe me.

'To this base uniform we will be adding burlap, a coarse cloth woven from jute. I will now show you how to use fishing line to sew knots that will go over the entire coverall. After the knots are in place you will use a drop of super glue to strengthen them.'

The specialist demonstrated, and everyone got to work. He walked around and offered advice. He then said to the group:

'When you reach your sniping location you will fill the net with vegetation from the local area such as twigs, small branches with leaves attached, and anything else that will make you and your weapon and gear indistinguishable from the local foliage. You will keep the ghillie as dirty as possible, even after each mission. You want to maintain a rich odor.

'Gentlemen, besides your spotter, your ghillie is your most important means of survival. If used properly, the enemy will never detect you, even if you have been stupid or unfortunate enough to let them come within three meters of you. Be aware that the ghillie will become extremely hot as a garment and that it is also flammable. I will inspect each ghillie to check that it is fit for duty. Good luck.'

The master sergeant was satisfied that the eight trainees had reached the competence level to begin live firing exercises.

Four men, including Cam, took a prone position with the rifle fixed to a bipod, and loaded a round. The master sergeant looked them over and was satisfied, for the moment.

'Ready on the right. Ready on the left. Prepare to fire. Fire.'

The rifles delivered a powerful kick.

'Gentlemen, as you know, the Army buys vast quantities of ammunition. As with any product, variations occur among various manufacturers and within batches of production. You will now be issued ammunition that I know is slightly different. You will fire three-shot groups using this ammunition and compare the results with previous efforts at sighting in your weapon.'

They observed the slight differences in the two different issues of ammunition as shown by the target groupings, even though the rifle had been accurately sighted in during the first exercise. It was mandatory to sight the rifle in again when issued with a new supply of ammunition in the field. The sniper could not be certain of his accuracy if this were not done. It was also a priority to sight in after a mission in case the scope had been knocked during rough traveling and use.

When the first four shooters were confident of hitting the target at 1200 meters, the entire process was repeated by the other four men.

All eight men trained as spotters as well as shooters. The spotter was the most important member of a sniper team and had a wide variety of responsibilities. When the team was moving, the spotter led and protected the team, and was in control of communication, carrying the radio. He called in artillery or air strikes if needed. He generally guided the team and carried maps. He also participated in building hides and creating diversions, often with explosives or mines.

The spotting scope had a mil-dot reticule, featuring duplex cross hairs with small dots at milliradian intervals in the field of view, for determining range and size of target, like the rifle scope. One milliradian equaled ten centimeters at one hundred meters. If the spotter sighted a human target 1.8 meters tall at three mil-dots tall through the scope, the target was 600 meters away.

They practiced using a spotting scope with a range of different magnifications from 20X to 60X. The width of the objective lens at 60mm provided good light gathering power in a straight-through scope, which can be hand-held if required.

As well as estimating the range to the target and confirming with the shooter that he was seeing the same in the rifle scope, the spotter determined temperature, humidity, wind speed, and angle of the shot – all passed on to the shooter, who made the proper scope adjustments.

Even though the spotter's job was complex and indispensable, the shooter was the team leader. He put the mission together and, once in the field, determined the route, positions from which to fire, the escape route and the extraction place.

Sniper and shooter depended on each other for survival as they most often worked between or behind battle lines. They had little or no support from anyone else. Cam liked the idea of making his own decisions and being in control of his own survival. Like every other large corporation an army had its share of bad managers, and he did not want one of those. Or anybody else, really, except his spotter.

Jon and Cam performed seemingly endless practice sessions, each doing the tasks required of a spotter while the other acted as the shooter. Cam struggled with the calculations and eventually worked out his own system for the way the scopes worked, and of determining range, windage, elevation and bullet drop, but was much slower than Jon. He thought this would probably be the reason he would be washed out and it caused him a great deal of concern.

At the end of their course, the drill sergeant addressed them:

'Gentlemen, you have now learned the fundamentals of a sniper team. However, you will not only be used to kill the enemy from a great distance, you will also do reconnaissance missions where you will provide your units with information about the enemy. You will be ordered to demoralize the enemy by hunting key officers, pilots on the ground, and key technicians. You will give support with blocking positions and destroying non-human targets such as radios, fuel and water supplies, and planes and helicopters on the ground, whereby the enemy's will to fight will be diminished. You will also take targets of opportunity while in the field should your mission allow you to do so.

'Through the use of special tactics you will do the damage of a larger force without engaging the enemy. You are a strategic weapon and a force multiplier.'

Two days after training had finished, the master sergeant called each man to his office. Cam's turn came.

'Campbell, congratulations on completing the course. Many don't. You have been monitored for good decision making and being an independent thinker. You can shoulder the responsibility of doing a sniper's job. The psychologist has evaluated that you are unusually calm about taking the life of another man and that you have slight sociopathic tendencies in this regard, which he believes may be the result of a lack of normal familial associations while you were growing up. However, he has passed you fit for sniper duty, which he has not done for two men in your class. They have already been transferred out.

'Your biggest deficiency is the time it takes for you to do the necessary calculations. We believe you will improve with time and practice. Rarely is a sniper called on to make split-second decisions unless he is under immediate attack, and then your rifle will be of little use anyway. We have observed that you and Daniels have formed yourselves into an outstanding team. He is much quicker than you with the calculations and is an excellent spotter. We are going to keep you together and put you on active duty. You will remain on this base until you are deployed to Vietnam, giving you time to hone your skills. I am pleased to tell you that you have been promoted to E-7 Sergeant First Class. Welcome to the world of the NCO, Noncommissioned Officer. Let me buy you a drink at the NCO club and introduce you to a few of your colleagues.'

Cam went to find Jon.

'You know we've been paired up for Nam?'

'Yeah, all right with you?'

'Just glad they didn't break us up after training so hard. You hear anything about an assignment?'

'Not a peep, but they have to assign us pretty quick because we're supposed to be on transport day after tomorrow.'

'You know, Cam, snipers aren't well liked by some of the troops. They think we just sneak around and don't face the enemy square on.'

'Don't even think it. We are the best of the best. Training to be an assassin is a bit like training to be a diamond cutter. You have to be very careful. You could end up with a pile of glittery chips that are only good to glue to a drill bit or you could find a scintillating small rock that you could cut glass and seduce women with. The second outcome is better and worth whatever some fool is willing to pay for. We are not cannon fodder, like the rest. We have the privilege of stalking the prey. The gooks are the prey, they run and hide, we chase. It's not how many of them we shoot, it's which special individuals we shoot.

'The nearest I can express my anticipation for getting in the game is a bit like studying the cultures of prehistory, you know, the Paleolithic, the stone age, the bronze age, the iron age. Those people functioned like we will, but you can't imagine what it must actually have been like. I can imagine it, but maybe it won't be like that. I've killed plenty of animals. Humans are just animals, after all. Don't stress, we're a team and a good one. We will survive this.'

The next day, the drill sergeant met them on the range for the last time. 'Report to the captain at 15.00. This should be your assignment. I recommended something tough because you can handle it.'

At the captain's office they stood to attention.

'At ease, gentlemen. I have your assignment. You have been assessed as outstanding and, therefore, you have been attached to the 1st Airborne Cavalry. They want to assess the efficacy of having sniper teams operate in conjunction with long-range reconnaissance patrols, LRRPs. Rangers are members, if you like, of LRRPs and called Lurps. You are to report to the commanding officer of Company H, Ranger Battalion, as soon as you are on the base. You will receive your orders from him and will also draw your weapons and equipment on the base. You will take the 700 and scopes that you trained with so as not to hinder your availability for deployment. I am certain you will not let the Army down in its assessment of you. That is all. Dismissed.'

They came to attention. 'Yes sir, thank you sir.'

When they had left the office, Cam said, 'Well, we appear to have done too well. Rangers are always behind the lines doing dangerous things and causing as much damage as possible. We'll have to think about it as a way to stay alive. We won't be in some grunt platoon led by a kid who has just graduated from high school and trained to march and drill, with just two weeks of tactics. At least we'll be with people who know what they're doing. Never know, we might even like it.'

They went back to the barracks to assemble their equipment. Cam cleaned his rifle slowly and carefully because for a year it would be his only tool. He had grown fond of it. He folded and packed his ghillie, hoping it would be the magical garment to keep him safe.

*****

CHAPTER SEVEN

Jon and Cam were herded onto the transport plane to Vietnam along with two companies of grunts they did not know. The interior of the aircraft was spartan, comfort minimal. The flight seemed interminable. Finally the pilot informed them that they would be landing in fifteen minutes. Catholics crossed themselves, Protestants prayed, and some Jewish soldiers put on yarmulkes and chanted.

The plane came in fast and high before dropping like a stone onto the runway – a maneuver designed to avoid rockets or heavy machine gun fire.

They marched off the airstrip to billets. The heat, humidity and smell were stifling. Cam hoped it was not like this all the time. It was, and it got worse.

An hour later a corporal arrived in OD fatigues and asked Sergeants Campbell and Daniels to report to Captain Parsons, the commanding officer of Ranger Company Q.

They went to his office and stood to attention.

The captain was a large man in camouflage fatigues with the red, black and white Ranger ribbon on his left sleeve. He looked extremely fit and like no one to mess with. He was armed with a .45 caliber Colt 1911 semi-automatic pistol in a shoulder holster.

'At ease, men. Welcome to the war. I'm going to get right to the point. I have been ordered to bring you into Company Q as an experiment. They want to ascertain if two-man sniper teams can add more effectiveness to long range reconnaissance patrol teams than having one man in the team acting as an occasional sniper. I am not happy about this; however, it may prove interesting. I have been informed that you were outstanding in training. Training is not experience of battle. My men have been in combat many times and are completely competent in their craft. They are trained in ways that the average soldier would never aspire to. You will be assigned to a team led by a staff sergeant. You both outrank him but to Rangers that means next to nothing. You will be guided by him. If you do not, I guarantee that you will be brought out in a body bag. Is this perfectly clear?'

'Sir, yes sir.'

'However, due to the unusual nature of these orders I will ask you to volunteer for this assignment. Do you accept?'

'Sir, yes sir.'

'Outstanding. I will issue an order to the quartermaster to supply you with equipment similar to LRRP issue. Once in the field you will find that there is no standard LRRP equipment. What works for each man is what is worn. There will also be a variety of weapons with which each man feels he can do the most damage to the enemy. As you can only kill from a distance with your weapon, you may choose other weapons for close-in combat when that occurs. I will follow your progress closely, and if I feel you are a danger to the lives of my men, I will relieve you. That is all.'

Once outside, Cam and Jon eyed each other, feeling like a rare species on the verge of extinction.

Cam broke the silence. 'Nothing like a warm welcome and gentle encouragement. Man, we have gotten into a situation and no mistake. I'm sure the LRRP team will be just as eager to have us along. Hope this is not a watch your back deal. I would like to have only the enemy plotting our demise.'

'Yeah, me too. Let's just go get our equipment and weapons. At least the captain was reasonable about that.'

The quartermaster's store was the first stop. They explained who they were and what they wanted to a supply sergeant who said, 'Jesus, are you some more of them crazy jungle running sum 'bitches? What do you guys do that for? Me, I'm staying right here behind my cozy little desk for my tour. Anyway, let's find what you think you need. I got a fair idea so let me show you around.'

He led them into a vast storeroom.

'I bet you two are Lurp virgins. You ain't got that look of the ones been running loose in the boonies. Now, I've kitted out some Lurp virgins before so let me assemble the basics of what you'll need.'

He gathered a bewildering assortment: camouflage fatigues, underwear, cushion sole boot socks and foot powder, a variety of pouches to be worn on a belt with a snap release buckle and a supporting H harness, tropical nylon rucksacks, ponchos and liners, ammo pouches, recon gloves, binoculars, a fixed focus camera, strobe lights with flash guards, flashlights, camouflage sticks, and other pieces of small equipment that Cam and Jon would figure out later.

'Now, you boys, I'm going to give you some advice for free. What you do with them recon gloves is you cut the fingers and thumbs off about halfway so you can shoot proper. They protect your palms because there are a lot of sharp nasty plants where you going. And each of you better take three of these two-quart canteens apiece. Water is very precious in the bush-bush. They give you water purification tablets, but they really don't work because the natural water is full of all kinds of ugly little parasites, and them damn pills just do not kill them. Next thing, take a handful of these here canteen covers. You jungle runners use them for carrying extra ammunition. I believe that will do for now. Every one of you boys has his own way of carrying his gear, I'm sure you'll find yours in a short time. Pack all that in these two duffels. Good luck.'

They lugged the gear to their billet. By then it was time for evening chow.

'Damn, this is a lot of equipment,' Jon said. 'After we eat let's see if we can figure out how to pack it all. There is apparently no correct way to do it, so we can experiment to see what is logical and, maybe, and I mean maybe, comfortable.'

The next day they chose their extra weapons. A corporal led them through the armory.

'I was told to let you have what you want seeing as how you are crazy Lurps.'

They toured around a bit until Cam saw a small shotgun with a pistol grip and a thirteen inch barrel, an Ithaca model 37. Having some experience with shotguns he decided to take one, two boxes of shells and a sling. He intended to wear it over his shoulder on his back. The next weapon he decided on was a Colt Python .357 Magnum revolver. Cam knew it had incredible stopping power and would not jam.

'You seem pretty interested in that .357. I can let you have that for thirty bucks and I'll throw the shoulder holster in.'

'You mean I have to pay for it?'

'It's not US Army issue. It belonged to a fellow who's back in the world. We sell anything that isn't US issue.'

'How much for ammo?'

'Two boxes for ten bucks.' Cam handed over the money.

Jon decided on a 5.56mm XM177E2 submachine gun, in the vernacular called a Colt Automatic Rifle-15, or CAR-15. This was basically a smaller more compact version of the M16A automatic rifle that he had trained with in boot camp. The corporal told him that there would be ammunition at the LRRP base, but he got three twenty round magazines anyway and filled them.

'They have any 7.62 NATO cartridges there?'

'Pretty certain they do, but you better take a full can with you.'

'Man, we are warriors now. Take over the entire base,' Jon said.

Later that day, they were more pensive.

'Think we'll embarrass ourselves?' Jon queried.

'I don't think we'd better or we probably won't come back. Sort of focuses the mind.'

Two days later they had loaded up and were on their way to the chopper pads for the trip to the LRRP fire base. With full packs and belt-held gear, plus weapons and ammunition, they were under a considerable load. Though they were fit men, they were thankful to have had all the hard training in basic. They carried the 7.62 ammo between them to offload at the base as Cam's first supply.

They loaded all the equipment into the Huey chopper and climbed in. Two gunners manned .30 caliber machine guns in each of the open doors. Cam had never ridden in a chopper, but as soon as it took off he felt a freedom he had never experienced before.

The flight was uneventful, which was not usually the case they had been told. As they approached the LRRP base, Cam could see a one-story wooden building which turned out to be the barracks, and another smaller wooden building – the operations centre. A communications bunker, tents of various sizes, and a chopper pad also came into view. Sandbags were piled high around two thirds of the base.

No one seemed to pay any attention as they off-loaded. They did not expect a welcoming committee but thought that someone would at least have been present to see who they were. It did seem like the place was going to be as unfriendly as predicted. They walked a little way into the base and a man in camouflage fatigues finally noticed them. He signaled to other men, all of whom walked slowly up to them.

The men were dressed in filthy, striped camouflage fatigues and sported hair longer than army regulation. One had a bandanna tied around his head. Another spat a wad of tobacco and pulled out a packet of Redman to reload his cheek. They spoke.

'Dear God, look at all the shiny equipment. Makes my eyes hurt. Where are my sunglasses?'

'Why do we always have to look after babies? I am not changing any diapers.'

'Let's roll 'em in the dirt a little so they have that lived-in look. Makes me want to puke.'

The put-downs kept coming. Cam and Jon had to take it, but it took a lot of restraint on their part. Finally one of the men stepped forward.

'Knock it off. We're stuck with 'em for a little while at least. We've got orders to let them hang around and we're not supposed to kill them. If Charlie does, not our problem. Maybe we can make them cry and they'll run home to mommy.'

'Which future body bag stuffer is Campbell?'

'I am,' Cam said.

'Then the other pile of puke must be Daniels. I'm the top dog in this LRRP team and what I say goes. We're not real sure what we're supposed to do with you. I don't need any more recruits, and I sure as hell don't need regular army. I was vaguely told about something to do with a sniper team, but you two don't look like you can hit your own asses in the dark. You want to tell us what you think you're doing here?'

'We have orders to merge with a LRRP team and find out if a dedicated sniper team can be used to effect with them. Our orders come from Battalion. Dedicated sniper teams are intended to be an additional support and will have participation in certain types of missions.'

'So the sniper team would be snipers first, LRRP second.'

'That is my understanding. Maybe two of these men would like to learn to shoot.'

One of the men took a step toward Cam, but the staff sergeant put his hand on the man's chest and stopped him.

'You must mean learn to shoot across more distance.'

'If you say so,' replied Cam.

The staff sergeant looked Cam up and down.

'Look, it has attitude.'

'Not really, just explaining what we are here for.'

The staff sergeant's hostility level had not gone down one notch following the explanation and the rest of the men looked ready for a fight.

'You'll have to sleep someplace, but there is no room in our barracks. Try the supply tent; it's the one on the far right.'

The Rangers walked off without another word.

The tent was full of boxes and ammunition, with little room to lie down.

'Nice to be wanted so much. Seems the boys are not happy. We'll have to swallow and get on as best we can. I don't think the two of us could win a fight against six guys at one time. Let's go and see about some food.'

The staff sergeant was still not friendly, but he did point out where the Lurp food was stored and where they could get water, and left them to it. Cam was familiar with the dehydrated food packages from basic and they had their pick of the eight meals on offer. They found out the next day that the Rangers had A-rations – thawed steaks, frozen pork chops, chicken and fish were also available, as were canned vegetables and canned fruit. Since Cam was used to getting practically nothing as a child he was not upset.

The next day Cam went to find the staff sergeant.

'Sergeant, I need to test fire some of the new ammunition I've brought with me to see if it affects the precision of the sight on my 700. Where can I do that?'

The staff sergeant looked at Cam like he was crazy.

'Why in the hell do you need to do that? We use what we're given and never had any problem with it.'

Cam patiently explained the difference in precision between a sniper rifle and the standard M16A1 assault rifle, and that he always had to test a new issue of ammunition. He added that he would have to test again after every mission in case the sight had been knocked out of line by even the slightest degree.

'All right, I'll show you where you can shoot. I want to see this. The rest of the guys will come along too, just for the entertainment value when you screw up and miss.'

'Bring some binoculars,' Cam suggested.

At the area, Cam and Jon first glassed for targets. A distinctive V of a tree limb at 100 meters was chosen, and a similar one at 800 meters, which could not be seen without magnification. Jon read out the numbers and it was good to go. Cam told the Rangers what the targets were. He loaded up a round, closed his eyes for ten seconds and took a shot at the 100 meter target. It did not hit precisely where it was aimed. The Rangers started laughing. Jon read out the numbers and he made the corrections. The next shot was dead on.

Cam and Jon conferred on how to set up the second shot.

Cam turned to the Rangers. 'Are you sure you know what I'm aiming at for 800? Identify it for me.'

The shot went in perfectly. The Rangers shut up.

'I've got a longer shot for you, bet you can't do it again,' a Ranger said.

They glassed it, and Jon produced the numbers. The target, at 1003 meters, disappeared. No comments at all from the Rangers.

They repeated their sighting exercise until they were as sure as they could, that the ammo would produce the necessary results.

*****

CHAPTER EIGHT

The next day the team received word that a mission had been assigned – to commence within forty-eight hours.

The company commander and the operations officer were in charge of mission planning. They maintained liaison with control headquarters, issued orders for team insertion and extraction, and closely monitored the mission from the command and control helicopter. They approved or rejected changes to missions, and requests for extraction, and coordinated fire support when required. Every mission was different but preparation was reasonably constant.

A chopper arrived carrying the captain of G-3 operations. The captain would have received his information from division-brigade G-2 about the proposed area of operation – located by previous units in the area. They planned to engage the enemy and take a prisoner.

The captain called the staff sergeant over. Almost immediately the sergeant began to gesture and get in the captain's face. Cam could not hear what was being said but he was fairly certain it was about them, the sniper team. These really must be odd units if the sergeant can get away with talking to an officer in that manner, Cam thought.

'Goddamn it, captain, why does my team have to put up with these two? They can shoot, I admit that, but they have absolutely zero experience in the boonies. They will at best slow us down and at worst get us killed. I want them out of here right now.'

The captain looked him up and down. 'When the hell did you get to own this piece of real estate? As I recall, you were a new guy about ten months ago. Nobody complained about you, and you were just as inexperienced. It appears, against all odds and my better judgment, that you learned what you needed to know and have survived, at least up to now. You would do well to shut up, extend some professional courtesy and do your job. Battalion is real interested in the outcome of this exercise and that means it reflects on you directly. Remember that. Collect the team and that means the snipers as well.'

The staff sergeant did not like it but knew when to go along to get along. It was the Army.

The captain handed out maps of the area of operation and map overlays. The map showed the primary insertion landing zone, LZ, the route to march, escape and evasion points, and the pick-up zone, PZ. They discussed these until there were no more questions. The maps and overlays were covered in combat acetate to keep them dry in the field.

The captain and staff sergeant started toward the chopper for the mandatory visual reconnaissance flight which would take them over the area of operation to confirm or alter the two or three proposed landing zones, the route to take, and the extraction zone.

To confirm his point about the sniper team, the captain motioned Cam and Jon to board as well. Already on board were two sergeants from company command. These men had assisted in mission planning and the production of the map overlays. They would fly aboard the insertion and extraction helicopters, or in the command and control chopper, to aid in the locations of the landing and pick-up zones.

Cam studied the route of flight on his map overlay. He attempted, with moderate success, to see himself on the ground following the same route. He doubted he would get lost if separated from the team.

On return to base there was another team session where answers to new questions raised by the visual flight were worked out. The pilot of the visual, who would fly the team in, confirmed the insertion time. Air support for both insertion and extraction would be supplied by the division Air Cavalry Squadron, normally utility helicopters, a light observation helicopter and AH1G gunships. The G-3 team cleared off.

The staff sergeant approached Cam and Jon, and said, 'I got my ass chewed over you two and have been ordered in the strongest terms to allow you to go with us. I never like to be ordered around like that.'

'Let's cut the shit about this assignment,' Cam replied. 'We volunteered for this duty, same as any Ranger does. We have our orders just like you. We could be on regular sniper duty, not with a bunch of crazy-ass Tarzans with a death wish. We are not less smart or capable than you. We just lack your experience in this particular specialty. Help us learn what we need to as fast as you can, at least for your men's sake. Teach us what to do and we'll do it, but stop being such an asshole about it. For all you know we might just turn out to be useful.'

The staff sergeant and Cam eyeballed each other until the sergeant backed down. He walked with them to where the rest of the team was discussing the mission.

'Boys, the captain made it clear we have snipers on our team so get used to it. What were your names again?'

'Future body bag stuffer.'

'Pile of puke.'

'Yeah, yeah, not the best greeting. Really, what are they?'

'First Sergeant Cameron Campbell. Everybody calls me Cam.'

'First Sergeant Jon Daniels. Everybody calls me J.'

The next day mission preparation began. There were no odors on them, just normal sweat. The enemy could smell anything unnatural from a long distance.

They test fired and cleaned their weapons. This was the first time for Cam to use the shotgun and the .357 Magnum. He decided he had made the right choice for close-in work.

For weapons, they were all issued with M67 'baseball' grenades, M26A1 fragmentation grenades, colored smoke grenades, and Claymore mines which propelled small steel cubes in a 60-degree fan-shaped pattern to a maximum distance of a hundred meters. Some of the men took M14 pop-up mines. One man claimed a 40mm M79 grenade launcher and another carried a XM203 40mm grenade launcher mounted under the barrel of his M161A.

They took Lurp rations, radio batteries, and a medic bag that included two serum albumin canisters and a snake bite kit. The two radio operators carried out a communications check, and received call signs and frequencies for primary, alternate, aviation and artillery. Jon checked the two hand-held radios.

The Rangers had relented enough to help them pack their equipment properly. They also got help with noise suppression. All gear with the potential to make noise was taped or padded or both. Cam had to remove the slings and swivels from his Remington 700 and shotgun and tie parachute cord on them instead. No metal-on-metal contact.

They boarded the insertion helicopter. They applied camouflage to face, hands and any other exposed skin. Weapons were sheathed in strips of burlap or tape. Cam used his sniper rifle ghillie cover for the 700. Any shiny metal was taped over or painted.

The team leader made a final inspection of men and equipment at the chopper pad. When he was satisfied, the team loaded onto the slick with the team leader on the side from which they would exit.

The slick, a Huey helicopter with the seats removed to carry a large number of troops, lifted off at the same time as the helicopter containing the operations officer and one of the sergeants from company command. A utility Huey, a Bell OH-6A light observation helicopter, affectionately called a Loach, and a Bell AH-1G Cobra gunship, also lifted off. The slick flew high and fast. It made fake passes at landing zones far from the designated one, as well as some closer in, and flew outside the area of operation to add more confusion if the enemy were watching. The gunship flew low over treetops to try and draw enemy fire. When nothing happened, the slick dropped in fast, flared and hovered about a meter off the ground. The team jumped out and ran as fast as they could into the trees. They stopped after about two hundred meters. The gunship continued to fly close to the treetops for a few minutes until the slick was safely away. After a few more fake insertions the choppers formed up and disappeared

The team kneeled down in a tight circle, weapons pointing out and ready. They remained that way for forty-five minutes, listening for sounds of movement or anything else unusual. Eventually the Rangers began identifying natural sounds. Cam and Jon did not know what they were supposed to be listening for but gradually heard what they assumed were natural sounds like rustling in the leaf litter, leaves blowing on branches and trees creaking. Cam tried to catalog the natural noises as he went along.

The team fell into a file, five to ten meters between each man. The senior scout acted as point man, M16 rifle set on full automatic. The team leader was second. Throughout the march the leader would direct the scout with arm and hand signals to confirm compass headings and any new directions required. The senior radio operator was third in line, followed by the radio operator. Fifth and sixth were Cam and Jon. The last man in line was the assistant team leader.

Each man had been assigned a sector for observation, every other man looking only right or left into his sector. They carried their weapons at the ready and for Cam that meant his shotgun. He was still trying to distinguish natural and man-made sounds. Due to his hunting experience he detected small movements in the undergrowth. He was well aware that the experienced Rangers would spot something wrong much quicker than he would.

At first it was surprising to Cam how slow and deliberate the team moved, but they had time in which to cover the assigned ground, and the need for stealth was paramount. Cam and Jon imitated the Rangers as they walked, careful not to tread on twigs, brittle dead leaves, or anything else that might make a noise. They seemed to cover two hundred meters each hour.

The team kept to areas where vegetation was thickest, following natural terrain contours and making frequent small direction changes. Cam had another surprise with the plant life. Soldiers called it jungle, but it did not resemble the tangled, dripping rain forests, choked with shiny-leafed trees and impenetrable vines that movies had made them believe. It was thick brush mostly, giving way to open forest of what looked like tall deciduous trees with a thick canopy. From the air the canopy seemed one great carpet but on the ground it was comparatively open. Occasionally, bare areas gave way to grass, often taller than a man, and welcomed by the team since they needed as much cover as possible. Every effort was made not to mark the terrain. They placed their feet in the steps of the man in front.

They used mostly arm and hand signals for communication. If a spoken message was required it was whispered down the line. Every four hundred meters a rallying point was chosen should men become separated from the team. They halted for about five minutes every hour to rest, look and listen. The team members kept scanning their assigned sectors.

The team moved until twilight, and then selected a place in dense vegetation, well away from the route, to spend the night. They placed Claymore mines in a 360 degree protective arc and at places that could be approached by the enemy.

Each man sat with his rucksack touching the next man's, with weapons ready at his feet. While in a tight circle, they ate a Lurp meal. During darkness, hourly check-in 'squelches' were made by radio relay, by pressing keys on the handset for a short time so that the transmissions could be picked up by helicopters overflying the area. Some tried to sleep for two hours while others stayed alert until their turn came.

Cam thought about Pines and Annie's food, and his little apartment. He wondered if he would be able to settle down and resume studies at Yale after the experience. He knew this was only the first of many missions where he would kill. It made him even more aware of how apart he was from his fellow students.

The earth beneath his boots was alive with possibility, very little of it good. It hummed, waiting for a sacrifice. A squadron of Cobra gunships flew over like dragonflies, across the face of a full, bright moon.

As dawn approached they checked their gear again and recovered the Claymore mines. The second day was a repeat of the first with no enemy contact or sightings. At 17.30 hours the team reached the area where they hoped to stage an ambush and capture a Viet Cong.

Jon surveyed the land and said, 'There's land to the east that is slightly higher than the trail here, about 700 meters away, which is good for us. We'll set up a hide with as good a view of the trail leading in both ways. We should be able to see any dinks before the team will.'

They snail walked to the higher ground and chose a spot at the highest point. They put ghillies on and busied themselves with stacking brush around a depression in the ground until they were satisfied it looked like any other bush around them. Jon broke out his spotter scope and lay prone in the hide. Cam lay down next to him. They both did sight checks on their scopes to get familiar with the terrain they would be glassing. Other than a blind spot about 300 meters to the right, they had good views of the ambush zone – 714 meters away.

'Cam, before it gets too dark I'm going to run the numbers on the one meter area thirty meters to the left of the blind spot.'

Cam picked it out and focused on an imaginary human-sized target within the space. Jon gave the numbers and Cam made the adjustments. They would have to repeat the sighting again at first light because of different atmospheric and wind conditions, but they had a preliminary.

'You want to tell the team where we are and where we think we'll shoot so they can take positions out of the line of fire?' Cam asked.

'Good idea.'

Night closed in. Claymores were laid. Jon and Cam stayed prone and shifted positions so that each faced outward and could visually cover a 120 degree arc.

They were awake well before dawn. They assumed their firing positions. Cam checked his loads again. He had inserted five rounds into the internal magazine of the 700 just before dark after carefully cleaning each round. He jacked a sixth into the chamber. As soon as they could see the trail, Jon ran the numbers and Cam adjusted. They repeated every fifteen minutes. In between they glassed both ends of the trail to either side of the blind spot.

Jon was the first to see movement on the trail coming from the right.

'I've got visual.'

Cam waited while he counted and counted again.

'I see six in Viet Cong uniform. Weapons AK-47, nothing bigger, some grenades. In a file, but sloppy, relaxed, talking. ETA to ambush ten minutes.'

'Remember we want a prisoner if possible, wounded is acceptable.'

Cam kept the leader in the center of the reticule as he advanced down the trail. Jon ran the numbers for the ambush point again. Cam visually followed the leader into the ambush zone. The second man in the line caught up to the first and started talking.

'J, I've got a two for one here.'

'I see it. Take the shot.'

Cam took a deep breath, exhaled slowly and gently squeezed the trigger. He had sighted on the lung area of the man in full view, knowing that the force of the bullet would drive through soft tissue into the man walking next to him.

Both dropped. The remaining four froze for a second. Two of their people were down and they had not heard a thing. Survival instinct kicked in. One man dropped straight to the trail, face down. Cam sighted on the back of his head, which was all he could see. Another had dropped and crawled halfway into the bush beside the trail. Cam sighted quickly just above the man's hip and he stopped moving.

The other targets had made it into the bush. They could hear no gunfire. A Ranger radioed. 'We've got two prisoners, both only slightly damaged. No shots fired by us.'

'Copy, good work.'

'Do we want two prisoners?'

'Keep them for now. We can always dispose of one. G-2 might be happy to have two.'

A few minutes silence. 'What the hell actually happened with you? We've got four completely messed-up bodies; we didn't hear a thing.'

'Sniper magic is all I can say. Tell you about it later.'

Cam recounted later that the first kills were like being served a plate of adrenalin along with a tall frosty, foaming glass of clear endorphins, followed by a rich, dark, velvety dopamine dessert. Cam had experienced pleasure in the craftsmanship. He knew all about the psychological explanations for killing. Cam had become a professional in a profession as old as time.

They dragged the bodies off the trail, stripped and searched the uniforms, and took useful papers and maps. They covered over the blood and brains on the trail with dirt and leaves. Two of the team decided to take an AK-47 and ammunition for themselves, regardless of the extra weight. They buried the other AKs. Wooden nickels, with an Indian brave's head on one side and the company identification on the other, were placed on the bodies. The Rangers wanted the enemy to know who had done the damage.

Since there was still plenty of daylight, they decided to utilize the ambush again in case more targets wandered down the trail. The first six had been very relaxed, so they hadn't been expecting any activity. More might come along in the same frame of mind.

They did, at 15.20 hours. Jon counted ten Viet Cong. Cam had reloaded with five in the internal magazine and one in the chamber and had been sighting-in every fifteen minutes, so when targets came into the kill zone, Cam was able to drop another four. The rest disappeared into the foliage.

Cam and Jon watched the fierce firefight through their scopes. It was not possible to distinguish the team from the enemy. All they could hear were faint firecracker-like sounds. Cam hoped to see another target but none presented. It was all over in about fifteen minutes. Cam reloaded the 700 again.

None of the team was injured and the Viet Cong were dead.

*****

CHAPTER NINE

They remained another night in the open, and Cam wanted the team to move to another location as far away from the ambush as they could before dark. If there were any other Viet Cong in the area they were likely to have heard the firefight and come looking. The Viet Cong National Liberation Front had even set up the 272nd Regiment Reconnaissance Company to neutralize Rangers, all of whom had a bounty on their heads. A Ranger's head, face camouflaged, had to be brought back for the bounty to be paid.

The two prisoners were tied and gagged. Two of the team would take one end of the rope at all times to prevent them sprinting into the vegetation. The team made clear, by signals to the prisoners, that if they were trouble of any kind they were going to die. The prisoners were small, young and very frightened. The myth that Vietnamese were all experienced jungle fighters was wrong. The Vietnam People's Army (PAVN) and the National Liberation Front (NLF) conscripted most of their soldiers from cities, towns and agricultural areas – young men who had no more idea about guerilla fighting than the young Americans who were opposing them. They were also not as fanatical as they were made out. The majority wanted to go home and live a peaceful life, just like the American boys did.

The prisoners had to watch the bodies of their comrades being stripped and wooden nickels placed on them. Cam thought the spectacle would be a very effective way of lowering morale and quashing thoughts of escape.

That night the team formed a prone circle, facing outward with boots touching. Nothing happened so at first light they made their way to the loading and pick up zone (LZ/PZ).

The extraction bird radioed, 'Mark your location.'

'Roger, popping smoke.'

A green smoke grenade landed on the pick-up zone. The team on the ground did not tell the command and control helicopter what color smoke they would be using in case the enemy was monitoring the exchange and tried to confuse the extraction chopper with the same color.

'Identify smoke.'

'Glorious green.'

'Roger, green.'

The extraction bird, with a gunship escort, flew in at full throttle, flared and set down. They ran to the chopper. The first two aboard took charge of the prisoners while the rest kept guard.

As soon as they were back in base they made their way to Operations and Intelligence for debriefing, where they handed over the prisoners. Operations and Intelligence were happy to get them and the documents. The entire team was debriefed, first as a group and then individually. Every small aspect of the mission was discussed and recorded. The debriefing forms were filled out.

The G-3 Captain motioned for Cam to stay.

'First Sergeant, it looks like this mission was a total success. Fourteen confirmed kills, eight of which are yours. Very good shooting. I believe the Rangers will have a different attitude toward snipers on the team. Battalion will certainly feel vindicated in attempting this exercise. What type of missions can best use sniper skills, in your opinion?'

'First, sir, it seems obvious that snipers are not going to help much with purely reconnaissance missions. We're most likely to be useful in combat missions like this one. Snipers need to find a shooting platform a long distance from the rest of the team where they can see the overall setup and pick the most useful targets. Maybe situations like outpost reinforcement, ambush patrols, raids on known enemy camps, stay-behind to cover a larger US troop movement, that sort of thing. If the sniper team is always a part of the LRRP, spontaneous uses for them are bound to come up.'

'Yes, I agree. I'll recommend to Battalion that you and First Sergeant Daniels continue in your duties here while a decision is made for training Ranger members as snipers. Carry on.'

Cam went to find Jon. 'How you doing, J?'

'Okay, I guess. Quite a shift in perspective, killing people.'

Cam thought Jon might not be as calm as he was trying to make out. A strained look on his face meant he was likely trying to convince himself that it was acceptable to put into practice the skills he had learnt.

Cam felt nothing concerning the deaths. Nothing. No elation, no remorse, no desire to put excuses together about doing his duty. The times, the moment, demanded that he kill human beings, and he did. He was clever, quick and merciless, an effective machine for wartime. He had actually felt something about killing those beautiful pheasants, which were works of art. Too bad they were so tasty. But people, not a twinge. He was curious as to where any feelings were but had no desire to psychoanalyze himself. He knew, however, he was not a psychopath as he could extend some empathy to other people he liked who were in trouble, but sympathy he could not feel. He knew the consequences of his actions. For certain he knew there would be no problem in killing again, until his participation in the war was over. He was quite sure he could turn the machine off when his skill was no longer required.

The Rangers seemed to have forgotten the animosity they felt when the sniper team had arrived on the base. A good body count seemed to cheer them up.

The next day the G-3 Captain flew in again. He was more serious than the first time Cam had met him, and was in a hurry.

'Men, we have a pilot down in an area where the VC can find him. We think he's still alive because his last transmission was that he was about to pop the canopy. We want you to be airborne within sixty minutes after the briefing.'

A large amount of information was exchanged in a short time. The objectives were to get the pilot out healthy if he were alive or bring his body back if not. The enemy would be expecting a rescue mission and would set traps around the downed plane and certainly around the pilot, if they had him.

Everyone had kept their gear loaded up and ready to go, so drawing ammunition, food, water and applying camouflage were about all that was required. They inspected their gear for noise control. Then they were airborne. The landing zone was expected to be hot, so two gunships flew alongside.

On approaching the landing zone, the choppers drew fire. The gunships opened up, chewing the bush around the landing zone with red tracers. As soon as the slick touched down, every man hit the ground firing. AK-47 rounds cracked after them. Instead of a defensive ring, the team spread out in a cloverleaf formation, and kept moving until they were no longer being fired on.

Everybody was accounted for, no-one hit.

They split into two teams and traveled a parallel march line, the sniper team 1000 meters to the right of the Rangers. They communicated their progress by squelches with the radio handsets every two hundred meters; otherwise, radio silence except for an emergency. No conversation.

Cam had to restrain himself from moving too quickly. They stopped to look and listen, every twenty slow paces. VC were in the area, of that they were sure, and they wanted to avoid firing until they were in a position to rescue the pilot. It took what seemed like hours to cover a kilometer. After six hours both teams had reached the area where the pilot was believed to be.

Cam and Jon set up and began glassing. It was difficult to see any distance because of heavy undergrowth, so they broke down and moved to a spot indicated on the map that was two meters higher than the surrounding ground. It was little better but allowed them to see any movement if it occurred. After two hours they had seen nothing so they moved on and circled around to come back on the pilot's presumed location from another angle.

They came upon a slight mound, where again they put their eyes to a scope. This time luck favored them. They could see the pilot. He had a rope around his neck which went down his back, around his wrists, and tied off at his ankles. He was in a kneeling position but poorly balanced. There was blood on his forehead and down both cheeks, but he did not seem to have any gunshot wounds or other serious injuries. While they watched, one of three guards strolled over and kicked the pilot in the kidney. He fell over but was immediately set back on his knees. The guard kicked him again, this time in the ribs. He fell over again and was set back up. The guard walked back to his companions, laughing. All three laughed. Cam was not amused.

Cam and Jon looked closely at the VC camp. There were two fires burning, sending up thin tendrils of smoke. The Vietnamese were busy with normal camp life – mending uniforms, cleaning weapons, smoking, talking, all very relaxed. Cam was amazed that there were no perimeter guards. Surely they would have heard of the firefight that had occurred when the team inserted at the landing zone. It appeared not. Counting the men in the camp was not easy as it was in heavy undergrowth, but they decided there were at least twenty, spread out in one direction from where the pilot was tied up. Cam was not assured of full body shots on the farthest out due to the scrub. He did have a head here, an arm or part of a torso there, which would be enough to gauge where the kill-shot portions of the body were.

'Damn it, one of the sons of bitches just kicked the pilot again,' Jon said.

'Seems to be their little bit of fun to relieve the boredom. Don't worry. I've got plans for them. Here's what I propose to do to get him out of there. I'm going to start picking off the ones farthest out. They're separated from each other in that thick bush so they may go down without the next one knowing. I'll keep working back until one of them figures out they are under attack, but even then they won't know the direction of fire. They'll start taking up defensive positions, which is when team two should sweep in with grenades and shoot anyone still capable of firing back. When team two engages I'll kill the three guarding the pilot. Team two can sweep him up and get the hell out of there. Doesn't matter if we don't kill 'em all.'

Jon radioed to the Rangers and explained what was going to happen. Since team two was not in a position to see the VC Camp, Jon laid it out and suggested spots where the team could engage.

By this time it was getting dark. The attack would have to wait until morning when it was full light. They would need time to acquire targets as the men would have moved during the night. The Viet Cong would not travel at night so the pilot should be in the same place he was the day before. Jon would make sure of his location.

A tense night passed. It rained as though a dam sluice had opened up. Although soaked they could not move for fear of being discovered. It stopped raining. It rained and stopped again. They lay there as wet as swimmers, and their ghillies steamed. An occasional sound came from the camp, but no one ventured to where they lay. As dawn broke they were on their scopes.

'The pilot is in the same place and the same position,' Jon said. 'Still three guards. The pilot probably won't be able to use his legs well since he's been in that trussed-up position for at least three days. He'll be cramped. It's possible they haven't fed him very much or at all, so he may be weak. And he just got his good morning wake-up kick.'

'It looks like they're getting ready to move – packing activity going on. Time to reduce the population some,' said Cam.

The Rangers moved into attack positions. The Viet Cong were good targets for Cam at 997 meters so Jon gave him the adjustments. Cam put the reticule on the man farthest out and took his first shot. No one seemed to notice when he dropped. He moved to the next target, and the next, and still no reaction from the camp. The next targets were between 820 and 550 meters and Jon gave him the changes.

The atmospheric conditions were just right for a bullet to form its own vapor trail, visible as a tiny shimmering cone expanding from the point of the bullet. Cam watched each round seek its target.

Since no alarm had been raised, Cam took time to reload five rounds into the internal magazine and chambered a sixth. After hitting target number six, a man finally recognized the wet smacking sound of a large caliber round hitting solid flesh, and the element of surprise had run out. They could see the man as he looked around wildly to locate the source of danger. He cried out. The VC started shooting blindly into the vegetation.

Team two started using the thumper to lob 40mm grenades into the camp. Cam immediately swung on to the three guards around the pilot and had to take a head shot on the first, no other choice, followed by two quick torso hits on the other two when they started to run.

Two Rangers swooped in and cut the pilot loose, while the other two laid down covering fire. Magazines emptied quickly. The wounded screamed.

Screams were not important for Cam. He did not hear them. More important was professional identity. He could not let a sound interfere with his craftsmanship. He was like a professional shell. It had nothing to do with him personally. He was equipped to put an end to the sound. Unavoidable violence, a soldier's violence, was not the limit, Cam reasoned. Gratuitous violence was the limit – a price had to be paid for it.

The pilot, as predicted, could not walk, so the Rangers picked him up by his underarms and half-lifted, half-dragged him as fast as they could.

Team two had no reason to be cautious anymore and started in the direction of the pick-up zone as quickly as the burden of the pilot would allow. The sniper team lost sight of team two but had to move out quick. They needed to reach the pick-up area at the same time as team two, so they moved with much more speed than when they had wanted to remain undetected. The Viet Cong would most likely chase team two, the only Rangers they had seen.

The sniper team encountered no enemy on the way to the pick-up zone. Approaching it they saw movement in the brush. Was it team two? They froze and then coming into view were canvas boots, typically worn by Viet Cong.

Cam pumped all his shotgun shells into the brush, pulled the shotgun around onto his back and pulled out the .357 Magnum. He rotated the wire safety clip on a fragmentation grenade, pulled the arming pin, watched the arming lever fly off and tossed it into the undergrowth from where an AK-47, with its distinctive rattle, had answered fire. The detonation drove a Viet Cong into his line of sight and Cam plugged him in the chest with a .357 round – devastating in its sheer power.

When dispatching with the rifle Cam concentrated so hard on getting a certain kill with a torso shot that all the visual he got through the scope was watching the body take the shock. He didn't see an exit wound unless the body spun as it tipped over. Using the revolver under twenty feet gave a much different spectacle. Bits splattered.

Cam saw himself as the very symbol of death – a mortifier, the face of death. How liberating and what a responsibility.

Jon rapidly fired semi-automatic bursts. He popped a can of white smoke to cover their retreat, and they sprinted in the direction of the pick-up zone.

They and the Rangers seemed to have scattered the enemy but they knew the Viet Cong would regroup and come after them. A Ranger paused long enough to set two Claymores on tripwires. Cam took the moment to reload the shotgun, Jon his CAR-15, the Rangers their M16s, and they were on the move again. They signaled the choppers, by popping smoke that included a red to indicate danger, to swoop into the hot pick-up zone.

The sonic cracks of the bullets indicated the enemy had begun shooting from two different directions, both slightly back of them, and on each side. A Claymore exploded behind them and then another. Cam thought of those 6mm steel ball bearings blasted out by 0.7 kg of C-4 explosive up to 250 meters, the blast wave and fragments alone enough to kill or maim them at 100 meters.

They made contact with the chopper and relayed the areas for the accompanying gunships to direct fire.

Cam heard the distinctive whack of the extraction helicopter and the sinister buzzing of the gunships. Tracers chewed up the entire pick-up zone perimeter. The sniper team dashed toward the chopper, where team two, already on board with the rescued pilot, hauled them in. AK rounds buzzed the air while a gunship fired rockets into the muzzle flashes.

The men in the team were unhurt, but the pilot would need immediate medical attention followed by evacuation from the forward base to the battalion hospital.

*****

CHAPTER TEN

The next day was a rest period for the LRRP team. Cam and Jon cleaned their weapons and carried out scope maintenance. Cam applied corrosion protective oil that did not have to be removed before firing. He was familiar with the smell from hunting pheasants with Pines, and liked it. He rubbed the oil onto the exterior metal of his weapons by hand. The weapons had become a part of him, almost like a living thing.

'Cam, what the hell do you really think we are doing here? I mean, you've killed eighteen men so far, maybe more in the last firefight. Is that making a difference to the war?' Jon said.

'I think you had better include your participation in that tally. I couldn't have wasted so many if you hadn't given me the right spotting. You're just as responsible as I am. You having guilt problems?'

'I'm not really sure. Maybe. I know our duty is to kill the enemy. That's what combat soldiers do, but I wish I was convinced it was going to make a difference to the outcome. We've become exterminators of pests, Cam. Because that is what they are to us, pests.'

'J, I am not a spectator. Carrying the weapons and the skills to use them make me a player. This is done all the time. I'm used to it. It's part of the game. There is nothing outside of myself that has to be served.'

Cam paused, but with no response from Jon, said, 'J, snipers are for nothing but killing, you know that. A grunt may or may not know he's killed someone in a firefight, and pilots, especially the ones in B-52s, never see the destruction they cause. We look right down the scope at high magnification and see the bullet remove most of a head or punch through a heart. Sometimes we see the bodies spasm and quiver, which is one of the things I could do without, but that's how animals react to their sudden, violent demise.'

'All right, all right, but you're getting off my point,' Jon replied. 'What is this whole thing about anyway? We are supposed to prevent the North from taking over the South. Stop the spread of communism before it expands all over South-East Asia, that's what we are told. We don't seem to be winning, or at least we're not being let to win. After I was drafted I read a lot about World War II. That was full scale, all out war, the allies knew they had to win and did everything they could, and I mean everything. There was no pandering to civilians at home like now and no mercy for enemy civilians. In fact civilians in the States and England were all behind that war effort or at least had the sense to keep their mouths shut, not like that Jane Fonda bitch. I mean, why are we here if we can't do everything to win?'

'C'mon J, this is a politician's war. You know that. They created this war and we are here to clean up the mess. Vietnam would have been one country if we had not sent the French back in after the Second World War. They stuffed the country up. We divided the country in two, and now we support a corrupt South Vietnam. They want us to protect them but don't like it when we do. Damn civilians. Bunch of old bastards who send young guys like us out to do their fighting and dying for them. Their inflated egos and ridiculous ideas make them believe that they are somehow qualified to tell the world what to do, but that's what gets us in trouble. And I don't mean just Nixon and that kraut Kissinger. Kennedy and Johnson, and others, were just as corrupt.'

'What should we be doing then?'

'We should just let Ho Chi Minh take over and be their leader. If he wants to run a communist country, let him. It'll fall in time. Just look at the USSR, China, East Germany, and Romania. They worked out well, don't you think? I mean, if some poor schmuck on the street had the notions of grandeur and a Napoleon-complex like the politicians in the US, they'd be locked up in a nuthouse and never let out again. Hell, Hitler and Stalin were as crazy as three bedbugs tied together and those Jap generals were just as bad. These politicians are all mass murderers; they just typically get young boys to do the murdering.'

'So, we are sacrificing our lives for these power players?' said Jon.

'Anyone with even a minimum of education, and I suppose I should include myself in that category because I have read a lot, must subscribe to the fact that before and throughout recorded history, people have been killing each other, mostly to do with land grabs and religion. It is the favorite pastime of what we like to call ourselves the most advanced animal on the planet. Care to name another animal that kills its own species for fun?'

'Well, hell, Cam, why aren't we in Canada or conscientious objectors, or some other sort of coward? When we got our draft notices we just showed up for the brainwash.'

'It's too cold in Canada, even colder than Wyoming if you can believe that, and I don't speak Canuck. Anyway, there's no guarantee yet that those boys won't get put in prison if they get caught when they return to the States, although politicians being what they are, I bet all will be forgiven when this thing wraps up. I spent seventeen years in a sort of prison and I don't want to be looking over my shoulder, waiting to see if I have to go back to one. I think it's better to take my chances here and have a shot at a normal life once I'm back in the world. I mean, that's why I volunteered for sniper duty, more chance of staying alive. Didn't you?'

'I'm not sure anymore, Cam. Suppose so. But you never seem to have any emotions about any of this, you're stone cold. I admire it and am proud to be your partner, but I hope you're not getting to enjoy it.'

'I'm not enjoying it in the usual sense, but if I do something, I like to do it as best as I can and be proud to do it right. I think the Rangers actually get their rocks off and more power to them. Where else is a certain kind of personality going to get the chance to be allowed to hunt the most dangerous animal on the planet as much as he wants? I'm happy to be with them, they're professionals.'

'Yeah, me too,' Jon said. 'Don't you feel anything, though? Don't you worry you won't be able to put all this killing into a compartment on its own once you get back?'

Cam shrugged. 'Well, I'm not brooding on it. After I scratched the first kill off the slate, I figure more aren't going to make a difference. I mean, is it worse if you kill many as opposed to one? Don't think so. This is what I was trained for, the US Army at least wants me to do it and so I'm doing it. Who knows, I might get a twinge in the night from time to time, some little niggle in the back of my brain. But I'll put it in its place and it will just be what happened, like every other major experience in life. I won't be making any excuses but I won't be carrying any guilt either. If every bad thing that happens to you goes on your back like a boulder, that boulder is going to get heavier and heavier and, finally, you won't be able to carry it. You'll go down, probably before your time. I don't intend to go down. I've had enough to last me a lifetime. Only way is up, brother.'

Jon let it go and headed for his quarters, seeds of doubt still festering.

For a time the Rangers were assigned some reconnaissance missions which were strictly non-engagement unless fired on by the enemy. They located and plotted new trail systems, analyzed terrain and made map corrections, and surveyed enemy infiltration routes and base areas. The sniper team was not required.

Cam and Jon were assigned temporary duty with a Navy SEAL team who were working the mighty Mekong River. The G-3 Captain flew with them to another forward base camp and then on to a US Navy cruiser in the South China Sea, where they would hook up with the SEAL team.

'J, this cannot be good. Why in the hell would the Navy want US Army snipers when they've got all those cocky marine snipers who claim to be the best in the world? Are we getting the expendable stamp?'

'I just hope they don't make us work from a boat. If I had wanted to float I would have joined the Navy. They do get better food than us, though, and seldom come into close proximity with the enemy. Thinking about it, maybe I made a mistake being a ground-pounding grunt, Cam.'

When they landed on the Albany class cruiser, the G-3 Captain shook hands with a baby-faced navy lieutenant who had walked out to meet them. The captain introduced them to the lieutenant.

'This is one of our best sniper teams, First Sergeant Campbell, shooter, and First Sergeant Daniels, spotter.'

'Pleased to meet you, I think. This is one weird situation, using army snipers with the SEALs. It seems that all the marine snipers are on assignments from which they can't be retrieved before this particular SEAL team needs to go into action. Might as well get it over with and make acquaintance. Hope you aren't insulted easily, you know how it is between elite teams from different arms of the service.'

They climbed down two narrow ladders to what appeared to be a small briefing room. Four very large young men filled the space. Cam thought maybe they had different physical standards for SEALs and Rangers. The Ranger personnel he had seen were fairly small, agile, and wiry with more muscle strength than one would expect. These guys looked like they lifted weights all the time.

As the army contingent entered, the SEALs stood to attention and saluted the lieutenant and the captain. They were a chief petty officer and one each of first, second and third class petty officers.

'As you were. These are the snipers that we've borrowed from the Rangers for your upcoming mission.'

'Looks like two sleeves to us, sir.'

Several thoughts passed through Cam's mind, none with pleasant consequences for the SEALs.

'That will be enough of that kind of talk. You will extend every courtesy to these gentlemen who, I might add, did not volunteer for this duty. The Army has been kind enough to offer their services in order for you to carry out your mission. I am given to understand that they are among the finest at what they do. You will cooperate fully; they may save your life. They have killed a great many of the enemy in very dangerous circumstances.'

'Sir, yes sir.'

'Good. Go on and give these men the briefing about what they will be doing alongside you.'

The chief petty officer pulled a map onto the table. Cam could see it was of the Mekong Delta and the smaller rivers feeding into it.

'Gentlemen, we will be conducting a river assault interdiction along the mouths of these rivers that empty into the Mekong from Cambodia. Our mission there is to interfere with supply and troop movement as much as possible and to capture enemy supplies. We will lay some mined wooden structures that will appear to be flotsam and driftwood if seen from a boat.

'We do not want to enter into firefights with the enemy, if at all possible. That is where you come in. We will bring you to shore at predetermined locations where you will maintain a search for any approaching military on the ground or water. When you spot them, you will apprise us of the situation and make a recommendation as to whether or not you should take them out with sniper fire or let them continue on their way. Since we will be either in the water or on the river patrol boat, our situation at any moment will be taken into account as you make your recommendations. Questions?'

'Do you expect a lot of foot traffic along the river banks? Can we call in artillery and air support?' Cam asked.

'Actually, there is usually a lot of traffic, especially where we're going. They come out of Cambodia where they feel relatively safe, either transporting something or personnel movement. You should have a few targets. We can call air support, but no artillery is close enough to help.'

Jon wanted to know the radio frequencies.

After a few more questions to clarify the mission, the navy lieutenant adjourned the briefing and escorted the captain to the deck for transport back to land. Cam and Jon were left alone with the SEALs.

'You boys look mighty skinny to be the warriors the lieutenant said you are. We'd rather have marine snipers, the best in the world. Having to put up with you army brats makes us nervous.'

Cam bristled.

'Okay, tough guys, just shut up and get on with the job. You sure aren't making any friends here who are desperate to keep you from becoming fresh killed in action. You four look big enough. Maybe we should call you elephant seals. All they seem to do is lie around on the beach, grunt a lot, and mate with ugly cow seals in their harem. You follow that regimen pretty much? Why don't you be good squids and show us to the galley? Poor army brats like us don't get to eat real steak, fresh veggies and ice cream like you.'

'Whoa, it is small but feisty. Okay, let's cut the crap. We're counting on you to keep us from getting plugged. It actually is mess call, so we'll treat you to that steak and ice cream. Maybe a beer, too.'

*****

CHAPTER ELEVEN

After a meal, a shower and a few beverages, Cam and Jon slept better than at any time they had been in the country. And after a complete breakfast with real eggs, bacon, toast and fruit juice, they were on their way with the SEAL team to an advance base where the water transport was docked. The base was as primitive as their forward fire base. It turned out though that the SEALs had much larger caches of supplies, especially fuel and ammunition. They were also able to make more autonomous field decisions than the Rangers, not having been given missions with all the checks and restraints.

They joined a river patrol boat, PBR, manned by four SEALs. A fiberglass, thirty-one foot long boat with an eighteen inch draft, it could go after sampans in shallow rivers. It was radar equipped, with twin .50 caliber machine guns forward, one .50 aft, a grenade launcher and an M60 machine gun for good measure. Top speed was twenty-five knots, so it could out-run and out-maneuver anything the Viet Cong had. Cam was relieved to see it was a boat that meant business. The six of them reported to the tactical operations center on base to get final instructions, one of which was that their areas were free fire zones. He could shoot any target he wanted, no identification required.

Cam and Jon checked each other's gear, put paint on each other and wrapped up for noise control. They stored their heavy gear on board until it was time to hump it into the jungle. Then they were on the water of the wide Mekong. A rather pleasant trip up river, Cam thought, and in better times he would drop a line and see what bites.

The patrol boat motored along for about two hours with one quick stop so the machine guns could be test fired.

'We're at the first drop off for you gravel crushers. Check coordinates,' one of the SEALs said.

The sniper team confirmed where they were and set up check-in intervals. They would report when they had reached a good vantage point for observation of both the river and its banks. Cam wanted a spot at least 1000 meters from the river and indicated to the SEAL team leader where on the map he thought this would be.

The patrol boat was driven as close to the east bank as it could get, but they still had to wade through thigh deep water.

The bank was thickly wooded, a good place to hide or stage an ambush. Cam and Jon dropped to one knee and waited for forty-five minutes to look and listen. With nothing other than normal bush sounds, they started the slow walk to their first hide, which took three hours. They could see reasonably well in both directions and had a clear view of the patrol boat. The SEALs were busy with something in the water close to the west bank. Nothing happened for a day and night. They returned to the river and transported further upstream.

The sniper team had no trouble getting into their second hide. Jon glassed upstream and Cam glassed down.

'Cam, I've got a big pile of what looks like flotsam and logs, but it's going too straight, it's not moving as the current carries it.'

Cam locked on and looked. The forest trash was too well placed.

'J, in the left lower quadrant, I think I see an arm and maybe a section of shoulder, what do you make of it?'

'Could be, but could be just a branch. Why don't you put one in anyway, good way to sight in if nothing else. Numbers coming and I'll let the squids know.'

Cam put the reticule on the target and squeezed off. The target jerked. A hand and lower arm fell out of the brushwork, made a fist and went limp. Jon was on the radio to the SEALs, three of whom manned the machine guns with the fourth steering into the channel in the direction of the log raft.

Cam put four more into the raft at intervals along its length at the same height as his first shot. The raft abruptly began to change course, much more controlled than a drifting pile of brush. A rifle barrel appeared and AK rounds raked the east bank to no effect as no one was there. Jon kept up a running commentary to the SEALs, who moved in close enough to put the forward .50 machine guns into action. The rounds chewed up wood and leaves. Cam reloaded. The raft made for the east bank and struck it hard. A black clad figure jumped into the waist deep water, but Cam removed his head before he made a step. Cam waited for more to jump, but none did.

The patrol boat had come close enough to fire a grenade, which made a dull thump but did not seem to do much damage. Smoke wafted out. More .50 caliber rounds went in and one of the SEALs prepared to board, carrying a 12 gauge combat shotgun, which he stuck between the branches and fired. No answering fire, so a second SEAL jumped onto the raft. Both crouched down and waited. After a few minutes they parted some of the foliage and looked in.

'We've got five dead Vietnamese in here, and that looks like all of them. There's one floating in the water so I guess you got that one at least, Cam. We're going in.'

The SEALs disappeared into the brushwork. Two minutes passed.

'Jackpot, gents, we've got a sampan full of drugs and medical supplies, probably on the way to areas around Saigon. We're going to tie this boat to the bank and set some C-4 around the place. You two keep a sharp eye out for any slopes coming to investigate.'

'We haven't seen any foot traffic following on either bank, but will make certain.'

The explosive was handed off the patrol boat and the SEALs got busy placing and arming it. A few boxes containing morphine were handed on to the boat. When all four were back on the patrol boat, they detonated. The result was a less than spectacular explosion of wood and debris, which carried quickly downstream.

They glassed the banks and trail for another two hours before calling the patrol boat to pick them up. When they got on board after wading waist deep, there were grins and back slaps.

'Maybe you two worthless army dickheads can be taught how to do it. I guess we'll keep you. We owe you some drinks when we get back. Tactical operatives at the base camp will be ecstatic.'

They moved farther upriver toward the next and last spot where the SEALs had to lay mined obstacles, which meant that three of them would have to be in the water for a sustained length of time, leaving one on board for weapons backup. Cam and Jon did the usual and reached their hide without incident. It was carpeted in what looked like spongy, slightly damp moss, soft to lie in.

After six hours the SEALs radioed their estimated time to completion as one hour. Jon called movement.

'Shit, Cam, Viet Cong moving north to south, fast. Platoon strength at least. Light weapons, but I see two RPGs. They will be in secure target range in fifteen. You think this might be payback for the sampan?'

'Doesn't matter, they'll still sight the patrol boat and they won't pass that up. Tell the squids I'm going to start dropping as many as I can. They'll scatter in the bushes, but it may be enough to slow them down so the patrol boat can get going. We need to get moving after I lose sight of them.'

Cam started making shots. The Vietnamese were in file, so he took five before they started to scatter. He took the time to reload even though he thought he probably wouldn't use the 700 again.

'No point in being sneaky now. Let's get the hell out of here.'

Running with a full rucksack was near impossible, but they weren't going to leave gear behind. Cam had swung his shotgun around and Jon switched to full automatic. About a hundred meters from the bank, they could see the patrol boat with about five hundred meters to go before they could wade out and climb aboard.

AK rounds cracked past them. Cam started pumping shells, hoping the wide spread of buckshot might hit pursuers. Jon also fired as he ran, having a hard time changing magazines as he went, and going empty fast. Cam pulled out a fragmentation grenade, armed it and threw it back over his shoulder without looking back, then did it again. He released the Python, the six shots it carried now his only defense. Rounds still whipped the bushes around them.

They were almost to the water when the SEALs opened up with the twin .50s and M16s. Cam slammed into the water first, Jon so close he almost pushed Cam under. They floundered toward the patrol boat, the weight from their rucksacks and weapons slowing them. The SEALs came on toward them in the face of withering enemy fire, reached down and hauled them in.

'Watch it, they've got RPGs.'

The boat slammed on to full power and skated away from the shore, aft .50 machine gun busy. Cam struggled to get the 700 back around, and brought the scope up to his eye. He could see a RPG being aimed at them so he shot the man, who reflexively pulled the firing mechanism on the grenade. It exploded in the water away from the boat. The enemy were now lining the bank and shooting fast. He picked off two more before hitting the bottom of the boat.

Catching his breath, he looked over and saw Jon doing the same.

'You two all right, you hit?' a SEAL called out.

Cam didn't feel hit but undertook a tour of the places he could see and reach on his body. When he touched the small of his back he felt something soft and squishy, like an extra layer of insulation. He felt the same thing when he reached over his shoulder. He dropped the gear and took his blouse off.

'Christ, Cam, your back is covered with leeches. It's disgusting.'

Cam could see leeches clinging to his front, too. They must have been in the wet moss where they were lying down, Cam thought. Jon's back was also covered with them.

'Get these blood suckers off now.'

Two SEALs began pulling the leeches off. Their mouths left circular welts that quickly oozed blood. Both started to tremble and sat down. The SEALs kept wiping them down and could not conceal the concern on their faces. The pilot revved up to full speed so as to reach base as fast as possible.

A medic was waiting at the dock and examined them. 'Jesus! That is undoubtedly the worst case of leeches anyone has ever seen. Maybe two or three get on board but nothing like this. Come along, I'm going to get you off to sick bay.'

The sick bay wasn't much, but it did have clean sheets on the cots.

They were grateful to lie down although the sheets stained quickly with their blood. Cam could see the medic talking to the SEALs.

The medic entered the sick bay and said, 'Well, they shouldn't have pulled those leeches off you. They should have burned them off. But hell, I know all of you were trying to get them off as fast as you could, so tough luck. See, the thing is, leeches in South-East Asia and Australia, so I'm told, carry a kind of virus that goes right to the nerve endings in the skin where they sit and wait for the right circumstances again. When that happens, they cause a nasty rash that takes a while to go away. It's not life threatening, just uncomfortable. Some guys never get it.

'Unfortunately, when they pulled off these leeches, more saliva entered the wound, giving you a double dose of the virus. What I'm going to do is give you a good scrub with an antiseptic soap and then put on some light bandages. We'll get you back to the cruiser as fast as possible where they'll want to give you at least a unit of blood. With all those leeches sucking on you for a few hours you probably need at least one unit. This is one story to tell your grandkids.'

Was there no end to this? Cam thought. They could nuke this place and put it out of its misery. The place was just a hole. No civilized person was going to miss it.

The sick bay on the cruiser proved a slice of heaven. They each received a unit of blood and antibiotics. The doctor wanted to keep them a couple of days to see if there were any secondary effects, which there were none.

They enjoyed the sea air and fresh food, and the beers in the mess restored their vitality.

'J, let's not tell the Rangers we were wounded by leeches. It'll just lead to an endless series of bad jokes and probably nicknames we don't want. I mean, it is a little embarrassing.'

'I'm with you on that, Cam. Snipers sucked dry by leeches. I can just see the headline.'

Sooner than they wanted, they were back on the LRRP forward base, where the Rangers seemed glad to have them back. Even though the Navy had spent time grilling them, the G-3 and G-2 captains wanted to debrief them again. They were especially interested in enemy movements that had come from Cambodia. They found out why the next day. They and the Ranger team were told to saddle up for some play time in Cambodia.

*****

CHAPTER TWELVE

They moved over the border into Cambodia on 26 April 1970, five days before the regular troops started to move in. President Nixon had authorized the South Vietnamese incursion, aided by American ground and air support.

The North Vietnamese had used Cambodia as a safe haven from which to launch attacks and move materiel to the South. The US Army discovered huge caches of weapons and ammunition in Cambodia that included vast quantities of anti-aircraft ammunition, rifle rounds, rockets and communications equipment. These were turned over to the Cambodian army. The North Vietnamese responded to the loss of their Cambodian supply route by seizing towns in Laos and opening up a wide corridor along the length of the Mekong River system back into Cambodia.

The LRRP team was assigned to normal duty, if there was such a thing for this elite group. Reconnaissance behind the lines was paramount to keep the regular soldiers informed of enemy movement and their whereabouts, but at the same time search and destroy was sanctioned as long as the primary task was not compromised. The sniper team accompanied the Rangers on missions to lend fire power to any contact situation.

During one excursion they had discovered a VC camp, possibly a temporary headquarters or supply camp. Their first surveillance revealed movement of men, medicine, food and arms into the surrounding area. They needed to find out more.

The LRRP team made their way to the location of the VC Camp and waited, watching movement. They observed three shelters, called hooches, made of thick mud and over a meter high with brush across the openings. No extra camouflage had been used, so it seemed the Viet Cong were relying on the thick canopy of mixed deciduous trees to prevent them from being seen from the air.

'Here's how we'll play this,' the team leader said. 'Cam, J, go set up where you want, just let us know where you are. The rest of us will split into three teams of two. Each team is assigned a hooch. At dusk the slopes eat the evening meal, sit around smoking and are not very alert. Cam, shoot as many as you can on my signal to set up panic. When they start moving, the rest of you toss a frag grenade into the compound and follow with a willy peter phosphorus grenade into the hooch. Spray the area as you go in. It would be good to get a prisoner, but paper is required by G-2. Cam, J, go get placed.'

Cam and Jon stopped at 1000 meters from the camp and radioed they were in position. They waited five hours until dusk.

'J, we're ready to go. Get Cam to drop a few.'

Cam singled out three definite targets and two more in reserve if he had enough time. He hit the three with torso shots, but after these toppled, the rest went for weapons and took defensive positions. The VC were not sure where the threat was coming from, and kept shifting. The fragmentation grenades went off, and the sniper team saw the Rangers go in. Bright, yellow muzzle flashes shone out in the deepening gloom. A white phosphorus grenade exploded in each of the three hooches with a distinctive crack. White smoke, peppered by tiny, glowing white stars, billowed upwards. Cam dropped one more before they scattered into the undergrowth.

The LRRP team took defense positions in case any of the routed VC decided to counter attack. The Rangers approached one of the hooches and stopped on either side of the entrance.

They smelled violent death and an odor of what seemed like barbequed meat. The bodies were smoking as the molten white phosphorous pellets burned deep into flesh – burning until the metal was depleted. No survivors. They stomped on a few embers so the hooch would not catch fire. Then they searched for items of intelligence.

The team did the same with the other hooches. In the third hooch, two VC were rolling around in agony from the phosphorus melting into them. One of the wounded men was hurt by the burning metal but seemed to show no other wounds. The other had been hit by an M16 round and did not look good for survival. They were both dragged out to open ground. Glassing the battle scene through the scope, Cam counted eighteen dead.

'There is a tremendous amount of valuable stuff here,' the team leader said. 'I've seen rice, arms, ammunition, medicine and other items. We can't deal with all this ourselves. We need some G-2 people in here to wrap it up and take it home.'

The LRRP radio operator told the sniper team to look for a landing zone on their way back and also call base with a request for help in removing the items.

Cam and Jon, spooked by having to make their way carefully back in the dark, made even more stops than usual to listen. Some of the VC had escaped and were undoubtedly still in a position to attack. They found an open area for a chopper to land, deciding they would reassess the area in the morning.

Although their position was well away from the combat area, it was likely the enemy would regroup and come after them, but nothing happened. They spent a tense night without sleep. In the morning the Rangers arrived and examined the proposed landing zone. It was tight on landing space but would have to do.

'Let's see what the fly boys can do,' the team leader said. 'We'll take up a position around the landing zone to keep the Vietnamese out. Tell them to bring gunships but not to fire unless we request it. We want to be extracted immediately, so they should bring regular army to protect the area.'

The leader looked hard at the prisoners. 'Cut the prisoners' legs loose. This one can walk, but we'll have to carry the other one. What is it, 400-500 meters? Easy.'

At the landing zone they set up a perimeter. The chopper landed and they piled in with the prisoners, and were away.

One prisoner was still smoking. Nothing could be done for him; he would just have to burn out. The medics could help him once he got to base, at least give him morphine. The other prisoner groaned, and blood spurted up in a fountain from his inner thigh.

'Shit, Sarge, I think some willy just burned through his femoral artery. Help me put some pressure on it.'

It was no use. It looked as though the phosphorus had taken a section of the artery about an inch long. After about five minutes, the man quivered twice, and a few moments later, lay dead.

The pilot radioed the base to see if they wanted the body brought in. They didn't. After a final search of clothing, the body was tipped out of the chopper door at 800 meters. G-2 was well satisfied with the live prisoner and the large haul of goods from the enemy base.

Cam and Jon had a briefing with the G-3 captain, who said, 'We're on our way out tomorrow to whack as many NLF officers as we can. Apparently there are some who are on the 'most wanted' list. Somebody's seen a few of them in Cambodia and we're on our way to meet and greet. You guys get to have no fun because you're not coming along.'

'Bullshit we're not,' replied Cam. 'You need us to make sure you don't get surrounded when you set up. I'm going right now to get the team on the detail.'

'Hey, up to you, we won't object. We get tired of looking at each other after a couple of days. J is not as cute as you seem to think he is.'

Maybe it was the team's record of success, but the officers were persuaded to let them come along. Cam and Jon were relieved to have them watching their backs.

The next day the team was inserted and began the hike to the last place the VC officers had been seen by a reconnaissance team. Creeping along, they came upon three heads of Asians on short spikes. It was hard to tell whether they were Cambodian or Vietnamese. The heads were fairly fresh, probably on the spikes for about thirty-six hours, and started to look like melted candle wax because of the heat. Maggots had already burrowed through the skin, peppering the face.

The spiked heads reminded Cam of the stories he had heard about cannibalism in South-East Asia. The Cambodians had enjoyed cutting out the livers of slain enemies and eating them. They had been doing this for hundreds of years and were probably doing it right now as a benefit from the allied incursion into Cambodia.

The team reached the specified coordinates without incident. Cam and Jon set up on a ridge overlooking a small creek in a valley, a natural corridor for men on foot. The Rangers set up at intervals around the observation post but no VC showed up that day.

Jon was the first to see movement early the next morning after the Rangers had dispersed to their defensive positions. Cam glassed the area and spotted three men walking quickly down the creek bank, away from the sniper team but diagonal to them, giving excellent shot exposure. The men were dressed in PAVN uniforms with officer tabs. Jon reported contact to the Rangers who dispersed to scout for any stragglers.

For Cam, the main question was which one of the Vietnamese to shoot first. The first shot would definitely be a kill, but the other two men might make it into the forest along the creek if they were fast enough, making sighting difficult. Cam had a gut feeling about one of the men who was taller than the other two. The officers had made themselves highly visible as targets. Why be so reckless as to advertise their presence? It didn't add up for Cam. He decided to take the tall man first. It was an easy shot at 907 meters. He was able to drop another man, but the third was quick and made it to cover before Cam could chamber another round.

Jon waited with Cam as they glassed the area for more VC and for the Rangers. Two Rangers approached the tree line where the last VC had entered. Within minutes they came into view, dragging a uniformed body between them. They had seen the VC trying to arm a grenade and had riddled him. The correct decision had been made about getting the tall man first. He was an older man, still fit. Papers confirmed, if not his exact identity, his seniority. He had a Czech-made Makarov 9mm semi-automatic pistol, the type carried only by senior officers and communist party officials.

A chopper picked them up. With no decent landing zone the bodies were winched on board with a sling. The sniper and LRRP teams were told to head toward an extraction zone twenty kilometers to the southeast. All normal extraction procedures would be followed. A 'hot' pick-up was not expected.

The team humped it to the landing zone when the point man suddenly crouched and motioned for the rest to do the same. They had stumbled on a nest of VC. None of the Rangers had registered any movement during the last look-and-listen stop. They had to engage because the enemy had seen them.

Cam brought his Ithaca around front as wild firing broke out. Jon had already run through one magazine and was jacking in another. Cam began firing shotgun shells at specific targets.

The buckshot made smacking sounds as they hit, like a baseball bat hitting a side of beef.

Cam dropped another VC that had been taking aim at a Ranger but didn't hear the right thumping sound that meant a solid kill. Cam ran over to finish the job, which he did, but out of the corner of his eye he caught movement. As he turned his head, something solid hit him across his left eye and cheek. He felt bone go and knew he was gone if he failed to recover quickly.

A Vietnamese had hit him with the muzzle of an AK, instead of the stock which could have killed him instantly. Cam had little recollection of what happened in the next minute. He blacked out for a few seconds and regained consciousness to see that he was on his hands and knees with blood dripping steadily from his face and nose. Half a meter away was a small, dead VC with his brains leaking out.

Cam could not clear his head or stand up. He looked up to see Jon staring at him and could tell from his face that he was badly wounded and might be dying.

'Shit, Cam, you got him good, but he got you, too.' The medic for the mission pulled out the field surgical kit and pressed a compression bandage against his face.

'Can you hold this by yourself?'

Cam tried and could. There was a lot of blood.

'Jesus, we've got to get you to a doc and a dust-off. Can you stand up?'

Cam tried but was not able. He sat for a few more minutes and tried to get his bearings. His consciousness kept flickering in and out. Finally, he thought he might be able to stand up, with help.

'Give me your hands. I don't think I can do it by myself.'

Jon gave him a hand and pulled him up, putting his arms around him to steady him. His gear came off. They tried to get his weapons off, but he resisted.

'No, by God, you are not taking my weapons off me. I need to fight. I need to kill 'em all.'

'Cam, we need to get as much gear off you as possible. You're in bad condition, you can't fight anyway.'

'By God, I can fight. Don't you tell me I can't fight, you son of a bitch. I'll fight you right now. Come on, you son of a bitch.'

Jon spoke quietly. 'Cam, tell you what, how about you keep your . 357? You can fight with that. We've seen you do it. C'mon, you don't need any other weapon right now.'

Cam accepted that.

'Okay, we got to get out of here. I'm going to call for band-aid and a bird.'

Jon realized the gravity of the situation.

'Cam, you got to walk out seventeen klicks to get to a good zone to get picked up. Can you do that? They won't come and get us here. I'm sorry as hell, but we can't give you any morphine now. You have to try to walk, and you won't be able to do that full of magic juice.'

Not have much choice, Cam thought. Areas of his face started to hurt badly after the initial shock, and he was unable to focus on anything.

Without speaking, he began to move as best he could. Jon supported him, but it was difficult to keep him upright. Eventually he found a semblance of balance and moved slowly.

He would never fully remember how he made it; he was severely concussed. He did remember finally reaching the landing zone. He remembered watching Jon fix the needle to a quarter-grain morphine syrette, slip the needle into a blood vessel in his arm and roll up the syrette like a toothpaste tube to push the morphine in.

Cam vaguely remembered the Huey landing and climbing aboard. He could not hear anything because of the rotor noise. Jon grabbed his hand hard, and then smiling, gave a thumbs-up. He would be all right. The LRRP team came up and each man shook his hand. The chopper lifted off, and he drifted blissfully into unconsciousness.

*****

CHAPTER THIRTEEN

On the ground, Jon and the LRRP team waited for their own extraction chopper and watched the one with Cam on board disappear.

The helicopter that had picked Cam up was a utility Huey. Since it was not equipped for evacuation of wounded as normal duty, they had laid him on the deck with no restraint, so he rolled from side to side.

Cam awoke as the chopper flared into the forward base. Waiting on the pad was a proper dust-off bird, a Bell UH-1H Huey, which could carry three stretcher patients, a trained medical corpsman and two pilots. Crews who manned dust-off choppers routinely flew into hot zones to retrieve wounded. The choppers were generally unarmed, although a few carried an M-60 machine gun on a lanyard.

Cam dragged himself to a sitting position and tried to regain balance. He rocked back and forth. The medic from the dust-off ran up and kneeled down beside him.

'All right, let's see what we've got here for fun.'

The medic recognized the symptoms of concussion. He looked at Cam's dog tags.

'Sarge, I'm a medic on the dust-off that's going to take you to the evac hospital. You have some severe injuries to the left side of your face. I need to wash off some of the clot to get a better look at what the damage is. Do you need another jolt of morphine to make the pain go away while I do that?'

'No, I don't need any damn morphine, and you leave my face alone. Who the hell are you anyway?'

The medic explained again and what had happened. He had to do this two more times before Cam seemed to realize what was being said.

'My face is injured? Let me look, how bad is it? I can't see much out of my left eye, is it gone?'

'No Sarge, your eye is still there. I think you have some breaks in the bone of your eye socket which is why you can't use that eye very well. You definitely have some breaks in your cheekbone, and your nose is mashed up pretty good, too. Will you let me wash some of the blood off now so I can get a better look?'

'Okay, but don't press on it so hard. Hurts like a bitch. Where is my team?'

The medic cleaned most of the blood off his face, and reassured him about his team.

'Sarge, the only thing I can do right now is put a fairly tight bandage on the left side of your face to keep any of the bone breaks from shifting. I'll have to cover your left eye, too, so don't get excited when I do it. Take it easy now and stay still. That will help me.'

The medic wrapped a bandage around the injuries. 'I'm finished now, no more poking you. I'll get a couple of the men and we'll put you on a litter and carry you to the dust-off.'

Cam tried to stand up but couldn't. The medic caught him.

'We will be carrying you if you don't calm down. Here, just lean on me until I see you can at least keep your balance.'

After a few minutes, Cam gained his balance enough for the medic to help him into the chopper.

'Here we are, Sarge. You get in there and lie down. I don't want you tipping over and hurting yourself even more. You crack that face again and you might have to go through life frightening dogs and small children. No more cursing me, you just get in there. We are on the way to the 93rd evacuation hospital at Long Binh so settle down and enjoy the ride.'

Cam had little recollection of the ride. A medic met him after they touched down, and he was placed in a wheelchair.

'Right, Sarge, welcome to the 93rd evac. These gents will take you to admitting. I know you will make a fuss about being carried on a litter, but you will be seated in this wheelchair for your ride. I think you'll come out of this in fine shape. Good luck.'

Cam was wheeled in front of a middle-aged NCO who chewed on the stub of an unlit cigar. An attendant handed him a file detailing his injuries.

'Head and facial injuries sustained in hand-to-hand combat. Well, from the looks of you, you probably won't die right away which makes my life easier. Do not make it more difficult by proving me wrong and falling over after I have processed you, because then I have double the paperwork, although it is easier to process a stiff than a live one.'

Welcome back to the real army, Cam thought.

A nurse took over and steadied him with a firm grip on his elbow without making it seem he needed the support. He made it to an empty, clean bed.

'Here's your home for the next few days, Cam. Don't take this wrong but you're pretty ripe. Maybe you'd like to get out of those jungle fatigues and take a shower. The showers and toilets are down there. I'll help you. There is a stool that I want you to sit down on while you shower. You won't lose your balance that way. While you clean up I'll bring you a bathrobe and a clean set of hospital issue.'

After he had soaped and rinsed off twice he shuffled back with the nurse.

'Get in bed please so I don't have to worry about you wandering off and getting into trouble. You can put your duffel bag underneath, it will be safe. I'd prefer it if you'd put that weapon into the duffel. You don't want to let an officer see it. They should have made you hand it over at admission.'

Cam put it in the duffel and hoped they would not mention it again.

'It doesn't bother me. I see in your records you've been with the Rangers and we all have some experience with you guys being a bit peculiar about a few things. I imagine I may learn about a few more peculiarities that you have. Now, do you want an aspirin?'

'Yes ma'am, five should help.'

'I'll give you two and see how you go. The doctor will be coming around in about an hour to make his bed checks. He'll give you a physical, and then we'll see what your routine is going to be. I'm going to take off your bandages so he can get a good look at your face.'

The nurse slowly removed the bandages. 'Goodness, you have a few places that are bleeding again. Sit still and I'll wash the injured areas. Here's a compression bandage, hold it on your face when I'm finished. The doctor should be along any time.'

Cam realized, for the first time with a more or less clear head, that whatever way they were going to fix him was going to take a lot longer than he had hoped. He dozed lightly, and the doctor woke him up.

'Ah, Sergeant Campbell, let's have a look at your wounds.'

The doctor pushed some magnifiers he was wearing on his forehead to his eyes and took Cam's face between his thumb and forefinger, turning it so he could get a close look at the left side. He didn't prod, just looked.

'Well, now, you have a cheek bone that's broken in at least three places. Your nose, and I suspect the sinuses behind it, are mashed pretty well, and some part of the bone that makes up your eye socket is at least cracked. Do you see one image when you look at my finger or two?'

'Two images, like I can't focus properly.'

'Move your left eye, up, down. Now back and forth.' He could not move the eye completely around.

'I suspect you have a medial wall fracture to your eye socket, or the orbit as it is called. Your symptoms, and the fact that your eyeball is recessed in the orbit, indicate that kind of fracture. Fixing your eye will require delicate surgery which we can't do here. Your cheekbone will also require surgery and your nose will as well. That's the bad news. The good news is that in my opinion you will regain full use of your eye and you may not be badly disfigured. More good news is that the surgery will need to be done by a specialist and that means a ticket back to the world. Your war is over. All we can do for you now is to bandage you back up so nothing shifts, and keep you as comfortable as possible with light doses of Demerol. Don't take any more aspirin. We'll put no aspirin on your chart.'

Cam didn't know how he should feel about this news. He decided to be content because he could return back to Yale and study for his degree. He had done his duty and it was time to get on with his life without anyone else telling him how to live it.

Three days later they loaded him on to a Lockheed C-141A Starlifter, one of the fleet taking wounded to the States. The aircraft had room for eighty litters, and seats for fifteen medical corpsmen or nurses. All sorts of wounded were brought on board, ranging from very serious to those like him who could walk. Spread out were intravenous poles with bags and bottles of blood, serum and clear fluids.

After they were in the air he was able to get up and walk the access aisle between the litters as long as he did not interfere with the medical personnel. Otherwise, he just lay on his litter and tried not to think about the operations he would have to endure. Looking at some of the other casualties made him realize how lucky he had been. Most of the wounded would never have a chance to live a normal physical life again. Limbs missing, organs shattered and removed, and more pain than anyone should bear. A waste of young men and their potential, Cam thought. The flight seemed endless. Cam walked as much as he felt he could without being a nuisance. Suddenly he felt a hand grab at his arm.

'Hey buddy, can I talk to you for a minute? I need to talk to somebody.'

Cam wasn't sure what the protocol was but couldn't see any harm in it. Lots of the guys probably wanted to talk if they were conscious.

'Sure man, what's on your mind?'

'You get shot in the face? Gonna lose the eye?'

'No, I'm told I won't.'

'You're lucky then.' The man started to weep. 'The doc told me they're gonna sew my asshole shut because I took a round in the guts. I'm gonna have to shit in a bag on the side of my belly. How am I gonna get married now? Why would any woman want to live with a man who shits in a bag? Christ, I wish that gook had just gone ahead and killed me.'

Cam had no idea what to say. He couldn't think of one positive thing that would help him. What could the Army do for him – his body, his mind? Who would accept him back? What a goddamned mess, he thought.

All Cam did in the end was let the guy hold his hand. Finally a corpsman gave the man a pain killer and he fell asleep. Cam admitted to himself he was relieved to move away.

Cam made his way back to his space, where he intended to stay for the rest of the flight. But the war intruded on him again. A man shook violently. A spreading stain of blood covered the bandages on his chest. Something was badly wrong.

'Doc, get here quick, this man is in trouble.'

A medic came running, took a look and yelled for help. Cam stepped out of the way as the medic worked on the man. After a few minutes the medic shook his head. The man had died. The medic closed the man's eyes and put a cloth over his face.

'What the hell, doc?'

'You still here? This man took some shrapnel in the chest. One piece nicked the pericardium, the sac that surrounds the heart. It was too delicate to operate at evac so the chest cutter put him on the plane and hoped he could make it to the States and a specialist. I don't know for sure, but the sac must have ripped and the blood poured out. Not a damn thing we could do, really. Just bad luck.'

Cam had seen more than enough. He stayed on his litter for the rest of the flight. He didn't pay much attention after the Starlifter hit the runway. He was glad to be on home soil but switched off the part that did the analyzing. He went where he was told, handed files over and received them, got in and out of vehicles, and endured another physical as well as more inoculations for the unknown. He asked for and received painkillers periodically. He was finally put into a ward, dedicated to service men with maxillofacial injuries requiring reconstruction, at the Walter Reed Army Medical Center in Washington.

The ward was pleasant and clean, and best of all was staffed by army nurses who were extremely dedicated and with whom the men fell in love. Attractive women handed out tender care on demand. The patients called them their angels.

He underwent more tests and X-rays. For a few days he did not do much except read, relax and enjoy the painkillers. Finally an officer with a major's insignia introduced himself as Dr. Stuart Campbell. He was a reconstruction specialist, or what many people called a plastic surgeon, although the major did not like the term. Cam's fellow ward inmates all had a high opinion of Dr. Campbell. They trusted him.

'Sergeant, do you want to have a look at what I'm going to make good as new again?'

'Yes sir. Might as well get it over with.'

The major handed him a hand mirror.

The side of his face had caved in where the cheekbone was shattered, and his nose was flat and pushed to one side.

The worst was his eye. It was webbed with red veins and pushed back into the socket. Looking at things made him dizzy because he saw double. The eye fell away and down to one side when he didn't try to move it. Made him look like a crazed psycho, he thought. He could star in a horror movie.

The major brought him back to reality. 'I know what you're thinking, you're thinking you will never look normal again and you won't be able to see properly. I'm here to tell you that I can reconstruct your face with latent scarring. Your eye is the most complex problem, but my prognosis is that I can return it to full function and normal cosmetic status. I'll have to do three separate operations, starting with your nose and then your cheek. There may be some collapse of a part of your sinuses that I may or may not be able to correct completely. It is rather like putting a honeycomb back into place after you have stepped on it – bit difficult. We'll fix your eye last. There will need to be a period of healing of a few weeks between operations, so get to feel at home here for a few months. The nurses will spoil you, they always do.'

The major went on to briefly describe in layman's language what he was going to do. He liked his patients to be as informed as much as their education and inclination allowed. Cam wanted to know as much as possible. The major brought in an anatomical plastic model of the head. Various parts of it could be removed to expose features relevant to his treatment.

The nose repair would be the most straightforward. The ethmoid bone and septal cartilage had been cracked and a septoplasty was scheduled. This involved simply pushing the bone and cartilage back into the midline and applying a splint. No major surgery to the frontal sinus was necessary as this would require peeling back the scalp and removing a part of the skull to access the sinus. The major was hopeful that the septoplasty would be all that was required, although it was common for mild symptoms of partial nostril occlusion to persist, as well as mild pain and bloody mucosal discharge from time to time.

Since Cam's cheekbone was broken in three places it would need delicate surgery. To expose the bone, a cut to the outside end of the eyebrow would be made, as well as another on the inside of the mouth through the gum above the back teeth, and a third cut in the skin crease just below the lower eyelashes. These would allow access to the cheekbone. It would be necessary to attach titanium plates and screws to hold the breaks in place. The surgeon would be able to determine if the bones in the floor of the eye socket were fractured as well.

The thin bone separating the ethmoid sinuses from the orbit was most likely fractured. Damage was also possible to the front ethmoidal foramina which direct nerves and arteries between the orbit and the cranium. The full extent of the damage would be assessed during surgery. Access to the orbit would be from the front of the eye. Any prolapsed soft tissue would be replaced into the orbit, the broken bone fragments would be reconstructed to their proper locations, and a reinforcing implant material placed to rest on the stable bones. After a period of healing, the appropriate muscles of the eye would be detached from the eye itself and either strengthened, weakened or repositioned, and reattached. This would allow the eye to move normally and cure the diplopia – the double vision. Normal binocular vision would be restored.

Performing these operations in sequence would leave him with a technicolored face from the bruising and swelling. The purple, blue, green, red and yellow tints would eventually fade. The men in the ward went through a chameleon phase as their operations progressed. The major was confident that his face would look normal under all but high magnification inspection.

The nose operation was easy and left him with raccoon eyes. Major Campbell let him rest for a few days and then tackled the cheekbone. The aftermath from that operation was a bit painful and Demerol tablets were welcome.

In between operations Cam wandered around the hallways of the wards above and below. A few days after his cheekbone operation, he decided to visit the ward directly above him. Halfway down the corridor he heard screaming coming from a room nearby. Combat veterans were familiar with screams caused by intense pain, but this time he felt he had to act. He burst into the room to see two nurses and a man.

'What the hell are you doing to him?'

One of the nurses turned to look at Cam. She had a jar of cream in one hand and a spatula covered with the cream in the other. She was about to smear this onto the man's burnt skin.

'Soldier, please go now. We're administering palliative ointment to this burns patient. He has forty percent second and third degree burns, and needs to have this on the burned areas. I know it is very distressing to watch, so please go and shut the door.'

'The hell I will.' Cam walked over to the man and extended his hand.

'If you can, take my hand and squeeze for all you're worth. Scream louder if you want, if it helps. Just look at me and try to block out the pain. Try hard.'

The man's left hand was not burned, so he snatched at Cam's hand and held on so tight it hurt. Cam held on to a rough and sweaty hand like it would save him from falling over a cliff. The man locked eyes with him and strained.

'Please go now, you've done enough.'

The man left off screaming and started shouting. 'Christ, let him stay! Let him stay! It helps! Oh Jesus!'

The nurses hesitated a second, but went back to slopping the cream onto the man. He kept a painful grip on Cam's hand but stopped screaming; he strained for words through clenched teeth.

'There is nothing worse than this, can't be. It's like having your skin peeled off a little at a time. I don't know how much longer I can last.'

'You can get through this. It's not the first time, is it? You can do it. Keep focused on me, squeeze my hand.'

The nurses worked on him for five minutes of unrelenting agony.

'Soldier, we want to see you outside.'

'I'll be there in a few minutes. Going to see this man settles down.'

The patient lost eye contact but kept his grip. After a few minutes the tension left his body and he breathed a bit better, not so shallow.

'Jesus. What a punishment. Don't feel I really deserve it. Thanks for that. I get that three times a day, do you believe it? All the men here have burns, this is the burns ward and most of them get this every day, too. I can hear them going through it. I know I'm going to be in line again soon. Wears me out, I can't stop thinking about it.'

'Don't you get something for the pain? Morphine or something?'

'Yeah, we all do, but the same dose gets weaker and weaker. They have to give us higher doses and those wear out too. Too much will kill us, so it's just maintenance. Most days I wish they would just give me enough to put me out while they work on me, but it's too dangerous. I might just go on sleeping forever. But sometimes maybe that wouldn't be such a bad thing, you know?'

'How long have you been in here?'

'Must be over a month, I lose track. Who are you anyway?'

'Call me Cam, everybody does.'

'Look, can you come back when they are going to torture me again? It really helped to have you here. Next session in about eight hours.'

'I'll be here if they let me back in. The nurses didn't look all that pleased.'

'Oh, they're all right, I like them, they can't do things any different. I know they hate having to give us so much pain, but without treatment more of us would die, no question. I'll ask to have you here, anyway.'

Cam left the room to face the music with the nurses.

'Just what the hell do you think you were doing in there? Burns patients have to have that treatment and we need to keep their environment as clean as possible. You may have dragged in germs. Who are you anyway?'

'I apologize if I did anything wrong, but when I hear screaming like that I generally tend to find out what's causing it. Funny little quirk that I have. Comes from being in combat too much. Anyway, I think that man benefited a lot by having me there. He calmed down, didn't he? He's also asked me to come back for his next treatment and I'm going to unless you bar the door. Here, take a peek at him now, he seems relaxed enough to sleep. Can't have done him any harm.'

The nurses had to admit that he was better than usual after a session of treatment.

While Cam recovered in hospital, the nurses allowed him to attend a number of burns victims, to encourage them and give them fresh hope for a new life – the 'crisp buddy system' as it became known.

A few weeks later, Cam's last operation was completed and he was discharged. He needed to keep a tight bandage on his eye and would have swelling and discoloration for some time, but his eye would look and function normally. The major advised to keep a bandage on to prevent any dirt getting in and to keep it from getting bumped.

The major told him that the 'crisp buddy system' had worked so well that it was going to be trialed on other wards with other wounds. He should be proud.

The major arranged a driver to take him to the bus station for the ride up to New Haven. He still only had a few possessions in his duffel bag, including his Colt Python which had survived everything. He liked traveling light.

*****

CHAPTER FOURTEEN

Cam arrived back at the Yale campus a week before the term officially started. A new dean welcomed him as 'the warrior returned'.

'I'm happy you called round,' the dean said. 'It's cocktail time. What would you like to drink? Scotch, gin and tonic, martini?'

'Scotch would be just fine.'

'Splash of soda? Capital. I'll call Pamela. She wants to meet you.'

Pamela turned out to be the dean's wife. A stunner, Cam thought. She extended her hand and kissed him on the right cheek.

'Again, welcome back to Yale,' the dean said. 'We are very happy to have you in one piece. You'll not have to tell us tales of war and we will never ask. You should know we have been rather thorough in amassing a dossier on you, so I am aware of your army affiliation and your citations. Let me say well done, even though Pamela and I are totally opposed to this war and wish it would damn well end soon. Nothing to do with you. You served honorably as a man must when called up. Just wanted you to know that. Chin-chin.'

'Thank you, Dean. Call me Cam.'

'Well then, Cam, you will dine with us tonight. Pamela has prepared her usual culinary delight. By the way, I have asked that you work in my office as your work obligation. It will be easy duty, just answering the telephone, messages and filing. I trust this meets with your approval.'

'Most definitely.'

The sumptuous dinner and company proved the best welcome. No talk about the war. No one wanted the truth, Cam thought.

At the start of the year, Cam met up with another Vietnam veteran. He offered his hand. 'Anton Mire. Pleased to meet you. Actually I'm relieved to meet another vet. I wasn't sure there were any except me.'

'I hadn't thought about it much,' said Cam. 'But you are right. It is good to meet somebody who was there and understands.'

'Yeah, I did. You?'

'I was a few months short of freedom when I got wounded. Spent the rest of my tour at Walter Reed chasing nurses.'

'The eye going to be in service soon or are you going to play pirate?'

'Only as long as I can get away with it. What college are you in?'

'Silliman. You?'

'Saybrook. Why don't we have dinner at Saybrook tonight and you can brag about your daring exploits. Damn good to meet you.'

'Likewise.'

At the end of the week, Cam found O'Malley's, a bar away from the campus. Anton joined him. They became regular weekend patrons.

On one Friday evening, Lieutenant Sullivan of the municipal police force walked in. Cam had assisted the police officer in apprehending a violent student who had been intimidating the females on campus.

'You ever heard of SWAT, Cam?' the police officer asked.

'No, Lieutenant.'

'SWAT stands for Special Weapons and Tactics. The Los Angeles police put a team together in '68. An inspector called Gates thought it up, but he wanted to call it a Special Weapons Assault Team. Ed Davis, the deputy chief out there, thought that sounded too much like the military, so he used the other name. Can't see the difference myself. The purpose of SWAT is to provide protection, support, security, firepower and rescue to police operations in high personal risk situations, where specialized tactics are necessary to minimize casualties.'

'Why all the info?' Sullivan cleared his throat. 'SWAT has been used for the last two years in California. First time was in a place called Delano where that Chavez guy and his United Farm Workers were staging protests. Wanted to keep the violence from breaking out. Second time was in '69 when those Black Panthers held off the Los Angeles Police Department for three hours. Three Panthers and three police officers were injured in the shoot out.

'Now, what worries me, Cam, is that we've had our own problems with Black Panthers. You probably don't know. You were in Nam, but a guy name Rackley was tortured for a week and then murdered by the Panthers. Nice bunch all round. Anyway, we arrested this Bobby Seale character, the founder of the Panthers, you know, and thirteen other Panthers. Had to let Seale go, which was a pity, but we did get three convictions on the murder rap. Problem was that demonstrations broke out here in New Haven and lots of Yalies were involved. The Yale administration made concessions to the protesters; otherwise it could have gotten real ugly. I thought at the time that something like the Los Angeles Police Department SWAT team would have come in handy. It seems to me that the world is going to get more violent, there'll be more armed crazies around, and we need to be able to deal with them.'

'I remember seeing the Panthers when I first arrived on campus, before I got drafted. Sounds like what you need are commandos. Your police are going to have to be trained to a new level, if you ask me. I'd be thinking Ranger or Special Forces training.'

'You'd be correct, Cam, which is why I have come to you. Chief and I had a little talk and we both came to the conclusion that we want you to train some of our officers to commando level so we can have our own SWAT team. What do you think? Take a minute. I'll get us a couple more pints.'

Cam didn't know what to think. He was flattered on the one hand but was concerned that the New Haven police didn't really know what to expect. He would have no problem training officers to a minimum Ranger standard, but a good deal of time in hard training would be required. He had submersed himself in his studies at Yale, but life had taken a dull turn, he thought. He could not relate to the students; he considered them spoiled and without experience. With this new venture, the fun might come back into his life.

Sullivan came back with the pints.

'Why don't you get some of the California surfer boys to come east and train your people? They obviously have the experience,' Cam said.

'I thought of that, but the chief doesn't want to ask for help when we have somebody like you to do the training. While you train our boys to be commandos, we can be sure that police procedure gets built into the system. We need your help, Cam.'

'Tell you what, I'll put together a list of what I need and you see if you can supply it. If I can meet you at your office on Monday afternoon after I finish in the dean's office we can discuss things further. You good with that?'

'I'm good with it. Chief will want to sit in. You're going to ask for expensive stuff, right? He'll need to get used to the budget taking a hit. I'll ask you not to discuss this with anyone until we get the green light.'

Sullivan and Cam shook on it.

Cam assembled enough weaponry to defend a small country, according to the chief of police. These included light automatic carbines, combat shotguns, Colt Python .357 Magnum revolvers, teargas, fragmentation and concussion grenades, and sniper rifles.

Lieutenant Sullivan agreed with Cam's suggestion to have his Vietnam friend, Anton, assist with the SWAT training.

After two months of intensive training, twelve officers were fit for SWAT duty according to Cam. Ten officers had dropped out or were considered unsuitable.

Cam earned extra money from his SWAT training activities and sent a money order to his friend Pines for the kids at the Rest on Thanksgiving and Christmas. He also provided blankets and mattresses for every bed so that they would be warm and comfortable in winter.

*****

CHAPTER FIFTEEN

Cam's life seemed like a blur of activity – classes, study, sport, and training. At a police request, Cam had made up a list of his activities so he could be found in an emergency. The dean was kind enough to act as a focal point for his whereabouts, and Cam exchanged a list with Anton so each would know where the other was.

The team performed well in their first encounters with two violent men in two separate incidents. The men were roughed up, but there were no injuries to the SWAT officers who subdued them. Minor scuffles, Cam called them.

Then, while carrying out an experiment in an organic chemistry lab, one of the campus officers on the SWAT team approached him. He was clearly agitated.

'We've got a big one this time, Cam. There's all kind of shooting going on at the college in Hartford, Emmanuel College. I don't know much yet, we'll be briefed on the way there by the lieutenant, but it sounds like at least two people are dead and three wounded. I was told to pick you and Anton up and drive you to the station. Do you know where Anton is?'

Cam did and they collected Anton. They stopped at Saybrook so he could collect his Python and shoulder rig, and the Remington 700. At the station it took forty-five minutes to assemble the team. As the team suited up and collected their gear, Cam checked them as though it was a mission in Vietnam. The atmosphere was nervous, like a football team before a finals game. Cam chatted and he checked people's eyes for anyone who might be overexcited and liable to make a mistake. The lieutenant entered the room.

'Gentlemen, we do appear to have a situation that requires the firepower and expertise of a SWAT team and you are it. The chief wishes you well and is confident you will do a fine job. Now, here is what we know so far, we'll get better intel once we're at the college.

'A student has holed up in a campus building and begun to shoot civilians indiscriminately, both on and off campus. The shooter seems to want the authorities to know who he is because he has taped a piece of paper with his name and what amounts to a suicide note on the door of the student union. He has written that he is going to take as many people with him as he can before he kills himself. He is failing his classes, and his girlfriend has given him the boot recently. He is known to have a history of amphetamine and alcohol abuse. A psychiatrist cum student counselor at the college health center has talked to him at his request. He is extremely hostile while he explains his frustration about his girlfriend and his grades, and has made a statement about feeling the urge to start shooting people on campus. A psychiatrist has prescribed valium without knowing about the other drug problem. When asked why he hadn't reported any of this to campus authorities, the psychiatrist replied that he saw 'lots of disturbed students and no one took them seriously.'

Cam thought that the shooter must be in a commanding position and using something high powered.

'So gents, this is a whacko of the first order,' the lieutenant said. 'He's already killed and wounded people. He fires at anyone that comes along his line of vision. When we arrive I want Anton and Cameron to assess the situation and decide on a course of action; they've been in deadly force situations before. The SWAT team is number one on this and the Hartford cops will enforce a perimeter and back you up, but what SWAT says, goes.'

No one on the SWAT bus knew anything about how the campus was laid out, and in fact did not know which building the student was in. The men sat on their seats in the bus like cats eyeing mice.

'Lieutenant, can you use the communications on the bus here to contact a cop fairly high up on the food chain?' Cam asked. 'We need to park where the guy can't see us arrive, and we need some intel about potential cover so we can get close enough to make a realistic assessment. He sounds like he knows how to shoot, and we don't know what kind of weapons he has. Everybody better have their armor on.'

The lieutenant made the call and got shunted from one cop to another. Finally a cop of equal rank answered the questions. They were told to park the bus behind the main library where the cops were supposed to have a command post. The shooter was in a building called the Chemistry Center, directly in front of the library about 300 meters away. Just great, Cam thought, with chemicals like acids and cyanide solutions. They had masks, but these may not be much good against a strong acid such as sulfuric.

As the bus rolled onto the campus a window broke inward and another round slammed into the side of the bus. Everybody piled into the aisle, tangled up.

Cam was first out while the team single-filed out of the bus, double time, and took defensive firing stances either side of the door, two men out and cover, run, the next two out. He crouched by the door, waving people out as they sprinted to a protective barricade – the inside wall of the library. More rounds hit the bus, and one passed a couple of inches to his right, punching a neat hole in the bus. He finally made the sprint when the entire team was huddled against the wall.

'Anybody hit? No? Okay, breathe deep, this guy may be a student but he's no amateur. Remember your training, you officially graduate today.'

'First thing we do is get our communications in order. Rob, could you link us all up?'

Rob did this in under a minute.

Cam could see that the Hartford city cops and state cops were in general disarray; they took cover where they could. First thing to do was for Cam to take charge.

'Hello gentlemen. My name is Cameron Campbell and next to me is Anton Mire. We are commanders of the SWAT team that has just arrived. SWAT is now in charge of the operation and we need to get sorted out.'

The officers appeared stunned, some looked over at them, but most kept looking in the direction of something they could not see. A cop in a Hartford uniform, hiding behind a fender, squeezed his face up in disgust.

'I ain't takin' orders from a boy and I sure as hell ain't takin' orders from no coon.'

The cop spat a gob of tobacco in their direction.

'That is entirely correct, officer. As of now you are relieved of duty. Get yourself back to the station where I'm sure your boss will want a word.'

The officer's face just got meaner. He left his cover and took two steps toward Cam, lifting his club from his belt.

'We don't have time for this. Come ahead but you'll be down in less than five seconds.'

A higher ranking officer stepped forward.

'Officer, you are relieved and now you face disciplinary action. Do I need to have you in cuffs? No? Get the hell out of here.'

The cop went red in the face and almost choked on his tobacco plug.

The higher ranking officer raised his voice. 'Listen up. SWAT is in charge of this disaster and we're grateful to have them. These two officers know more about assault tactics than anyone here, and that's what we need to do, assault a building and take the son of a bitch down. You will obey their orders immediately with no back chat. Am I making myself perfectly clear?'

He was, but not to the state patrol. One of them spoke up. 'Let me get this straight. SWAT is out of New Haven but is now in charge here.

Do they have state jurisdiction? I mean, do we take orders from them, too?'

'You do. I suggest the highest ranking state trooper here get on the horn to headquarters and the big boss. He can verify from the governor's office that SWAT is in charge. In the meantime shut up and get to work. Detective Campbell, get on with it.'

'Thank you, sir. I see a few plainclothes people here. Would those of you who are civilians please raise your hands.' Many of them did. Cam pointed at two officers.

'Officers, please relieve these people of their weapons and escort them off the campus.' There were general noises of disapproval.

'We have enough to do without having to protect civilians from their own incompetence. Thank you for your enthusiasm, but you must go.'

'I'd like to introduce you to Sergeant Rob Taylor, the SWAT communications coordinator,' Cam said, addressing the officers. 'He is in constant touch with every SWAT member and I want you to liaise with him for all communications. He'll be receiving and sending updates to officers that need it and will pass on to you anything that SWAT wants relayed. No idle chatter. Rob could quickly overload, so report only what is important. Any communications people here? Good, get going with Rob.'

'We need a map of the campus to show us where to deploy people. We also need a blueprint and elevation drawings of the Chemistry Center.'

People looked doubtful at each other until someone finally spoke. 'I don't think anyone knows how to find those kinds of drawings.'

Well, call some campus officials, the maintenance department, anybody, but get them here fast. We need to know how the building is constructed before we clear it. Less chance of one of us taking a hit.'

One of the state troopers got on his radio. After waiting, a map appeared.

Cam wanted to scope the chemistry building from several other buildings to see if there were good positions for the team snipers. Two cops took Cam and Anton to a vantage point on the left hand side of the library, the left front corner. Cam flattened down on his stomach and carefully put his head around the corner. The Chemistry Center was fronted in reddish-brown brick and shaped like an L, similar to the style of an old English campus. There were three stories with windows at meter intervals in each story. On the long part of the L were decorative pyramids built up from the top story. Directly behind the pyramids was a square tower, with a window on each face a small way down from the tower roof. Cam pulled his head back around the corner and knew that the sniper was holed up in the tower.

'Cam, this is no picnic,' the higher ranking officer said. 'There's open ground on all sides of the building and four windows where the shooter is high enough to see the whole campus. If he is even close to being anywhere near as good as you, he could shoot way beyond the campus, so let's hope he is just targeting what he can see more or less directly below him.'

He wasn't. He had already wounded two people off campus, in the town.

Back at the makeshift command post they examined the map. The Chemistry Center formed part of a much larger complex of buildings that appeared to form a continuous three-sided square. On the bottom end of the square was the tower that could support a sniper. Another higher tower, on a building that formed the arm of the square farthest from the library, would almost certainly have a direct line of fire into the chemistry building. Filling up the three-sided square was an expanse of lawn with some trees and foot paths. From one side of this green to the other was about 300 meters in all four directions. Devoid of cover it was almost impossible to cross without being seen.

'All right,' Cam said, 'let's tighten down this campus. First, I want officers on every entry and exit of every building on the Chemistry Center end of the campus. No one in and, especially, no one out. Set up only on the sides of the buildings away from the green, the killing zone. If there are students in the buildings, keep them in until this is over. Many will be panicky and some might try to make a dash to freedom. Be sure they don't. Second, I want barricades on every street exit and entry on the entire campus. Absolutely no vehicles in. For cars already in and moving, I want them directed to exits as far away from the Chemistry Center as possible, and the means to get into the Chemistry Center on foot absolutely blocked. Detective Mire is an expert at setting up perimeters, so please work with him.'

Cam prepared to inspect the towers in the other buildings. He walked back to the team and picked up his 700, checked it over and mounted the scope. He told the team members what he was going to do, described the building and surrounding terrain, and what help he wanted from them.

'Squads One and Two, you are going to help me and Anton crack that building when the time comes. Squad Three, you are going to start laying down suppressive fire as of now. One of you is the spotter and the other three are going to fire two round bursts from CAR-15s at the tower windows any time the spotter tells you to. Spotter, you will order fire only when you see a barrel of any kind come out of the tower windows. You will be able see the windows from where I place you. We don't know if he's got anyone with him up there, so do not fire at body shapes, only at barrels.'

Cam ran with squad three to the left foremost corner of a building about 200 meters to the left of the library where they could see two windows in the center tower. As they took position, Cam radioed Rob with the plan and told him to inform all the other police so they would not react badly when firing started.

Cam planned his overland crossing to the buildings in which he wanted to place snipers. There were only two areas of about thirty meters between two buildings where he might be exposed to the shooter. He could sprint from the library to the next building and then again. After that he would be able to stroll to the buildings with the towers.

'Rob, listen up good. Get on the radio and apprise every cop that I'm coming through in the next couple of minutes and to hold their fire. Describe me. Do it now.'

He did.

'Keep me on a direct open line to you and squad three. I'm going now. Squad three, fire immediately if you see a barrel in the tower.'

Cam stood up, shielded by a corner, and pushed off. He heard a burst of shots. The shooter had tried to shoot him. A few cracks went past his head. Clods of grass popped up around his running feet. He slammed into the side of a building.

The tower in the second building faced the chemistry building directly, and made an ideal hide for a sniper. He would need to climb into the second tower to check the hide. While jumping into the open space leading to this building he heard two more bursts. Two rounds pocked the wall behind him as he came around it. He skidded into the wall of the second building and crawled around to the entrance.

The second tower made an ideal hide. He heard four shots as he came back down. He recognized the report of a high caliber rifle, something in the .30 range, maybe a 30.06. He ran back to the vantage point he had just left and glassed the killing zone. To his dismay he saw two bodies sprawled on the green, one a little farther away than the second. The first was a young woman, probably a student, and from the way she lay sprawled, he was certain she was dead. He had seen enough bodies to know.

'Sir,' an officer reported, 'that young woman just got away from us, she ran like a deer out this door when we had our backs turned.'

The second person down was an officer in uniform, and he was still moving, if feebly. Both had come out of one of the buildings farther down from the one he was in. This could have been avoided if the snipers had been in place, he thought.

Cam moved around to the back of the building from where he thought the victims had come. He found another officer crouched in an open doorway.

'Goddamn it, that's my partner out there,' he said.

'He's still moving,' Cam said, 'and we have to get him out and the body too, if we can. Sit tight, I'm going to set it up. Go find some other officers to work with.'

'Rob, we've got two people down on the opposite side of the chemistry building from where you and the team are. We have to get them back and the only thing we can do is use suppressive fire. Keep communications open to squad three. Send the two snipers along the route I've just taken and for god's sake order the cops again not to shoot at them. They almost got me.'

The snipers made it to the station and set up. Cam motioned the police officers that now surrounded him to pay attention.

'Okay. Rob, here is what we're going to do. The shooter is probably waiting and hoping that someone is going to come after the two bodies. When I give the order they are going to run out and collect the two victims. Fire continuously until I stop you, two round bursts, new magazines, and don't waste ammo because you won't have time to reload. Accurate and methodical. Shoot rounds at will, but you only have six, so watch the tower and the progress of the officers. This may be a chance to nail the perp. I have a bad angle but I'll shoot the window frame. All copy, please.'

All copied. Cam turned to the officers. 'You ready for this?'

They looked tense but nodded.

'Teams, on my mark. Go.'

Shooting began and four officers sprinted to the bodies, two for each, and picked them up by the shoulders and legs.

'Cease fire, we've got them. Anybody see the shooter?'

'All negative.'

The young woman was dead, one round going in at the right side of the chest and exiting from the left hip. Probably through the heart and lung, dead seconds after she was hit. The officer had been hit in the thigh, probably shattering the femur. He would live but was never going to walk normally again.

Cam ran the gauntlet back to the command post and gathered the team. Nobody shot at him.

'We didn't get the shooter so we are going to have to clear the

Chemistry Center building. You've seen the drawings, so you know this is going to be tedious and by the book. My current thinking is that the shooter is alone, but we are going in as if there were more armed men. We've gotten a bit of luck because even though we have three floors to clear and numerous rooms, there is only one junction at the base of the L, so we have that much less chance of running into an ambush. I want to use two-man clearing teams. Anton and I will each be point man on one of the teams. Two men from squad two will take second position in the clearing team. Squad one is the four-man firing team behind the clearing teams. The firing team will use the serpentine formation, number 1 man at center front, numbers 2 and 3 on each side slightly behind, and number 4 as tail gunner. We have rooms on both sides of the corridor. Each clearing team will sweep rooms on one side of the corridor. We will do this simultaneously as most of the rooms are equidistant from each other across the corridor. We will be using two police officers to defend each of the stairwells once we have cleared them. The remaining two men from squad 2 will act as escort for these officers as they are needed. You will report to Rob when officers enter the building and are in place. Do not contact the clearing team directly unless there is a dangerous unforeseen situation which requires team attention.'

Cam paused for a few seconds so they could take in what he had said. 'Any questions? Good, everyone arm with a shotgun because the carbines will be of less use in this tight situation. Take a canteen of water and strap it down so it doesn't make noise.'

Lieutenant Sullivan had attended the briefing.

'Seems like you've thought this through,' he said. 'How long do you think it will take to clear the building?'

'No way to tell,' said Cam, 'but it is not going to be quick, that's for sure. And there is always something you haven't thought of that bites you in the ass, but I believe we're good to go.'

'Okay, I'll stay with the Hartford force and let the brass know what your plan is.'

'I'll tell you what I think,' said Anton. 'I think he is alone in the tower and barricaded. I vote we toss a couple of concussion grenades in when we get that far and shoot at any pieces that are left. Don't have my hero costume on today.'

'Fine by me.'

The team, under suppressive fire from squad three, made it intact to the ground floor entrance at the foot of the L, on the side the shooter couldn't see. The Catholic members of the team crossed themselves.

'Corridor fire team, you're up when we get to the first set of doors, and Anton and I take point. Let's rock.'

There was nothing unusual about the inside of the building. Linoleum floors, solid walls painted green to hip height, and cream or tan to the ceiling. Wooden doors with a glass window. They would have to enter and sweep each room, overlapping their fields of fire.

When finished with clearing a room, Cam and Anton softly called out 'room clear'. The team reached the L junction without incident. The clearing teams fell back, and the corridor fire team then proceeded to clear the junction. Men 1 and 2 took up parallel positions at the edge of the junction, number 3 kneeling. On signal, man 3 turned right around the corner, keeping low and aiming down the junction. Man 1 stepped forward while turning right, keeping high and aiming down the junction. Men 2 and 3 continued to move along the corridor. As man 2 passed man 3, man 1 shifted laterally to his left until he reached the opposite corner. Man 2 turned to aim down the junction between men 1 and 3. Man 4 did not pass the junction and continued to aim backwards down the corridor he was in. 'Clear' was called and the entire team resumed their original positions to clear rooms in the new corridor.

The team came to a stairwell leading to the next floor. To clear it, Cam climbed four steps and swept up and to his left. The next man joined him on his left and swept up and to the rear. That way the second level of the stairwell could be covered in case of any firing from it. Nothing happened and the team proceeded to clear the first floor.

The first floor was mostly laboratories. This made it more difficult to clear because there were a number of benches that people could hide behind. It was impossible to view the entire room. Each aisle between the benches had to be walked through and searched.

It was in one of the labs that two students were hiding. When Cam had gone in he had seen a flash of a hand – a small hand – before it disappeared behind a bench. He was fairly sure it was a woman's hand. That didn't mean it couldn't be dangerous. A woman could come up with a firearm or a bottle of acid as easily as a man. He kept the shotgun at the ready position and signaled to his backup with a head gesture.

'Police. Show yourself now by rising from behind the bench. We will not hurt you, but do not make a sudden movement. Begin to rise now. Slowly.'

Nothing happened, which meant a person was waiting until Cam moved into a pre-chosen ambush. Cam didn't move.

'Show yourself now or we will retreat and clear the room with a grenade. Last chance.'

Slowly two heads, both with long hair, peeped over the bench top.

'Show your hands.'

Four arms came up in the right places. This did not mean that there wasn't another person still hiding.

'Stand up, slowly.' Cam was looking closely to catch eye movement that would indicate that there was another person still on the ground. Both sets of eyes looked directly at Cam, wide with fear. What materialized were a male and a female, presumably students.

'Place your hands on top of your heads and step into the aisle, one of you on each side of the bench.'

The pair did as instructed.

'Halt and remain absolutely still.'

Cam spoke into his radio.

'We have two students that need collecting, Rob. Get two uniforms in here on the double.'

No other incidents occurred as the team cleared the rest of the first floor and most of the second floor. When they arrived at the stairway that led to the tower, Cam called a halt. They faced one long flight of stairs that they knew from the elevation drawings led to a second, slightly curving, smaller stairway that accessed the tower. Their target was definitely in the tower.

Unfortunately, two bodies lay at the foot of the smaller stairway. Cam called this information in.

'Right. Anton and I are going to take a look at what's beyond the smaller stairway.'

The team took up position, ready to follow if there was gunfire. Anton and Cam stood on either side of the stairs, and began creeping up. They climbed three flights of stairs and saw the tower entrance blocked by two large, thick wooden tables, upended with the table tops outward. By good fortune a small space above the barricade could accommodate barrels or grenades. No sound could be heard so the sniper had not detected them or was deliberately keeping silent. When they came back down, Cam raised Rob on the radio.

'Rob, get me our snipers. Sniper 1, you have not had a shot, correct?'

'That is correct. I have had only partial sightings.'

'Sniper 2, are you also a negative?'

'Correct, only brief partial sightings.'

'So, no joy for a quick end to the whole mess. Rob, get me Lieutenant Sullivan and the top brass from Hartford.'

'Gentlemen, we have cleared the building and are now at the foot of the stairway leading to the tower. There are two bodies, a male and a female at this location. I have conferred with our snipers and they report not having been able to get a secure shot. We will have to assault the tower. It will be extremely dangerous to make this assault as it must be done full frontal and there is a barricade between us and our objective. We do have space to use grenades. At this time we believe the shooter is alone. Do you agree with our assessment of using grenades?'

After a brief conversation, Lieutenant Sullivan said, 'You have permission to use concussion grenades. I repeat, you have permission to use concussion grenades only.'

Anton turned to Cam. 'You want to do the so-called decent thing and give him a chance to surrender?'

'Hell no. Those concussion grenades are going right in there. It is our civic duty to prevent the use of taxpayer funds to support a long and costly trial which will likely use the insanity defense, possibly allowing the scumbag to live a full and happy life in an institution and then get out on parole at the age of sixty-five, ready for a nice retirement. He is, as they say, proverbial toast.'

'Good argument. Shall we get this done? I'm getting hungry.'

'Another good argument, I'm peckish, too.'

They passed their shotguns to a team member and released their Pythons. Each carrying a grenade, they made the slow walk up the stairs to within two meters of the barricade. The team took up positions behind them. At a nod from Cam they armed the grenades, waited two seconds and threw them. Both grenades sailed through the slot in the barrier. At the same time, Cam and Anton turned their heads away and held their hands over their ears. The explosions in the small space insured maximum force. A second after the explosions, Cam and Anton ran up the last flight of stairs, the team right behind. The barrier had more or less disappeared and a double door behind it had partially disintegrated. They both hit a side of the doorway and grabbed two more grenades off their webbing. Armed, the grenades sailed through the shattered door.

After the dust settled Cam took a furtive look into the room. A heap of clothing with legs sticking out lay on the floor. Cam put two rounds of .357 Magnum into it. No gunfight. After that there wasn't much left to do but the autopsy. The medical examiner would have to assemble the pieces.

The team trudged out of the building. Cam asked Rob to relay the order to the uniforms that they should remain in their positions on the stairwells, exits and entrances until their Hartford commander released them. Because of the lockdown on the campus there were no representatives of the press to bother them. They received hearty congratulations, handshakes and back slaps from the cops. SWAT had come through their trial by fire, and Cam was proud to serve with them.

When Cam returned to his room at Saybrook later that night after debriefing, he found a note from the dean under his door asking him to come to their apartment as soon as he read it.

The dean and Pamela, both looking shaken, met Cam at their door. Pamela grabbed hold of him for what seemed like a full minute.

'Cameron, was it terrible? We were so worried about you. There was an update on the radio and television every fifteen minutes. We could practically follow your progress. How awful for the victims and their families. At least you saved those two students trapped in the chemistry building. We are just so happy to have you back safely.'

No mention of taking down the shooter.

'Pam, let the man go and get him a drink, I'm sure he needs one.'

'No need to worry about me, but thanks for the concern,' Cam said.

After a few drinks Cam made a courteous escape.

*****

CHAPTER SIXTEEN

The director of the CIA met with the head of operations in the Middle East at Langley, Virginia.

'What do you think?' the director asked. 'Is he our man?'

'Well, he comes with excellent US Army credentials. Resourceful, likes a challenge and excitement, good tactician, a natural leader, excellent sniper, intelligent …'

'But you have reservations.'

'From what we know, he has sociopathic tendencies.'

'Is that a problem?'

'He could gun down the enemy – commit any type of violent act – without feeling guilt or remorse. They say the more effective soldier shows remorse and empathy; he doesn't violate the rights of others and performs with better judgment.'

'Didn't he show compassion towards the burns victims of our soldiers in Vietnam?'

'An isolated incident, we think.'

'Well, I think he's our man. He performed well leading the SWAT team on the Yale campus… becomes a liability, we can deal with that.'

'He hasn't quite finished studying for his degree at Yale.'

'Don't worry. We can fast track his degree. We will squeeze the dean – we have something on him.'

Cam and Anton made their usual appearance at O'Malley's on Friday. This time there was no applause or cheering, because the patrons knew this one had been rough, involving civilian murders and wounding. And they had to take out the bad guy. There was a good deal of sympathy for the victims and their families.

They made their way down the bar to the two stools that were by proclamation kept open for them on Friday and Saturday nights. Beverages and food appeared quickly on the bar.

'Lads, there were two guys in here yesterday looking for you,' the barman said. 'You're not in any strife are you?'

'As far as we know we're golden. What'd they look like?'

'Kind of skinny, both dressed in dark gray suits, white shirts and little black ties. Good shoeshine. Short hair. Sound familiar?'

Cam and Anton shook their heads. 'They'll find us when they find us,' Cam replied.

They did.

Two days later, the two men, sporting buzz cuts, in gray suits, skinny black ties and shiny shoes, stepped into the doorway of the dean's office where Cam was working. He recognized them from before as CIA men.

'Can I help you gentlemen?' Cam asked.

One of the men approached Cam. 'Actually, you can help us. We have a job for you.'

'Well, gents, I need to finish my degree. I've got a few months to go.'

'You have your degree as of today. We've arranged it.'

'You what!'

'Here is the citation from the university.' The CIA man handed him a letter of confirmation and a Yale degree certificate.

They must really want me, Cam thought, for that kind of leverage.

'You're studying biochemistry, right? We want you to finish up,' the man said. 'We need your expertise and your martial arts skills.'

From his army experience Cam needed to know as much intel as possible.

'What's the job?'

The CIA man explained: 'Egypt is building up its military might on the west bank of the Suez Canal, and Syria is doing the same on the Golan Heights. We may have to support Israel to stabilize the situation. We have promised them arms but haven't delivered yet. We know the Soviets are supplying the Arabs. A change in the balance of power in the Middle East could affect America's interests. If the Egyptians and Syrians gain the upper hand in an attack on Israel, Prime Minister Golda Meir might authorize the ultimate option, to arm their Jericho missiles with nuclear warheads. We want someone in Israel to keep us informed about this highly volatile situation.'

Cam swallowed hard. 'How on earth can I do that?'

'Fortunately, we have secured an agreement with Israel that we need an observer and an intel gatherer. They prefer that person work with Mossad, their intelligence and special operations organization. It's their way of making sure that person is not a security risk. Another bonus for them is your operation and sniper skills in countering terrorist threats. If you work for them, and they are satisfied with your performance, they will give you top level security clearance. Well, that's the theory. And that's what we want – for you to let us know what's going on.'

Cam had no illusions about Mossad. They were an efficient and ruthless organization. He would have to prove himself in the field if he were to be accepted.

'Sounds like I will need extra skills in diplomacy if I'm to be accepted,' Cam said. 'All right, I'll buy in, but I want my choice of weapons.'

'What kind of weapons?'

'My choice of handgun is the .357 Magnum Colt Python revolver. And if I am going to go sniper duty I want a Remington model 700, chambered for the 7.62/51 Nato round and fitted with a Leopold 3 9×50 variable scope. The 50 mm lens lets in enough light for twilight conditions.'

'We'll see what we can do about the weapons.'

Before his orientation Cam made sure Anton would take command of the SWAT team. He said goodbye to his friends at university and to the dean in charge of his residential college.

Nothing surprised Cam at 'The Farm' with its special activities. At the end of the first week, the skills trainer came over to him and said, 'Cameron, we don't think you need to undergo more training, especially as you are a decorated Ranger with plenty of confirmed kills, the commander of a SWAT team, and have trained others. In fact, we might ask you to help with our training at some time in the future.'

'A pleasure,' Cam said.

They took him to John F. Kennedy International Airport for a flight to Ben Gurion Airport in Tel Aviv, Israel. The security police had been forewarned about his handgun and let him pass.

After refueling in Portugal at Lajes Airport and crossing Spain, the plane flew over the Mediterranean Sea, escorted by American jet fighters. About 200 kilometers from the Israel border, Israeli air force Phantoms and Mirages escorted them into Ben Gurion Airport. The CIA had made sure he would arrive in one piece.

A stocky, muscular man met Cam as he stepped off the plane. Two tough-looking guys flanked him, as he introduced himself as Amzi Edelstein, an officer with Mossad.

'Welcome Mr. Campbell. We have a full file on your experience and think you will do well in this exercise. We have been advised that you have brought your own weapons with you.'

'Please call me Cam, everyone does.'

'You may call me Amzi. We are quite informal among colleagues.'

They entered a small room with four chairs and nothing else. An interrogation room, Cam thought. Amzi and Cam eyed each other for a few moments, sizing each other up.

After the mutual scrutiny, Amzi smiled. 'Shalom, Cam. You'll do.'

'Shalom, Amzi.'

'I was worried that you would be facially deformed given your Vietnam injuries. A worry for us because you could be more easily recognized, even with a disguise. You must have had a good surgeon.'

'Yes, he was very good.'

'We have confidence in your skills, not only from the US Army Rangers as a sniper specialist, but also from your training of police teams in special weapons and tactics. And congratulations on receiving your degree from Yale University.'

Was there anything they did not know about him? Cam thought.

'We are going to Sderot, a city in the semi-desert region of southern Israel. We have your Remington 700 there, fitted with your choice of telescopic sights. Quite a rifle and you have used it well, I believe.'

They climbed into an armored personnel carrier. The driver had an Uzi on the seat next to him. Another officer had one as well.

'Have you fired one of these, Cam?'

Cam knew that the Uzi was the most popular machine gun in the world. It fired 9×19mm rounds with an effective range of 200 meters. 'No, but I've got the hang of it already. Simple and effective.'

'With your experience I believe you can use it well, no problem.'

As they drove, Amzi explained that Sderot was only a kilometer from the Arab town of Beit Hanoun in the Gaza strip, from where the Arab terrorists launched their attacks. Sderot housed about fifteen thousand people and every household was armed in one way or another. It served as a transit camp for Kurdish and Iranian Jewish immigrants who had to live in tents and shacks until permanent housing was completed in 1954. Sderot was built on the Arab village of Najd, which had become occupied by the Israeli Army in 1948, causing the villagers to flee to Gaza. Twenty-five years later the Arabs remembered with bitterness the loss of their family homes and committed acts of hostility.

Amzi finally let Cam know his mission. He had intelligence that three leading terrorists were going to hit Sderot in the next few days. Cam's job was to snipe them.

As they passed through the Negev, green patches of field crops dotted the barren landscape. The Israelis had also established fruit orchards with water piped down from near Tel Aviv to irrigate the trees.

They arrived at Sderot and pulled up at a small house constructed from pebbles and concrete. A communications set-up kept Amzi in touch with headquarters.

'Are you hungry, Cam?' Amzi asked.

'I could do with a bite.'

Amzi motioned to one of his staff who prepared bagels with cream cheese and fish paste. They tucked in.

'All right, Cam, let's get down to business. Here is a Mossad warrant card, identifying you as a senior agent. It will open most doors in the military and police, but I hope you don't need to show it often. I, or one of my people, will be with you at all times as you do not speak Hebrew. Just show it if you think you need to, and don't say anything.'

'Don't I look a bit young to be a senior agent?'

'Not in Mossad and not necessarily in the Israeli military. No one will question it.'

'I need to fire the Remington 700 to verify the accuracy of the ammunition,' Cam said.

'There is lot of desert out there. We can pick a spot.'

They did. Everything was in order.

'Don't take offence, Cam, but we know you have some difficulty with mathematics so we will provide a spotter – a good one. Meet Aviram, we call him Avi.'

A lean, tall man of about thirty, with thick, curly black hair, reached out to shake hands. His deep blue eyes were deadly penetrating, but in lighter moments, sparklng with amusement.

Cam suggested they take some practice shots from at least 800 meters so that the subsonic effect would confuse the targets. If the enemy could not tell where the firing was coming from, they were more likely to panic and do things they should not do.

Since the intended incursion was not for two days, Avi and Cam decided to take a look at the lay of the land.

A seasonal watercourse, a wadi, afforded some cover for the terrorists but could not conceal them completely. A small mound fortunately provided a viewing point and enough height to be sure of head and body shots. Almost perfect. Visibility in the desolate desert was practically unlimited. Cam could lift and turn the rifle a full 360 degrees if the terrorists came in from a different direction. He could take them out at 1200 meters.

'Terrorists tend to try and cross at dawn,' Avi said. 'If they made it to Sderot they would fit in better with the locals than if they crossed at night when they might be challenged by security forces.'

'I think it best if we set up tonight and for two more days after the intel date. With ambushes it is always better to have a larger window of opportunity than given by intel. I learned that in Nam,' Cam said.

Amzi agreed.

The plan was for Cam to kill all three, but Mossad personnel would be spread around in case one got away.

Cam spent the rest of the day cleaning the Remington 700, the

Python and the Uzi. He also inspected, oiled and polished the ammunition for all three weapons to prevent the likelihood of jamming. When the Mossad boys observed him doing this, they did the same, although it probably was not their practice. But hell, Cam thought, dust was one of the worst things that can happen to a weapon.

Cam slept for a couple of hours before putting on desert camouflage, including a thermal vest to ward off the cold of the desert night. They wore desert boots which made it easier to walk in the sand.

Amzi wished them good luck.

They settled in for a long and uncomfortable wait.

As dawn broke, they both glassed in 360 degrees, each of them taking turns with the spotter scope to prevent eye strain. They stayed there until mid-morning, but no one showed.

They repeated the exercise for the second day, but again no response. On the third day, three bearded men appeared in typical Arab dress. They carried AK-47 assault rifles. Avi advised base and asked for permission to shoot.

'Cam, take the shots. Amzi says it doesn't matter if they aren't the men we are waiting for. They are obviously terrorists, so three less is always a good thing.'

The men walked down the wadi in single file so Cam put the scope on the leader. Avi gave him the numbers. Cam adjusted and squeezed off a round. The Arab fell. The other two did not know what had happened. They froze. They knew something was wrong. Cam took that brief moment to shoot the second man. The third started to run back down the wadi, but he had nowhere to hide. Cam shot him with ease.

Amzi and the crew came out to view the bodies and identify them. Comparing the faces with photographs confirmed that they were the ones they had been after.

'Great job, Cam,' Amzi said. 'We had been told you were good, but that was exceptional. You and Mossad are going to have a long relationship.'

Cam did not take that acceptance for granted, but it was a start. He knew there would be further tests.

He thanked Avi and told him he would request his help on any future mission. Avi said he would be delighted.

Amzi had arranged for a helicopter to take them to Tel Aviv, where he lived. He had not seen his wife for several weeks.

When they landed an armored car took them to his apartment.

Amzi's wife, a trim-looking woman with a smooth complexion, and large brown eyes with an oriental touch, met them at the door. Cam hoped she had an unattached sister.

'Hello, I am Ahuva. Welcome. Come in and be comfortable.'

'Pleased to meet you. Amzi is a lucky man. Call me Cam, everyone does.'

'And call me Ahuva. After what you have already done for Amzi and Israel you must consider yourself part of the family.'

Ahuva did not bat an eyelid at the weapons they carried, so Cam assumed she had become used to them. They propped up the Uzis in a corner of the room along with the 700.

'We are both sabras, born here in Israel,' Ahuva said. 'Sabras are like our prickly pears – hard and prickly on the outside but soft on the inside. You will find out.'

'How did you meet?' Cam asked.

'We met at university in the United States. A strange coincidence, is it not?'

Cam agreed. Ahuva served a three-course meal that started with chicken soup and matsah balls – a kind of dumpling made from bread, eggs and oil. Eggplant stuffed with fish paste followed, then orange and brandy grilled chicken, a green salad, and finally a sweet yoghurt and blueberries. All accompanied by red wine.

'Delicious meal, Ahuva. You'll make Amzi fat if you keep that up.'

'No chance,' Ahuva replied.

Later in the evening Amzi apologized that he could only offer a sofa for the night. 'Looks fine to me,' Cam said. 'I've slept on worse.'

Cam slept soundly for three hours. A phone rang, and he could hear Amzi talking, urgently.

Amzi hung up and walked over. 'We appear to have an emergency. We will take a chopper back to the Negev, and I'll explain on the way.'

As Cam started out the door, Ahuva put a restraining hand on his arm. 'Cam, please help protect him. With your experience and skills I know you can.'

'I think it's more likely the other way round,' Cam replied. 'He is extremely competent, and I'm still learning about this part of the world. We will look out for each other.'

Ahuva looked deeply into Cam's eyes and hugged him as he left the apartment.

*****

CHAPTER SEVENTEEN

On the way, Amzi explained: 'Our informant has warned us that Arab terrorists will stage an attack on the Negev Nuclear Research Centre, located southeast of the city of Dimona. Officially, I have not told you any of this, but you have been cleared at a high level by the Office and the Company, and I want you to know what you will be defending and how important it is. Since I have seen you in action I plan to have you play a major part in the operation. We will bring in three sniper teams from the army. They are supposed to be among the best. I want you to be their commander. We'll know more and do more when we get there. Avi will be your spotter again as you work well as a team. He made a good report of you so he is looking forward to working with you again.'

One of the pilots of the chopper had brought aerial and ground photos of the nuclear facility. Amzi handed them to Cam who gained an impression of a large installation with processing and storage areas. Surrounding it was desert, which would make it easier for snipers to get clear shots, but the enemy could see what was going on. Cam calculated that the nuclear centre was too large to be guarded by three sniper teams. He shuddered to think of a bunch of rabid Arab terrorists taking over a nuclear weapons facility.

'Amzi, please contact the army. From these photos I can see we need at least two more teams for adequate coverage. The Arabs can attack from any and all directions because we can't channel them into one or two approaches. It's just flat desert in every direction. Get the two additional teams here as quickly as possible.'

Amzi hopped into the pilot's area, put on headphones and spoke animatedly, using hand gestures as Israelis often do if they cannot see the person they are talking to. Handing back the phones, he turned to Cam. 'Done. Expected time of arrival is about two hours.'

'Excellent, makes a better chance of success. We have about an hour until we arrive so I'm going to take a nap. Who has been guarding this place and how are they armed?'

'Two platoons of regular army with Uzis, assault rifles, and 40 mm M79 shoulder-fired, single-shot grenade launchers we got from the US, plus some rocket-propelled grenades, or RPGs as you know them.'

'Good, I like thumpers.'

Cam slept well.

He woke up as the chopper set down on a purpose-built helipad. As the rotors slowed, Amzi, Cam and Avi jumped out and headed towards a tall, bald man in his mid-forties, wearing a sports coat, tie, soft-looking trousers and desert boots. A squad of army soldiers stood close by.

'Good to see you again, Amzi, but I wish it were under better circumstances,' the bald man said.

The man introduced himself to Cam. 'I am Emmanuel, director of this center. And you must be Mr. Campbell. Your reputation precedes you, and you are most welcome.'

'I am pleased to meet you, sir. Please call me Cam, everyone does.'

'Let's proceed to my office, and I'll give you some background about this place.'

They entered a cabin outside the facility, furnished with a desk and several chairs. A large filing cabinet fitted with a dial lock stood in one corner, a safe in another.

'Please be seated, Cam. Some tea?'

'Tea is fine.'

'Cam, let me give you a brief history of the center. Amzi has told me you have high level security clearance. But I must emphasize at the outset that the information is never to be repeated. Our conversation never took place. You have a free run of the outside walls and perimeter, but your clearance is not high enough to allow you to go inside. There are also safety issues with nuclear stations with which you will not be familiar.'

'Fine with me,' Cam said. 'I don't want to glow in the dark.'

The director smiled. 'Now then, construction started with French assistance in 1958. As you may know, the French at that time decided to launch a gigantic effort to build a series of nuclear reactors at various places around their country in order to have the majority of their electricity produced by these reactors. In time they were hoping to generate so much electricity that they could sell it to other countries. With French expertise our center was built in the utmost secrecy. French customs were told that the parts were for a desalination plant to be built in Latin America.

'Our reactor became active in 1963 with the possibility that a hundred or maybe two hundred nuclear weapons could be produced by the year 2000, based on the power of the reactor. We had weapons ready before the Six-Day War in 1967. Our government refuses to confirm or deny our capability.

'When the CIA discovered or believed they had discovered the purpose of our site in the early 1960s, your government demanded that we agree to international inspection. We could hardly refuse due to our close relationship and our dependence on the US for military support. The Israeli government agreed, but only if US inspectors were used to carry it out, rather than inspectors from the International Atomic Energy Agency, and that we would receive advance notice of any inspection. Since we neither confirm nor deny our weapons capability, Israel has not signed the Non Proliferation Treaty, which would naturally confirm that we have nuclear weapons.

'Some claim we rigged the inspections because we knew the schedule of the visits and were able to hide the purpose of the site by installing temporary false walls and other such things. The US became frustrated, declaring the inspections useless, and ended them in 1969, although the CIA believed we had at least one nuclear weapon. In fact, we had several at that time.'

Cam did not ask the obvious question but guessed that they had more than several at this time.

The director rose from his chair. 'Let us now go to what we call the situation room that Amzi has set up outside.'

The situation room turned out to be a trailer packed with communication equipment. Avi, Cam's spotter, came forward and bear-hugged Cam.

'When you two have finished, I will show you what we have here,' said Amzi.

Amzi produced a topographical map, covered in plastic. The three of them bent over the map to determine the strategic points around the nuclear facility. Cam decided that he and Avi would set up directly in front of the center, while the other teams would take a corner of both the large and smaller complex. He planned overlapping fields of fire for maximum coverage in the flat desert country where visibility was practically endless.

Cam suggested to them that all teams would set up 700 meters out from the facility and start shooting when the enemy crossed a 1700 meter mark further out. A competent sniper could handle a range of 1000 meters. He knew he could handle the 1700 meter mark, but if the army sniper teams were reluctant they could pull back to a lesser distance. Cam chose likely spots to cover that eventuality. He regretted not having a hill for maximum advantage.

'We are not going to use mortars or small cannon,' Amzi said. 'If the enemy captured these, they could use them to breach the center.'

Cam nodded and turned to Avi. 'Let's go out there and check the choices. I've got my Uzi, do you have yours?'

'Before you do,' Amzi interrupted, 'we need to explain our plans to the army lieutenants who will take command of the teams.'

Laying the topographical map before the lieutenants, Cam pointed out the chosen spots for hides with overlapping fields of fire that would cover both sides and corners of the two buildings.

'All sniper teams will be equipped with Uzis in the event of the enemy breaching our hides and getting too close,' Cam said.

Cam continued with the briefing: 'This brings me to your plans to set up a perimeter at close quarters around the center during the operation. Talk among yourselves and when you are prepared, please let me know. If you determine that you require more men, now is the time to get them, and as soon as possible. Then Avi and I would appreciate a walk around the site with the lieutenants so that we become aware of where your forces will be, should we need to call on them for support.

'I would like to point out that the sniper teams will be in full desert camouflage including face and hand paint. All members of the perimeter platoons must be made aware of the sniper positions because, if we have done our job, they won't be able to see us any more than the enemy will.

'Avi is the communications chief, responsible for coordinating all communications among the snipers and the other army personnel as well as spotting for me. He needs to meet with all radio operators so they become familiar with the set-up. Any questions at this point?'

After clarifying points raised, Cam turned to Amzi. 'Do you have anything to add?'

'Only to emphasize how important it is to have a complete victory. It would be an unmitigated disaster for not only Israel but for the whole world to have terrorists damage the building or, God forbid, enter and occupy even a small portion of the center. They do not know how to operate it and would likely, true to form, try to blow up at least a portion of it. This is one of those times in which a small number of men take on a great responsibility. I know you will acquit yourselves well.'

'I'm hungry, let's go check out the mess,' said Cam.

The sniper teams arrived an hour later and Cam assembled them outside Amzi's trailer. They drew to attention and saluted. Cam walked down the line to inspect battle-hard, fit young men with the Israeli equivalent of jump wings. In each man's eyes, a steely coldness showed they had volunteered for duty and had known what it meant to kill an enemy that could not see the assailant or fight back. The sniper watched him die through his scope. The Israeli Army said they were the best, and Cam did not doubt otherwise.

'Gentlemen… I am Cam, in charge of the operation. Avi and I are officers with Mossad, which I am sure you already know. May I speak English as the mission language or would you prefer a translation in Hebrew, which Avi can do?'

One of the officers stepped forward. 'Permission to speak, sir?'

'Of course. But I should point out that this team will be an informal one. Snipers are very independent or they would not be snipers. I find we all work better when we work informally. No need for attention and saluting, all that is over. Relax, but not in the field.'

The men responded with a feel-easy look.

'Sir, we all speak reasonable English because we are often on missions overseas where English is the only language in which men from various countries can communicate.'

Cam was about to tell him to drop the 'sir' but decided to let it go. 'You are not all from the same outfit, and I hope you will get to know each other well. As a supplementary weapon we will be carrying Uzis in the field as well as our rifles. If you don't have one, we will get you one from the armory. Avi is in charge of all communication and of patrolling the facility.'

Avi briefly explained how the communication devices operated, which was really a refresher for the men since they were all experienced. They tested them in the field to ensure there were no problems. The men then became familiar with the map, hide positioning, and tactics for the operation.

To be clear about the hides, Cam said, 'As you have seen, we have hides directly in front of the large building, on the left and right front corners of the large building, one on the rear right corner of the large building, and one on the left hand corner of the smaller building. I have designated these in an anticlockwise fashion, starting at the center hide as number five, and then on until the hide on the left corner of the large building becomes number one. We will use these numbers as call signs among ourselves. I've randomly assigned your teams to each of the hides. Avi and I will be number five, center. Is everything clear?'

It was. 'I don't need to say anything about weapon care,' Cam said in his final words, 'but I would ask you to do one thing you may not have done before. Please take these cloth bags and put sixty rounds in them. Oil and polish each round to help prevent jamming in these dusty conditions. Okay, let's go eyeball your positions so that you can get an idea of your field of fire.'

Avi and Cam walked back to the situation room to report to Amzi.

'Are you both satisfied with the men?' Amzi asked.

'Very. They will need no training, so it is straight on to the job.'

'Excellent. The director has invited us to share the evening meal at 18.00 in his quarters.'

The next day all the snipers, including Cam, sighted in their rifles. As they prepared, each man put on camouflage fatigues and painted the face and the hands of his partner, and checked the gear in individual rucksacks. They taped down anything likely to make noise and wrapped the barrels of the rifles in camouflage cloth. Cam checked all the men who, being professionals, were more than ready.

They each carried three two-quart plastic canteens. For food they had a choice of eight different types of freeze-dried meals.

Before they left Amzi chanted a Hebrew prayer. The men started towards their hides, but the hides in reality were little more than small desert bushes. Moving across open land offered perfect targets for both the enemy and Cam's soldiers.

The teams covering the front and sides of the building spread out in a staggered V formation with about fifty meters between each to prevent getting picked off by automatic fire all at once. After glassing the area for over an hour, they simply ran like hounds to their assigned locations. Cam hoped the Arabs had not kept the ground under constant surveillance. Did they have their own snipers? Cam wondered.

When they reached their respective hides they hit the ground hard. Avi made contact calls to confirm everyone was in place and ready. They settled in for a long, cold night. The two men in each team alternated with two hours sleep while his partner glassed 360 degrees. Cam knew that the men needed whatever sleep they could get; a tired sniper did not perform well.

Everyone was alert by three am and ready for the dawn. Nothing happened on the first night and morning. The snipers waited with infinite patience – a practiced skill – but nothing happened on the second and third nights and mornings.

By the third day they were running out of water and double-timed it back to camp, carrying the six canteens allocated to each team. One man from each team in turn carried his Uzi while the other teams monitored him closely. Cam made the dash as part of team five, having chosen the most vulnerable position in a frontal attack.

At the next dawn, the Arabs finally appeared.

Avi and Cam sighted them at the same time at 200 meters out from the 1700 meter fire line.

'I count fourteen, Avi.'

'I count sixteen.'

'I'll take your word for it.'

They alerted the other teams. Teams one and four had marked them at the same time. The rear teams had not sighted anyone coming towards them from the other direction.

The 50 mm lens on the Leupold 3-9 x 50 scope, mounted on the Remington rifle, allowed Cam to see the enemy clearly in the predawn light. They wore a light green uniform, not desert camouflage. Cam thought they might be Syrian regulars. The one-color uniform presented a perfect silhouette for a sniper. Cam lined up one of them coming directly towards their position. The intruder crossed the fire line.

'Open fire and make it count. Fire within your assigned overlap-area unless you can help other teams,' Cam ordered.

Cam squeezed off a round and the man catapulted backward. He took aim again and knocked another man down. Teams one and four scored several hits. The Arabs had nowhere to hide. They were all within the firing area and, even if they had turned and fled, they had no time to escape from the deadly sniper fire. Soon it was all over. The Arab fighters lay still on the ground.

'Avi, can you confirm all sixteen dead, no survivors.'

'Yes.'

'Teams one and four, can you confirm no survivors.'

'Yes.'

'Avi, please radio the situation room to inform Amzi.'

Less than a minute later, Amzi came on air. 'Excellent results. My congratulations. What are your plans?'

'We are going to stay here for another day and night in case they try again. If it is a larger force we may not be able to get them all, so some may get by us. I advise you keep the camp on high alert.'

'Okay, Cam. Will do.'

The teams stayed alert and performed their routine.

When all appeared calm in the desert, Avi grunted with surprise. 'I can't believe this. They are trying again in broad daylight in the morning – almost unheard of. Looks like platoon strength, about forty men.'

'Team two reporting. We have company on this side as well. Also the count is close to forty.'

The enemy crossed the fire line, not in organized formation – a big advantage to the sniper teams. If Cam had organized them he would have sent them in four separate squads in arrow formation with fifty meters separating each squad. They were walking. They should have been running. Snipers preferred a walking target to a running one. Runners were about three times harder to hit.

Cam spoke. 'Teams two and three, if you start to get into trouble I'll have team four help you. Commence firing when they are 1000 meters into the 1700 line.'

The snipers kept picking targets and dropping them. The Arabs panicked. Some hit the ground which did not help them, while others looked for cover and found none. It was too easy and pitiful.

They stopped advancing, having made about 500 meters within the firing line.

'Teams two and three, do you need assistance?'

'Not now, we have them confused for a while and they still can't figure out where the firing is coming from. We have accounted for as many of the target as we are going to get. The rest have started running like rabbits back the way they came.'

'Spotters, please make a visual count.'

The teams had taken out forty-eight Arabs.

Amzi came on line. 'Cam, this hardly seems possible. A sniper rifle is not an automatic weapon. I have not heard of anything like this before. No one at the Office is going to believe this.'

'The enemy was unprofessional, poorly trained and poorly led,' Cam explained. 'They presented perfect targets because they were not in proper defensive formation. They did not know who was firing and from where. The only thing the enemy can see are their colleagues going down for no apparent reason. This tends to panic even the most experienced soldier. Will he be next? There is no enemy he can see to fight. There is no cover. The ones we didn't kill ran away as fast as they could. It might be a good idea to send your people out for a sight count so they can prove to the Office what happened today. Our team will protect them.'

'A good idea. I'll get back to you as soon as I can. What are your plans?'

'We'll remain on duty tonight and for one more day. It's going to get pretty ripe out there in the hot sun, so if you want a visual count it will have to be soon. I have a proposal for the bodies.'

'Let them rot,' Amzi said, quick to respond.

'Amzi, I know you hate them, but Israel does not need its enemies to have more fuel for the counter campaign. Here is what I propose. Let them into the kill zone to collect their dead. They can bury them in the time specified by the Koran, which may not bring much goodwill, but at least would be good propaganda. And we get rid of the bodies.'

'Yes, but that means we have to let them within a few thousand meters of the facility, and that seems too dangerous.'

'The bodies are between 700 and 1000 meters from my position, which is plenty of space if they decide to try something, which I doubt they will after this fight. They would only be making more bodies to recover. Remember, they have no idea how we killed so many without them hearing or seeing anything. The snipers would be ready for any mischief.'

Amzi mulled over what Cam said. 'Okay, I don't like it, but you have a point. I'll check it out at the Office.'

'Make it as quick as possible. The Arabs will want the bodies as soon as possible, and I don't want any activity out there after dark.'

Half an hour later, Amzi came on line. 'The plan has been reluctantly approved, provided you guarantee no Israeli will be injured.'

'I'll do my best. How will you get word to the Arabs that they can come and get the bodies and it is not a trap?'

'Let me worry about that.'

An hour later, about thirty Arabs arrived with carts and wagons, and some with donkeys. They loaded up the bodies and took them away.

The Arabs, Cam learned later, had decided that the nuclear center was defended by Djinn, a fierce kind of demon.

Amzi decided that they would rest overnight at a kibbutz and drive to Tel Aviv the following day.

*****

CHAPTER EIGHTEEN

Kibbutz Shoval lay at the northern end of the Negev desert. Founded in 1946, the kibbutz typified the fulfillment of the Zionist dream to make the desert bloom. About 300 Kibbutz members worked together as a village-type community to raise dairy cows, sheep and chickens, and grow potatoes, wheat, barley, apples and oranges.

After showering and a dip in a half-Olympic sized swimming pool, they made their way to the communal dining hall. A tall, dark-haired man in his late thirties welcomed them and introduced himself as Yehuda Bauer. 'I will join you,' said Yehuda.

As they sat down for their evening meal, Amzi informed Cam of Yehuda's background.

'Professor Bauer is a historian at Hebrew University and is researching the Holocaust. He is especially interested in anti-Semitism and the Jewish resistance movement during the Holocaust years.'

'I did not know there had been an active resistance movement from the Jews,' Cam said.

'Most people do believe that Jews had gone to their deaths passively. But what is surprising is how much resistance there was, not how little,' Yehuda replied.

'How could this genocide occur?' Cam asked.

'The genocide was the worst in all history and targeted the whole Jewish race. Hitler was the key figure who caused the Holocaust. There was no real evidence of a master plan prior to the war and nothing noted about genocide in Hitler's book Mein Kampf – lots of invective, of course, against the Jews. Himmler had written down in his notebook towards the end of 1941, "What to do with the Jews of Russia?" Hitler's response, according to the notebook, was "Exterminate them as partisans." His plan to exterminate Jews had evolved during the Second World War. Hitler was solely responsible for that decision.'

Cam tried to comprehend the deadly combination of Hitler's evil and power – power to manipulate the German people and to forge a new empire without Jews.

'Is there a possibility that genocide could reoccur if the Palestine people became stronger and regained Israel?' Cam asked.

'Yes, but not just from the Palestine people.'

'You mean that Israel itself could…'

'Why not? If faced with the prospect of extermination again, the Jewish people will take extreme measures. We have returned to our land not to lose it. We may have to take the ultimate option in defending ourselves.'

'That is extreme,' Cam said.

'I am a Zionist. We support the establishment of a Jewish state in the Land of Israel. The United Nations partition in 1947 endorsed this, not just for the Jews that lived there at that time, but for all Jews to consider Israel as their true home, and to settle in Israel if they wished. We will do whatever we have to do to stay in our land.'

'How does this help the Palestinians?'

'We hope that they, too, will have a state which will be their home.'

'Will that happen soon?'

'That depends on negotiations and their cooperation, and the willingness of the Palestinians to accept the Jewish state.'

A kibbutz member handed a message to Yehuda.

'You must excuse me, as I have to attend to university matters,' Yehuda said. 'It's been a pleasure meeting you, Cam, and to know that you have helped Israel.'

'Likewise a pleasure, sir. I hope we can meet again and talk more about the history of the Jewish people.'

'I look forward to that, Cam.'

'You know that the kibbutz life is unique in the world as a communal type of settlement,' Amzi said, after Yehuda had left. 'Professor Bauer, himself, acts as a leader of groups of young people coming from overseas countries, so they can experience firsthand what it is like living in a kibbutz – usually a three-month stay.

'We have some two hundred and thirty kibbutzim scattered throughout Israel and most have more than three hundred members. We pool our efforts and skills in a democratic way to farm the land as well as carry out other types of work, and although we don't get paid, all our needs are met. We play an active part in political life, and many of our leaders come from kibbutzim. Our first prime minister, David Ben-Gurion, had his home in a desert kibbutz. Both Avi and I have grown up in a kibbutz. One day we will return to the kibbutz way of life. That is our hope.'

'Can anyone join the kibbutz?' asked Cam.

'Sure,' said Amzi. 'If you are Jewish it helps. You can try it out for a few months to see if it is to your liking. You take part in the work and cultural activities and you can learn Hebrew. Most of those from cities in Israel, though, who have tried living in a kibbutz, go back to city-life – it's too foreign for them. You really need to grow up in a kibbutz to feel it is right for you. Are you thinking of joining?'

'You never know. Israel is starting to grow on me.'

The next day after breakfast, a helicopter picked up Amzi, Cam and Avi and they touched down at the section of the Ben Gurion airport in Tel Aviv reserved for Mossad operations. Army regulars guarded helicopters, light fixed-wing planes, large transport planes and Mirage jet fighters; they also patrolled the razor-wire topped perimeter fence.

A uniformed officer saluted Amzi but not Cam and Avi in their battle-stained dress and full firepower.

When they arrived at the Office, two officers escorted them to a spacious reception where an attractive woman, the personal assistant to the head of Mossad, supervised a large desk with a selection of telephones. When she saw Amzi, her eyes lit up. She leapt up to hug and cheek-kiss him. A burly man in uniform stepped forward.

'Gentlemen, will you please release your weapons into my care. They will remain here under my guard until your business with the head is concluded, at which time they will be returned to you.'

The personal assistant caught a whiff of battle odor and flexed her nose. Amzi explained in Hebrew the reason.

'Welcome gentlemen,' the assistant said, 'I hardly recognized you, you are so filthy. You must be agent Campbell. I have heard a little about what you did in the Negev. Thank you on behalf of Israel.'

'It was our duty, nothing more,' Cam said.

'You are too modest.'

A light flashed on the desk.

'The head will see you now.'

The personal assistant punched a code and opened the door. They entered a large office, paneled in wood. A tall, slim man with thinning black hair rose from behind a polished wooden desk. He walked with confidence around the desk and embraced Amzi. A light banter followed which ended in laughter.

The head repeated his greeting ritual with Avi, then stood before Cam and said, 'Welcome, agent Campbell. It is my pleasure to meet you and welcome you to the Office. You have made Mossad and the agency extremely proud. I am a man who gets directly to the business at hand. At Amzi's request I have spoken to the director of CIA to secure your continued availability to Mossad when we require your particular expertise. He has agreed and also sends his congratulations on a job well done. This will be ongoing for an indefinite period. Do you accept?'

Cam thought for a moment about working for two agencies at the same time – the challenge was too appealing. 'Yes sir, I accept wholeheartedly.'

'Excellent. Of course, you will continue to perform missions for the

CIA and act occasionally as liaison between the CIA and Mossad. For convenience we have assigned you to technical operations, but that is for the record. You are basically a free agent and will be used where needed. You will report officially to the deputy head, as does Avi, but Amzi will continue to be your handler.

'I have a new warrant card for you. It allows you the second highest security clearance in the Office, just one behind the level that Amzi, the deputy head, and I enjoy. With this card you can gain access to anything in the civilian police and military organizations. You may also, if you feel justified, directly issue orders to members of these organizations. You have demonstrated exceptional judgment and lateral thinking, and we are certain you will make the right decisions. In Israel, especially in military and police matters, it is not unusual for young men to hold powerful positions.'

'By the way, the Negev incident never happened and will never be mentioned in the press or anywhere else,' the director said, in a more serious tone.

Cam and Avi both acknowledged his directive.

'Now, I'm sure you gentlemen would like to get washed and get into some clean clothes. These are ready in the quarters we have made available for you which are close to this office. Avi knows the way and will be in the accommodation next to you, agent Cameron. I understand that everyone calls you Cam and I hope you will permit me to do the same.'

'Of course, sir.'

'Very well, that is all for now. We will meet again shortly. Good day and thank you again for your service.'

At the reception area, the chief's personal assistant stood with a tray of three teacups and a finely engraved China teapot. 'I was certain you men would like some refreshment before you go to your quarters.'

'I thought we were too disgusting to be allowed in polite company,' Avi responded.

'Oh, you are, but I can put up with you for fifteen minutes. You will be too handsome to resist when you are cleaned up.'

After refreshments, Avi showed Cam to a spacious unit with comfortable chairs, a radio and television, a double bed and an immaculate ensuite. Civilian sabras, carefully vetted, cleaned the room daily and changed the bedclothes.

After a shower, rest and a change of clothes – a sweat shirt, a pair of jeans, and a new pair of desert boots dutifully placed outside Cam's door – they met for drinks at the in-house bar.

Avi poured three large measures of Johnnie Red. They touched glasses. 'L'chaim.'

'We are pleased to have you in Mossad and expect to have a long relationship,' Amzi said.

'I'm pleased to be accepted. It is always a pleasure to work with professionals, less chance of getting killed.' They laughed and made small talk about the Negev operation. On moving to the dining room a white-jacketed waiter recited the day's menu. Cam ordered a fillet mignon with roasted rosemary potatoes and mixed vegetables. A bottle of red wine accompanied the meal.

After the main course Cam cleared his throat. 'Gents, I need to tell you something. I am not going to be a Mossad mole in the CIA, and there will be no information from them to you or from you to them, without clearance, at least at the deputy head level. The exchange of information will be on a case by case basis as required to carry out a mission or for the national security of both countries. I will, however, be happy to act as liaison between the two agencies as the head has asked.'

Amzi and Avi looked at each other with stern faces, then brightened into smiles.

'Cam, you have passed the last test,' Amzi said. 'We were wondering when you would bring that up. We can trust you with classified information and we appreciate your integrity.'

After a restful sleep Cam reported to the head's reception area for his appointment with the armorer.

The armorer, a nondescript man wearing rimless glasses and having a slight stoop, welcomed Cam. 'Good morning, sir. I hope you slept well. Please follow me to the armory.' He led Cam to a large and impressive array of weapons. Cam caught a glimpse of a tattoo on the armorer's arm as he spoke. The armorer had been in a concentration camp.

'I understand you are very fond of the Remington 700 as your sniper rifle,' the armorer said. 'It is a fine weapon and you have used it to good effect, so I am told. We use a different sniper rifle, but when one has become accustomed to a certain type it is best to continue using it.'

Without waiting for Cam to reply, the armorer continued, 'I must address the issue of fitting your 700 with a suppressor.' Cam flinched with the thought of someone altering the rifle.

As if reading Cam's thoughts, the armorer said, 'The head of operations has ordered the modification as you will be performing sniper duty for dignitaries such as the prime minister. Do not worry. I will explain that this will not degrade your rifle or its accuracy. I am proposing a titanium suppressor that may be detached from the rifle. For this I will need to create the grooves for a left hand threaded attachment on the end of the barrel. I promise this will not interfere in any way with the performance.

'This suppressor is quite typical, allowing the expanding gases to be trapped inside a series of hollow chambers. The trapped gas expands and cools, and its pressure and velocity decreases as it exits the suppressor. You will be using baffles, and a single, larger expansion chamber located at the muzzle end will allow the gas to expand considerably and slow down before it encounters the baffles. I will install fourteen baffles which should be sufficient for your 7.62 caliber. The device will be 383 mm long and 51 mm in diameter.

'Further, I will use a two-point mount that supports the suppressor at the threads in the muzzle. If a small error in alignment should occur, it will not progress into a much larger error at the suppressor's muzzle.

'Please have just a bit more patience. I am almost at the end of my lecture. As you know, when a weapon is fired it produces torque that twists the barrel in a left hand direction. With the two-point mount and left hand threading, the barrel mount will remain in place, zero creep will remain zero, even after the suppressor has been removed for cleaning and replaced. There will be no cold shot shift after a day, a week or a year.

'Last, a properly designed baffle will strip and deflect the high pressure gas that surrounds and follows the bullet, resulting in an increase in practical accuracy. Also, the weight of a heavy unit tied to both the center and end of a rifle barrel does beneficial things for harmonic barrel vibration, contributing to an increase in the practical accuracy of a suppressed rifle.'

There was little Cam could say to this sort of expertise. He had known it was only a matter of time before he would have to accept suppressors, not only on the rifle but on semi-automatic pistols. He opened the case and stroked the rifle. It had been a good weapon over the years and he hoped that this craftsman would take good care of it. He had to believe that.

'When will I be able to get it back?'

'Two days at the most. I understand how men using weapons professionally become fond of them. I'll be careful, on that you can rely.'

'Thank you. May I have a can of regular 7.62/51 NATO and a can of armor piercing? I will have to sight in, with and without the suppressor, using random rounds from both cans.'

'That will be arranged when you collect your rifle. Avi will take you to the range and I will have a word with him.'

After the appointment Cam decided to wander around Tel Aviv to get a feel for the city. He showed his warrant card to the guard who came to attention and saluted as he passed the threshold.

Cam spent most of the day sightseeing. He found Tel Aviv to be a curious mixture of modern buildings and ancient landmarks but, in general, it looked like any big city in the modern world. He observed ultra-orthodox Jews wearing black ankle-length overcoats and fur hats.

When Cam returned to headquarters he took a closer look at the aging six-story brick edifice with no distinguishing features. No one would look at it twice. And no one would guess it housed one of the most efficient and deadly clandestine operations in the world.

Cam went through the warrant card business at the entrance with a different guard, who also came to attention and saluted. At his room he showered, shaved, performed his usual calisthenics and took a nap. He was not used to such leisure but lapped it up.

At 18.45, Avi knocked on his door. 'The car should be waiting and we don't want to keep Ahuva waiting. I've fasted all day in preparation for the feast she will put on. Hope your appetite is functioning.'

Ahuva welcomed them at the door with hugs and kisses. Cam thought Ahuva was absolutely stunning. Amzi shook hands and said, 'Welcome to our home for the evening meal. Let us be seated, we can talk as we dine. Some dishes must be eaten immediately as they are prepared.' A prayer was recited in Hebrew.

During a succession of dishes, Cam learned about recent politics and the ever present danger from the Arabs and other Muslims in the surrounding countries. Israel, it seemed, was under threat every day from every quarter.

The meal came to a comfortable end before Amzi briefed them:

'Cam, Avi, we will be going to Jerusalem tomorrow so that Cam can get an idea of the situation of the Knesset building. Cam, you need to help create a plan to use snipers and ground personnel to protect the prime minister and the one hundred and twenty members of the government. We at Mossad have not been satisfied recently with the current protection and feel we need a fresh view, and you can bring it. In fact, we are considering appointing you and Avi as advisors to security. You will not be identified as such; there will be a man covering as chief of security, but he will report to you. I will collect you at 08.00 tomorrow.'

*****

CHAPTER NINETEEN

At CIA headquarters, a few kilometers west of Washington D.C., the director met with the head of Middle East operations.

'How is our man doing in Israel?' the director asked.

'He has won favor with Mossad after a successful counter attack on Arab terrorists. He now has a high level of security clearance.'

'That's excellent. Is he able to inform us of what is happening militarily?'

'Under the agreement, his report passes to us as well as to Mossad.'

'And what if we don't want the Israelis to know?'

'We have a secure line.'

In Tel Aviv, ten high ranking military officers and Mossad spooks assembled in a conference room adjacent to the head's office. The head spoke in Hebrew, but Cam surmised that he was delivering the same information as he had heard about their mission. At one point, heads turned in their direction. Cam hoped the grim expressions were for the plans taking shape and not for them personally.

As Avi and Cam left the briefing, the personal assistant to the head of Mossad stopped them for cheek kisses. She held out her arms, palms up, and chanted a Hebrew prayer. Cam asked Avi what she had said.

'It is a prayer for our safety and our success in defending the chosen land. She has called us the Lions of Zion and mighty warriors, and has called on God to protect us and help us achieve victory over our enemies.'

Cam could hardly argue with that. He needed all the help he could get. An army general approached and extended his hand. Cam shook it.

A driver picked Amzi, Avi and Cam up outside the Office for the drive to Jerusalem, only forty-one kilometers from Tel Aviv. On the way, Cam wondered why anyone would want to wage a war over such an uninspiring landscape, but Cam knew that Avi and Amzi, and a whole nation like them, were dedicated body and soul to the preservation of a Jewish homeland. He could not find fault with that, considering how Jews had been treated over the centuries and, certainly, during the Second World War. Millions had died simply because they were Jewish.

They arrived at the Knesset building, located in the quiet Giv'at Ram neighborhood of West Jerusalem. The final design had yielded a large square structure of several levels with a terrace leading to the main entrance. It sat on a small hill, surrounded by a park. The location meant a security nightmare, with exposure on all sides to mortar attack, or strafing from the air, as well as providing easy access for a lone Arab gunman. Making matters worse were the daily tours conducted in many languages, including Arabic. Anyone could get in.

'Amzi, the place is totally exposed. What sort of security is there now?'

'It is currently guarded by the Knesset Guard. They are armed.'

'But not trained in counter terrorism…just a sort of a rent-a-cop operation, isn't it?'

Amzi looked embarrassed and uncomfortable. 'Yes Cam, you are correct. I have been pushing for a more professional approach, but the government wants to maintain a low profile. They want to make the Knesset friendly and, therefore, make Israel appear friendly. Thousands of tourists come through yearly.'

Cam appeared deep in thought before speaking. 'First thing, I would want trained army personnel in the Knesset guards' positions. We can hand pick them. They can still wear the same Knesset guard uniform. They should ideally be able to speak Arabic or a European language so they can eavesdrop on visitors' conversations to detect suspicious phrases. I would need a metal detector at the main entrance and that will be the only entrance that is available to the public. Anyone who beeps coming through the detector, especially those that look Arab or Muslim, will be gone over with a wand. There should be two interrogation rooms close by the entrance for detaining visitors who match profiles. Psychologists and the army should create the profiles. And we need someone who can recognize furtive and out-of-character behavior. We have to keep the prime minister and the members safer than they are now. I'm surprised nothing has happened since the building opened. Just luck, I imagine.'

Cam continued: 'The building needs to be sectioned and I would want two guards patrolling each section constantly. The guards should wear side arms. I don't care how unfriendly that looks. Weapon lockers would be installed every two hundred meters on every floor and corridor; these will house Uzis, combat shotguns and ammunition. Locks should be quick-opening but not easily penetrable, other than by those authorized to carry a key. It should be possible to find locks that will jam if the key is not inserted and turned in a certain way. The security people can make recommendations. I also would want those newly-developed motion detectors installed. Some big brain has come up with a device that uses ultrasonic pulses, whatever the hell they are, to measure the reflection off a moving object. I don't understand the science behind this, I've just read about it. We'll need to get the proper eggheads in technical to research a source for the device. I'd like the engineering group who does the maintenance around here to recommend where motion detectors could be useful, and we can take a look at their suggestions.'

Cam requested a walk around the building and surrounding garden area. It was all completely exposed, although in a crisis it provided a good staging area – helicopters could offload troops. Next he investigated the surrounding neighborhood. Good places to hide snipers were Wohl Park – Gan Havradim, the HaMenora Garden and the First Old Jewish Cemetery. All were within 600 meters of the Knesset. Buildings close to the Knesset were the Central Bank of Israel, the Ministry of the Interior, and the Supreme Court which was directly opposite the Knesset and next to the Foreign Ministry, all the buildings high enough to offer snipers a good vantage point. They would have to look at the security of these buildings as well. If Cam thought that they were good sniper hides, so would the enemy. Cam anticipated a security set up much the same as for the Knesset. He was not going to be popular with bureaucrats or departments, which would have to find the money to do the work.

The final worries were the approaches to the Knesset: Kaplan, Rothschild, Derech Ruppin and Sderot Ben Tsvi must be closed within minutes of an incident. The necessary barriers and other equipment would have to be brought in and ready for use. Two select army units needed to become familiar with the closure procedures.

'This is a tough one, Amzi. No one could have selected a more exposed location. At least somebody was thinking when the committee rooms were constructed at an angle so the southern wall, a security wall, did not face directly toward a Jordanian armed position. Do you think you can convince the government to spend the money to upgrade the security?'

'After your assessment, perhaps they will listen to reason. The surrounding Muslim nations are more vocal and belligerent. I'll need your help to explain what is required.'

'My pleasure. Anything to add, Avi?'

'No, but I would like to be part of the discussions and the planning.'

'Of course, both of you will be supervising the makeover. Let's get back, give a briefing and start setting up meetings.'

An army general approached them.

'May I address you as Cam?' he said. 'I have been assured you know what you are doing, although you are younger than most officers who would be leading such an action. The head has full confidence in you and Avi, and so must I. When we exit the building you will find two platoons of my men, very hard men, veterans of much combat, who will be manning the barriers you have selected around the Knesset. Your sniper teams will also be present, including the men who served with you in the Negev. They speak well of you. Please follow me, and I will introduce my junior officers to you.'

The officers were young and equivalent to Rangers, so Cam knew he could count on them. They already had the locations of where to set up roadblocks on the approaches to the Knesset and were ready. Cam's sniper comrades greeted him, and Cam told them he would be making position assignments when they were at the Knesset building. The general looked more relaxed.

Cam and Avi returned to Tel Aviv.

*****

CHAPTER TWENTY

Prime Minister Golda Meir; the chief of operations of the Israeli Defense Forces, Moshe Dayan; the head of Military Intelligence, Eli Zeira, and the chief of staff, David 'Dado' Elazar, met to discuss the latest military build-up by the Egyptians and Syrians.

Golda Meir expressed her concern:

'King Hussein of Jordan has advised me that the Syrians have increased their military strength on the Golan Heights and could be preparing for a strike against Israel. Egypt could join forces with Syria. Are we ready for that scenario?'

'King Hussein doesn't know the real military situation with Egypt. We are watching the Syrian build-up,' Moshe Dayan replied. 'Don't worry. If they attack on their own they know we would defeat them.'

'I agree,' said Eli Zeira. 'The Syrians would never act alone and the Egyptians don't have long-range bombers.'

'All the same,' said Golda Meir, 'the build-up is cause for alarm and we should mobilize Israel's reserves.'

'We did that five months ago and it cost us thirty-five million to cover a false alarm,' said Dado.

'I am against any mobilization unless the Arabs attack,' said Dayan. 'Let them be the aggressor.'

'But we need to be ready, especially on Yom Kippur, the national holiday, which would be an ideal time for Syria and Egypt to strike,' said the Prime Minister.

Later that day, the ministers of the cabinet endorsed Golda Meir's concern and gave her authority to call up the reserves on Yom Kippur if she saw fit.

On the eastern shore of the Suez Canal, 450 Israeli infantrymen and 300 tanks faced a build-up of Egyptian forces of 100 000 Egyptian soldiers and 1350 tanks. On the Golan Heights, Israel's two infantry regiments and 177 tanks faced a Syrian force of 45 000 and 1500 tanks.

On the afternoon of Yom Kippur the Egyptian and Syrian armies attacked and overwhelmed the Israeli forces. The superior military might of the Syrian and Egyptian armies included anti-tank missiles, SAM-2, SAM-3, and the new SAM-6 missiles, all supplied by the Soviets to target Israel's air force.

Golda Meir met with Moshe Dayan and Dado Elazar. Full of

remorse, Moshe spoke first: 'I was wrong. The destruction of the Third Temple is at hand. I offer my resignation.'

Golda Meir could not believe what she was hearing. She could not countenance a resignation which would send shock waves throughout Israel. A national hero resigning at such a critical time was inconceivable. 'No, I won't hear talk of resigning. Israel needs you.'

Dado rejected any notion of retreat in the Sinai Peninsula and while he acknowledged the initial setback by the overwhelming attack from the Egyptian and Syrian armies, he was confident in his forces striking back effectively with everything they had. Dayan, on the other hand, preferred to abandon their present position, regroup, and offer a defensive stand.

Later that evening, the ministers of the cabinet endorsed Dado's strategy.

The head of Mossad called Avi and Cam into his office early the next morning.

'Cam, I want you to be in Jerusalem within the next two hours to coordinate the safety of the prime minister and the members of the Knesset. I will convene a broader briefing with armed forces personnel within a few minutes, but that will be conducted in Hebrew. I will introduce you to some of the key players so they know who you are.

'The situation is this. Egypt and Syria have invaded the Golan Heights and the Sinai. We have been caught off guard, I am afraid to say, and even though we have mobilized, the Arab armies have moved forward with unforeseen speed. We are under considerable stress and need further supplies. Fortunately, our ally, the United States, is willing to provide airlifts of military supplies and equipment. El Al is already flying to a US Navy base in Virginia to begin transport. Ben Gurion airport will be used to collect the materiel.

'Prime Minister Golda Meir has unprecedentedly authorized the assembly of a number of twenty-kiloton nuclear warheads on Jericho missiles and F-4s, ready for deployment against Syrian and Egyptian targets. This is not an idle threat. We will use nuclear force if the situation calls for it. The European nations have declined to aid us, the anti-Semitic bastards, but the States will help us. I am reluctant to say that the Soviets have begun their own resupply operation to Arab forces by sea, which will be aggressively resisted by our naval forces. This is a very serious situation. Israel prefers not to go nuclear, but our nation is at stake, and we will never give it up.

'The prime minister will meet with her cabinet this morning. We want to ensure her safety at the emergency meeting.'

When Cam and Avi arrived in Jerusalem, the regular army had firmly established the barriers for the approaches to the Knesset. Cam traveled to every outpost with the same message. He told them he knew they would rather be at the front line, in active combat, but he received the same answer every time from the junior officers and the men, especially the non-commissioned officers. They all felt privileged to protect their seat of government. These people were ready for anything.

Cam placed the snipers in the parklands and buildings previously selected. They were just as fired up as the regular army men, but he hoped that their skills would not be needed. Meetings had been scheduled between the Israeli Prime Minister and various foreign diplomats and negotiators, so the teams were prepared to stop any terrorist activities, the Arabs having learnt how to set off bombs rather than fight.

Avi and Cam set up in the Supreme Court Building. Avi took control of overall communications among the various teams they had deployed. After an hour they had settled in.

Cam described the set up to the deputy head of CIA, his US boss. That information would be passed on immediately to the director and, through him, to the White House and Joint Chiefs of Staff. His boss rang off with best wishes.

He had already sighted in the Remington 700, with and without the suppressor, and knew what to expect in performance. With the suppressor it pulled a little, but this was easily compensated. Accuracy was excellent, especially within the short distances of shooting in a city, and no need for shots over 1000 meters. He kept the breach open so he could load an armor piercing round if needed. The magazine held the normal five rounds if he wanted to drop people and not a vehicle. He advised the other sniper teams to set up in the same way.

Avi made a circular motion with his hand, meaning something was happening. A convoy of armored military vehicles escorting Prime Minister Golda Meir to a high level meeting at the Knesset was approaching the barrier on Kaplan. The prime minister's vehicle was in the middle of the convoy and the escort vehicles were pushed in tight, only two meters between the bumpers of each vehicle to prevent unwanted guests from sliding into the line.

A small, battered white Toyota pickup veered off Derech Ruppin onto Kaplan, traveling at high speed. Cam spotted a large plastic barrel in the bed of the pickup. The Arabs had lately decided a mixture of fertilizer and diesel was the explosive of choice and, even though extremely crude, bombs made of the stuff packed serious explosive force. A device as large as the barrel in the little pickup could be equal to a kilo of C-4 plastic explosive.

The pickup's approach was well-timed. The Kaplan barrier had opened up to allow the prime minister's convoy through. It could not be closed until at least half the convoy was through since the prime minister's car was sandwiched in the middle.

The little pickup raced toward the convoy. Apparently, the vehicles behind did not respond. The driver of the pickup realized there was no way to break into a tightly packed convoy. Instead, he drove the pickup onto the verge of the road in an attempt to come alongside the prime minister's car.

Avi clicked on to the situation in a flash and yelled into communications. The entire convoy put on a burst of speed, and two of the escort vehicles flanked the prime minister's car to prevent the pickup from coming alongside.

The troops at the Kaplan barrier formed a defensive line, Uzis at the ready. It was a futile as the barrier could not be closed without shutting out the prime minister's car. A bomb could be detonated before the prime minister's car could pass through the open barrier.

Cam chambered an armor piercing round into the Remington, having another ready to reload. Through the scope he could see two people in the cab of the Toyota. A woman was driving. It was not a particularly easy shot at a swiftly moving target. He had to estimate a lead on the pickup. He took the shot, putting the round through the engine block, then reloaded and shot again. Smoke billowed from under the hood and the pickup shuddered to a halt. The prime minister's convoy streaked through the barrier, which was immediately secured.

Another problem loomed. The occupants of the pickup might blow themselves up anyway. Avi screamed into communications. He ordered his group to secure the pickup and the people in it before they had a chance to detonate. They surrounded the vehicle.

'Avi, I want the occupants alive. Don't let the army kill them, we need to interrogate them.' As Cam watched, the army received the message. They rough-handled the occupants and removed them from the cab. Damaged goods to be quizzed, thought Cam.

Cam and Avi double-timed it off the roof of the Supreme Court Building and headed for the Knesset garden. A squad of army soldiers dragged the prisoners to where they waited.

Cam would interrogate the prisoners; it would not be pretty. He wanted to know who had recruited them and organized the attack. He asked to have the assistance of two soldiers who would not flinch from dirty duty.

Two, physically solid and mean-looking, non-commissioned officers arrived on the scene. They came to attention and saluted.

'No need for formalities, gentlemen. Get these prisoners into a secure room here in the Knesset where no sound will be heard.'

The NCOs located a suitable place and soon had the prisoners bundled into it. Cam had scopolamine as a routine item in his kit. No one would admit to having it for use in interrogation, but he knew the Israelis would not care if he obtained the information he needed. He also had the only antidote known – physostigmine – to bring them around again.

The male prisoner was clearly frightened. The woman, however, was as fierce as a cornered wildcat, thought Cam, and kept screaming insults in Arabic.

Cam filled a syringe.

'Hold her secure. I want her done first. The other one may just have to be taken away, he seems of little use.'

The woman cursed and spat in his face. Cam wiped away the spittle and tapped a vein in her arm as the NCOs held her down. The injection went smoothly and within two minutes she was semi-conscious and susceptible to suggestion. Three minutes more and she revealed the name and location of the terrorist who had organized the raid on the Knesset and what he was planning in the near future, which was a series of bombings in Israeli markets and other crowded places. Even drugged, the woman spouted hate at Jews everywhere in the world, including the United States. Cam would have to make Mossad and the CIA aware of this growing threat. Muslims, incompetent at fighting, had geared up to use explosives.

The mastermind terrorist was holed up in the Gaza Strip but made occasional forays into a small town in Israel called Kefar, located just over the border. Cam would make plans to deal with him when he next spoke to Amzi.

After a few hours there was no more information to be gained from the woman. Cam had the NCOs haul the man and the woman off to Tel Aviv, where they would be imprisoned.

Amzi was on the line to Cam: 'Prime Minister Golda Meir would like to meet with you as soon as possible.'

A short time later, Cam and Avi were ushered into the prime minister's office.

Golda Meir addressed them: 'Please, we are most honored to meet you. Mr Cameron Campbell and Aviram, may I introduce you to Moshe Dayan, David Elazar and Eli Zeira, but I am sure you know of them well.'

'We are privileged to meet you,' Aviram said.

'And we are in debt to you. What you have done this morning in preventing a terrorist attack at a time when we are facing a serious threat to our way of life is most commendable. Mr. Campbell, we acknowledge your special contribution in upgrading the security level for the Knesset. If the terrorists had succeeded in undermining the heart of our government at this critical stage in our existence, the consequences would be unimaginable.'

'I am happy to work for the security of Israel in whatever way I can.'

'Thank you. I will be frank with you, Mr. Campbell. We are in dire straits. We have been caught napping, as you say. The combined strength of the Syrian and Egyptian forces could overpower us in the next few days. We desperately need the arm supplies promised to us by the US. For some reason, Henry Kissinger, Secretary of State, is delaying the supply. You must realize how important these arms are in preventing a full scale onslaught. We will defend ourselves to the last drop of blood if we need to. But at this moment we need your help to avert a catastrophe.'

'You want me to ask the president of the United States to speed up the supply of arms?' Cam said, picking up on the prime minister's line.

'No, Mr. Campbell. We don't wish you to ask him anything. We would like you to tell your CIA contact something.'

'Tell something? I don't understand.'

'It's simple. All we want you to say is: The Jericho missiles are armed. I know we have no right to ask you to do this, but we are in desperate times.'

'I… I will do what I can to help.'

'Do you have a secure line?'

'I have a secure line. Under the CIA-Mossad agreement, a copy of my report to CIA is also handed to Mossad.'

'No, I mean, do you have a secure private line?'

'I…'

'It's all right, Mr. Campbell, you don't have to explain. We just ask you to send this message on your private line.'

*****

CHAPTER TWENTY ONE

A day later, President Nixon called an urgent meeting with Secretary of State Henry Kissinger at the White House.

Nixon said, 'We have a situation in the Middle East that threatens our interests as well as the State of Israel. We are playing a dangerous game by not supplying arms to Israel.'

Kissinger replied, 'I don't think we should be too keen to concede to their demands. We will invite condemnation from many countries including the Middle East. It could also lead to an oil embargo.'

'That will happen whatever we do. I repeat that we are playing a dangerous cat and mouse game. And now we know from our agent in Israel that the Jericho missiles are armed with nuclear warheads. I have no doubt that Golda Meir will use that option if she feels there is no other way to save Israel from annihilation.'

Kissinger said, 'That sounds like blackmail.'

The President responded, 'Blackmail or not, we can't afford to take that chance. We must restore Israel's fighting capacity and reduce the risk of Israel taking up the nuclear option. Supply them with what they need and immediately.'

'Yes, Mr. President.'

'We must promote a ceasefire agreement with Israel, but it has to be in a better position to bargain. She will still need to make concessions.'

'Yes, Mr. President. I will see to it.'

Even before a response from Washington, the tide started to turn for Israel with successful counter attacks.

Kissinger ordered a massive airlift, but it had to fly through Lajes Air Force Base in Portugal, the only European country that would permit the aircraft to land. Traditional European allies refused to allow resupply aircraft to land for refueling or even overfly their territory. Aircraft had to fly an exact airspace border between the hostile Arab nations to the south and European nations to the north, down the middle of the Mediterranean Sea to Israel. American jet fighters from the US 6th Fleet escorted the transports, C-5 Galaxy, and the C-130E Hercules, to within two hundred kilometers of Israel, where Israeli Air Force Phantoms and Mirages escorted them into Ben Gurion Airport.

Supplies were not all that was delivered. In the opening days of the war the Arabs had been surprisingly efficient in destroying significant numbers of Israeli aircraft with the new Soviet surface-to-air missile, the

SAM-6. The US sent F-4 Phantom II fighters from the 4th Tactical Fighter Wing, the 33rd Tactical Fighter Wing and the 57th Fighter Weapons Wing. These were flown into Lod, where American pilots handed the aircraft over to Israeli pilots, many of whom had trained in the States. The USAF insignia was changed to the IAF insignia, and aircraft were in the air and in combat within hours of arrival.

Israel launched successful counter attacks on the back of the US resupply and the war was over within days of the resupply mission. The Arabs seemed incapable of sustaining a hostile action, even with the Soviets airlifting 15 000 tons of supplies, much of which went to Syria, and another 63 000 tons arriving by sea. It was another decisive victory for Israel in the face of a superior force that could have been the victor.

A major consequence of the war was a complete oil embargo on the US by the Arab countries, which resulted in the 1973 fuel crisis. The US, however, learned a valuable lesson about the need for staging bases overseas. Their air force greatly expanded its aerial refueling capabilities and made long-distance sorties the standard rather than the exception.

Back at the Office, Amzi was pleased but grim-faced, knowing of the explosives tactic the Muslims had adopted. A plan was put in place to deal with the man in northern Gaza who seemed to be in charge of terrorist activities in that area.

'Cam, we want you to take this man out when our agents have had a chance to follow his movements,' Amzi said. 'He seems to change his location daily, but we will know when he crosses the border from Gaza. This will be the best location for you as you cannot pass for an Arab or an Israeli, but you only need to get close enough to put one in his brain, no tricky disguises needed. Our armorer has taken a liking to you and has produced a weapon he says will suit perfectly. Please see him as soon as possible, as we will have to call on you at a moment's notice when the Gaza individual plans to cross the border. We also want you to take a short course in Krav Maga, the Israeli style of martial arts.'

He continued, 'Before you get beaten up by our Krav Maga experts, I'd like to explain a few things. Contrary to some of the press stories, Mossad takes great care in using termination as a viable option. The approved execution list exists only in the safe of the prime minister and that of the head of Mossad. Every prime minister is required to review this list. If he or she initials a name, we proceed on a time line. The prime minister can insist on being consulted before each new mission and sign an new execution order. There are three groups – the few remaining senior Nazis; all known terrorists, mainly Arabs and other Muslims who have already killed Jews or we know are planning to, and lastly people working for Israel's enemies who represent a great danger to Israel and her citizens. If a hit is requested, the prime minister will pass the matter to a judicial investigator whose identity is closely guarded. If the request is confirmed it goes back to the prime minister for signature. One of three Kidon teams will then carry out the assassination. This sequence of events occurs well before you are assigned a mission. You must not think that you are acting without the full support of the government.'

'Thank you, Amzi, but I wasn't worried. I have no reservations.'

At the armory, Cam shook hands. 'Welcome again, Agent Campbell. Allow me to offer you another weapon for your close-up work, a .25 caliber semi-automatic pistol affectionately known as the Baby Browning. It is only 104mm long with a barrel length of 54mm. It carries a 6-round magazine and weighs only 254 grams. You can put it in a trouser pocket and no one will be able to see it, it is that small. I have fitted it with a suppressor that is quickly removed. Firing it will only produce a popping sound, less noise than opening a can of soda. It is only accurate up to two meters, but if I have the correct information about you, you will put it directly against the head of your target. Please also accept this shoulder holster especially adapted to the pistol, if you wish to carry it in that fashion. No one will detect it under a jacket or suit coat. You will be able to free it easily even with the suppressor attached. I wish you good hunting.'

Cam thought it an elegant piece of equipment. He had heard about this weapon but never seen one. To use it he would walk up to the target from behind, push the suppressor against the first vertebra and fire, using a full jacketed round. The round would sever the vertebra, essentially killing the target immediately, but just to be certain, the next round in the magazine would be a hollow point, fired into the back of the skull. The bullet would shatter on impact, scattering tiny particles around and through the brain, mincing it. Effective and ninety-nine percent certain of a clean kill.

Later that day Cam reported to a gym in the Office, where he met a rough NCO, a 9th Dan in rank in Krav Maga, the highest achievable, who would take him through his paces.

'I know you have had martial arts training but nothing like you will receive here,' the NCO said.

Cam was still grateful for the unarmed combat training he had received with the Rangers because this guy looked like he meant business.

His first opponent, a latex dummy, represented a complex structure of skeletal joints and fluids to duplicate the human body. He proceeded to break the dummy's neck, the trachea, the sternum, and any other critical points he could think of, including foot and ankle bones, elbows, and hands. The dummy had the resistance of a real human body, so it was hard work. He ended up panting.

'Just passable. You will now enter my world and the world of the Middle East. I know you have had your face rebuilt so I will not hit you there. Everywhere else is fair game. I will now explain some basic principles. First and foremost, Krav Maga, or KM, is not a spiritual exercise as so many Asian martial arts are made out to be. KM is attacking preemptively to the body's most vulnerable parts such as the eyes, jaw, throat, groin and sternum areas. Neutralize your opponent as quickly as possible by responding with an unbroken series of counter attacks. There are no sporting rules. People trained in KM are not limited by techniques that avoid severely injuring opponents. It is just the opposite. We want to severely injure the people we are fighting. You will learn how to execute strikes, including punches, hammer fists, elbows, various kicks and use of knees. You will learn defense against takedowns, chokes, bear hugs and other possible attacks, including defending against knives, guns, metal bars and the like. KM includes techniques from traditional Eastern European street fighting, military combat, Kung-Fu, karate, boxing, Muay Thai, Judo, Aikido, western wrestling and Ju-Jitsu.'

The instructor paused for Cam to digest all that, and then continued. 'The first thing you need to know is to measure the aggressiveness of the target and to identify the vulnerable points. Most targets will tighten their stomachs or upper torso, leaving their necks and skulls weak. You will now learn how to penetrate these vulnerable points.'

The instructor proceeded to teach him.

Training went on for two hours almost every day for three weeks. The instructor and Cam had become good friends by that time, and he had bruises in various colors all over his body to prove it.

'Well learned, my friend, after only a few weeks. You need a hell of a lot more practice, but I can now recommend you for full Mossad service in the use of Krav Maga. You are most welcome into the fight for Israel. Please come back for continued training at a more serious level.'

Cam thanked his instructor but was not so sure of the next level.

Finally, Cam received word about his target in Kefar, the one who had masterminded the assassination attempt on the prime minister. He reported to Amzi, who had a photo of the target and a dossier. To Cam, he appeared like a nondescript bearded Arab that no one could pick out from a crowd.

'Come on, Amzi, how am I supposed to identify this guy out of the rest of the population?'

'We have people in place to be certain to identify the target. They will point him out to you, no question.'

'If you have people in place, why don't they do the deed? Too squeamish?'

'It is not their job, Cam. We need a cold professional for this, like you, someone we can trust to do it and just walk away.'

Cam arrived in Kefar in less than an hour. They told him to stay around a certain street corner and take time to apply some CIA trade craft to ensure no one was interested in him. The Baby Browning nestled under his left arm, and he carried a Gerber Mark II fighting knife in a sheath on his right ankle. He hoped no Arab would try to speak to him.

Two men dressed in traditional Arab clothing, but not Arabs, approached him. They were suitably grimy. One used a prearranged hand signal to identify themselves as the Mossad contacts. No greetings were exchanged. They walked down the street. Cam followed two hundred meters behind. They suddenly turned into an alleyway and he followed them. Emerging, they turned left and arrived at a tea stand. One of his guides pointed to a middle-aged, bearded man wearing a red and white checkered keffiyeh, the traditional Arab head scarf, and black agal – a black cord to keep the scarf in place on his head. He was alone and sipping a glass of tea – his last. The men disappeared around a corner of a building.

Cam found it surprisingly easy. He simply walked up to the man, drew the suppressed Baby Browning, put the initial round into the first vertebra and the second in the back of his head, and walked calmly away. He did not need to look back. He was dead before his forehead slammed into the table top. The two fake Arabs were waiting and escorted Cam to their vehicle. Then back to Tel Aviv, mission accomplished.

*****

CHAPTER TWENTY TWO

Cam met Amzi. 'Well done, another rat eliminated.'

'Amzi, why am I getting these exercises? Surely you have your own people to do this. I have met many hard men who don't need my help.'

'But they do, Cam. You are a machine that we require, and the Company has authorized every step.'

Cam did not like the term 'machine', with its connotation of being controlled like a robot – having no mind, no feeling. It dehumanized him. At the same time he recognized the truth in what Amzi said. His tough upbringing and predisposition to violence had been reinforced by his role as a sniper in Vietnam and by being an assassin with Mossad. He remembered what his friend and mentor, Ralph Pines, had said: 'They will try to turn you into a machine. Don't let them do that!'

If he were a machine, could he be switched off? For the first time in his war-torn life he doubted it. He felt as though life had gripped him in a vice and would not let go. Any hope of recasting himself as a peaceful, compassionate person had been erased.

Amzi, sensing that he had touched a raw nerve, said, 'Why don't you come round to our place for dinner tonight. We are celebrating the festival of Hannukah. You will meet Adiela, Ahuva's sister.'

As soon as Cam met Adiela he knew he was in trouble. She looked stunning, with a touch of the orient like Ahuva. He admired her thick, raven-black hair, dark amber eyes, slightly slanted with small gold flecks, translucent skin, straight nose, just perfect for her face, high cheekbones, about five-six in her bare, perfect little feet. Adiela, meaning Ornament of God, or the diminutive Adi, meaning Jewel, seemed just right for her, Cam thought. She was in her last year of her course in political science at Tel Aviv University. Over dinner, Cam made conversation about her studies; she might go into law.

After the first night of the eight-day festival, and back at their quarters, Cam asked Avi how one went about getting to know a Hebrew girl of Adi's age.

'Ha, got it bad haven't you? You make polite conversation. Israeli girls aren't shy; she'll let you know if she's interested. I think you have to be a little careful with the boss's sister-in-law.'

Amzi and Ahuva invited Cam and Adi to their home each remaining night of the eight-day festival, when a candle was lit in a nine-branched candelabrum, a menorah. They sang a Jewish song to commemorate the history of the Jewish people. They dined on traditional Hanukkah foods, fried or baked in olive oil, which included potato pancakes, jam and jelly-filled doughnuts, and fritters.

In the last day of the celebration, Avi told him it was time to ask her to go out during the rest of her leave.

Following Avi's advice, Cam invited Adi to walk on the beach and dine on the terrace of cafés. They talked about her almost certain conscription into the Israel Defense Forces, IDF, and how she wanted to spend her twenty-four months of service. She meant the Intelligence Service. Like her brother-in-law and sister, keep it in the family. She was careful not to ask too much about what Cam did. Ahuva might have hinted that a relationship might not be a stable one, Cam thought. Cam made it plain he would like to see her the next time he was in Tel Aviv and that seemed all right. He told her he would see her as much as he could before he left and that seemed all right, too. The day he went back to training she gave him a light kiss on the lips. He parted with a new spring in his step.

Adi was stationed at the Camp in Kirya, central Tel Aviv. The Camp housed the Military Intelligence Directorate – the place for her since she had decided to become involved in Intelligence during her conscription. Ahuva assured Cam that Adi would get some leave and Cam could spend as much time with her as her roster allowed.

Cam signed out a car and drove to Kirya. At the gate he showed his warrant card, was saluted, and allowed to enter. When he parked the car in an official spot he took a walk around the campus, having a good look at the place. Security was tight, which he was pleased to see. Even though he wore fatigues, he was challenged several times, and not just by obvious security personnel with automatic weapons. Men with side arms also approached him and demanded to know his business. Not knowing enough Hebrew was a disadvantage, but the warrant card transcended all languages, and explanations were carried out in English. He was generally saluted and asked if he needed any assistance. He loved the card. One man, on examining it, said, 'Oh, you are him. Welcome, sir.' Cam didn't know what that implied.

Ahuva had arranged Cam's first meeting with Adi at an administration building, not at her barracks. When he entered he could see her through a large window – she was pacing back and forth in a room he assumed was used as a second verification area. She was not allowed to greet him until his identity had been proven.

After more standing at attention and saluting, a guard opened the door and politely motioned Adi out.

Adi was dressed in customary Israeli olive green fatigues – a pressed blouse with a white T-shirt underneath, sharply creased trousers and highly polished combat boots. Women could wear their hair long and Adi's was pulled back and secured with a gold clasp. She had brushed her thick raven mane until it shone with a luster. On her left sleeve was the insignia of a private conscript (Hogrim Turai) – the lowest rank – which was normal as all conscript ranks were elevated purely on time served. She looked the professional female soldier, Khayyelet, and she could not have been more beautiful. She smiled as they shook hands – perhaps for the benefit of onlookers, Cam thought.

They did not make conversation as they walked to the car. The guards at the gate came to attention and saluted them. Cam was certain up to that point Adi had never been given a salute, which was what she did for people above her rank – everybody, in fact.

They motored along for a few kilometers before Adi told him to pull over. Cam had no idea what to expect. She leaned over, put her hand on his face and stroked it. She was trying hard not to cry.

'I want to go to the beach and get an ice cream,' she said.

They parked at the beach and, within two steps of the car, Adi grabbed Cam in a tight hug and, finally, the tears came.

'You look absolutely terrible. Are you starved and sick or just starved? How many kilos have you lost since coming to Israel?'

'It is very nice to see you, too, and thanks for noticing,' Cam said. 'Don't you think I look stylishly thin? Remember, you can't be too rich or too thin. I think some movie star said that. It must be all the fresh air and exercise, don't you think? You, on the other hand, look stunning.'

'Oh, shut up. My sister and I are going to feed you until you pop and you can be sure my aunties will as well. You will have so many women bothering you, you'll want to go back to America, but if you try that I will get my service weapon and shoot you.'

'Just what I needed. Words of endearment. How nice to be threatened by someone other than an ugly thug who drags his knuckles when he walks. I shall treasure your warning forever.'

Adi kept hold of Cam, as she stood on tip-toes and kissed him lightly on the lips. 'Enough, I want my ice cream.'

They walked hand in hand along the beach to a terraced café. They sat at a table, shaded by a blue and white striped umbrella, Israel's colors. The colors matched the IDF flash on Adi's right sleeve, a blue Star of David on white in the upper left corner, and a gold sword with olive branch supported by a gold-stylized Star of David in the lower right corner, the whole flash surrounded in thin gold braid.

Not wanting to be conspicuous but proud of it nonetheless, Cam wore a dog tag with the Mossad flash embossed on it. The flash showed a silver menorah on a black background, the menorah surrounded by the motto 'kee betachbulot ta'ase lecha milchama', translated as 'with clandestine terrorism we will conduct war'. Beneath the menorah the motto was 'Ha-Mossad le-Modiin ule-Tafkidim Meyuhadim, translated as 'Institute for Intelligence and Special Tasks', the Israeli intelligence agency commonly referred to as Mossad.

'I'm hungry. The food on base is not all that bad but not what I get at home. I want a burger with fries,' Adi said.

'Welcome to the army. I would prefer a chicken matzo ball soup.'

They sat for a while, relishing each other's closeness.

'You know,' Adi said, 'we do everything the men do in training. It's standard for all conscripts. We could pick up a rifle and go to war.'

'Aren't you exempt because you serve in Intelligence?'

'Not necessarily.' Cam held her hand a little tighter.

'But what about you?' Adi questioned. 'You don't need to be here. You can go back to your profession as a biochemist at any time.'

'You know about that? I graduated in biochemistry at Yale University, but I have yet to practice. I could have lived a quiet existence in a laboratory, but how unexciting. In any case, I love it here in Israel. How would I have met you?'

'That's the best part for me, but I fear for you. What does a biochemist do anyway in a laboratory?'

'Well, we carry out routine tests – on blood, for example, to assist doctors in the diagnosis of diseases. Or we carry out research, which might help those suffering from diseases like cancer.'

'So, a biochemist deals in life, and here you are in a foreign country, taking on our problems and dealing in violence and death.'

'I know, Adi. When I came to Israel I was looking for excitement and purpose. I have found that but, more important, I feel as though I belong here, and I have a special bond with the Jewish people. Of course, I will defend that home like everyone who have settled in Israel.'

They walked along the beach until the sunset draped a marigold glow over the horizon. Afterwards, at a restaurant they ordered fish and two glasses of white wine. And then it was close to Adi's curfew, so Cam drove her back to base, but not before they embraced and kissed passionately.

Cam and Adi met three more times that week.

'Aren't all these day passes raising some eyebrows?' asked Cam.

'Let them get their own high ranking Mossad officer,' Adi replied.

*****

CHAPTER TWENTY THREE

'I must tell you,' Amzi said, 'that I have seldom met two men who are as rough and uncouth as you. You may take that as a compliment if you so desire.' The atmosphere became more relaxed as the three of them consumed more tea and whisky, but Cam could sense that something else was on the agenda. Amzi cleared his throat.

'I have another assignment for you – a short interlude, if you like – which has already been cleared with Mossad and the CIA, so it is a done deal, as you Americans put it. This assignment is more of a favor to CIA so that we will remain on good terms for any military assistance we might need from the US in the future.

'The Malaysian government has identified Chinese triad involvement, and verified that heroin, morphine and raw opium paste are being transported through Burma to the Thailand and Malaysian borders. A major drug manufacturing laboratory and distribution organization have been located in the Banjaran Titiwangsa mountain range along the watershed of the Perak River. Despite the ongoing but low level dispute about the sovereignty of the Pedra Blanca, Middle Rocks and South Ledge Islands, and the territorial waters surrounding them, the Malaysian armed forces claim not to be in a position to carry out an operation in this area. Their government has requested help from CIA to eliminate this drug operation. And CIA has passed it on to us, knowing we have you on board.'

Cam and Avi exchanged a look that conveyed disgust.

'This is some kind of diplomatic connivance where both governments can disavow any knowledge of our presence there if we mess this up and get killed,' Cam said.

'I do not know myself how this transpired, but evidently it has to do with international relations between the US and Thailand. Unidentifiable personnel are required to carry out the mission and you two are the best in the area at the moment. My apologies, but in this case I am only the messenger.'

'Great, sounds like super spook stuff thought up by a desk jockey at Langley with no field experience and thick nerd spectacles.'

'My information is that you will be transferred to Takhli air force base within two days. You may request what weapons and ammunition you require from our armory. I have not been informed of further plans. I wish you good luck.'

Takhli had been used as a CIA airfield for some time so it made sense for them to touch down there first. Cam and Avi found the military transport uncomfortable and boring. The flight seemed interminable. They had stocked up on weapons and ammunition in Singapore before departing, not being sure what they could get in Malaysia. They had acquired a 40mm grenade launcher, Uzis, Czech CZ-70 pistols, and Cam had been sure to obtain an Ithaca 37 combat shotgun. Altogether they were heavy with ammunition. From Takhili they were transported to the Malaysian Special Forces staging area at the Kuala Lumpur air base.

From Kuala Lumpur they were trucked to a remote location supposedly near the drug lab. Heat, flies and sullen Asians kept them company. Cam and Avi had discussed the possibility at least some of the Malay military were connected to the triads and were less than happy to see them. Lots could go wrong in the jungle.

They were dumped by the roadside with the promise that a chopper would show up before first light to let them survey their area of operation. They were more than skeptical, but at least they had a map.

'This is another fine mess you have gotten us into, Stan.'

'What, you're doing your Laurel and Hardy thing again?'

'Very good Jewish slapstick comedy, which just about suits our situation at the moment. You have any idea how to get us out of here alive and still expend lots of grenades?'

'Yeah, I think just lay down as much firepower as possible and hope some exotic bug unknown to science doesn't bite and inject us with poison to kill us within minutes.'

'I just happen to have smuggled in some bug repellent, so we might as well break out the gourmet dried rations, get comfy, and hope it doesn't rain.'

A bottle of Scotch appeared and was duly put to rest. Against all expectations, a Bell 204, a knockoff of the Iroquois UH-1, descended, and the copilot gestured them to come on board. The Company might be of some use after all.

After a five kilometer-ride, they spotted the drug lab in a small compound that had been fire-cleared of vegetation. They could see fifty-gallon barrels, presumably filled with base – ripe for exploding – and apparatus consisting of glass vessels and copper tubing.

'Primitive, but what do we know about base refining? Time to get busy,' said Cam.

The Bell dropped them off and they retrieved their weapons. They flipped for who would carry the grenade launcher and Avi lost.

'Don't get your knickers in a twist, I'll carry half the load of grenades,' Cam said.

'You sure as hell will, and you had better be ready to pass them quick smart when I want to light them up.'

They hiked the short distance to the lab and set up 100 meters away in thick vegetation to observe the routine. Two days of observation was enough.

At the lab everything seemed relaxed. A group of women arrived at 08.00 and carried on with various duties that made no sense to Cam and Avi, since they did not know how to make drugs under a primitive set-up. Later, at 16.00, three men in a battered Toyota mini-truck arrived at the drug lab and made a cursory inspection.

Cam and Avi rested and set up the next day to carry out their attack after the men had arrived in the Toyota for their daily check. They wanted to be certain in taking them out. Cam thought it a pity that the women had to be collateral damage – they were probably just trying to make a living.

As predicted from the two previous day's observations, the Toyota mini-truck arrived on schedule, and Avi started in with the grenades. Spectacular explosions occurred with the flammable solvents, all in technicolor. No survivors and no more drug lab.

They congratulated each other on how easy things had gone and made for the designated extraction area, hoping no one would meet them.

As usual, things did not go to plan. The drug lords deployed a deuce and a half with a mounted .50 to randomly chew up the jungle in the hope of hitting them. The chopper would not pick them up in a hot zone, so there was nothing they could do but return fire.

Cam and Avi shifted position every few minutes to avoid being spotted, and to make it look like there were more than two of them. Finally, Avi got a clear shot with an incendiary grenade that put paid to the deuce.

The chopper came in, but for some reason would not touch down. They had to climb up rope ladders to board.

'I don't know about you, Avi, but I can use some R and R. Sitting by the Med in Tel Aviv seems good to me at the moment.'

'Beratzon. We have been in the desert for much too long. I want to look at the sabras on the beach. L'chaim.'

Back in Tel Aviv, they relished a clean apartment, clean sheets, clean toilet, a shower, and mini fridge stocked with tasty beverages.

Cam knew it could not last.

*****

CHAPTER TWENTY FOUR

Head of MI6 – We are concerned with the increase of arms shipments from both Libya and the Palestinian organization, Fatah, to the IRA. The IRA is using an Active Service Unit (ASU), a cell of four men to carry out the operation. We would like to neutralize this cell, but we prefer to outsource this operation to Kidon.

Head of Kidon – We can carry out this operation in return for information on the IRA which might threaten the security of Israel, and, of course, any other support which you can unofficially provide.

Amzi pulled Cam out of the Office and they sauntered along to a quiet, unobtrusive street in the Tel Aviv neighborhood, but home to what looked like an expensive law firm. In fact, it was home to one of the most concealed operations in Mossad. People said it was not even real; it was a figment of the collective imagination, designed to terrify and appall the leaders of the enemies of Israel. The headquarters of Kidon, the 'bayonet' or 'tip of the spear' was known as Caesarea until the mid-1970s; its function was assassination and kidnapping.

Part of the recent myth was the mayhem it carried out on the Palestine Liberation Organization, PLO, in Beirut. Operation Wrath of God was payback for the massacre of Israeli Olympic sports stars in Munich in 1972.

A well dressed, handsome man greeted them at the entrance and introduced himself as Michael Rivkin, the officer in charge of Kidon.

'Welcome, gentlemen, welcome. I know Amzi very well and I am most pleased to meet you, Mr. Campbell. Your reputation precedes you because otherwise, frankly, you would not be here. As it is lunch time I have taken the liberty of ordering for us. I hope you find medium rare roast beef sandwiches acceptable.'

'Please call me Cam, everyone does. A roast beef sandwich sounds tempting.'

As they ate, Rivikin related information about Kidon. 'All candidates are recruited from Mossad's ranks and normally training takes two years at a base in the Negev. Assassination teams usually consist of four members of which some can be women. One team member is responsible for target tracking. Another is the transporter who safely and secretly moves the team to and from the target. The other two members are the executioners. In addition to the core team are agents known as sayanim, helpers. Over time team members simply fade away due to the nature of the work and the psychological and emotional stress. They are aware of the dire personal and familial consequences if they reveal anything at all about their time with Kidon.

'From your psychological evaluations and your past performance, we in Kidon are convinced that you will not be troubled by assignments from this office. You are more than suited for us and do not need training. In fact, we have something for you now, if you want it, and the Office can spare you. Allow me to explain. It is an action against an Irish Republican Army Active Service unit. While we would normally not be overly concerned or involved with a uniquely British problem, that government has asked Mossad, and from there to Kidon, to provide assistance.

'Israel is concerned because Libya is directly involved. Dear Colonel Gaddafi has been cuddling up to the Soviet Union for some time and receiving military aid. Collections and the Research Department estimate that Libya will have received some US twenty billion dollars in sophisticated arms, tanks, other material, even submarines, although how sand staffers could learn to operate a submarine stretches the imagination.

'Of further concern are the ties that the Irish Republican Army, or IRA, has with the Palestinians, particularly Fatah. They have held these ties with each other for some time and Fatah has trained IRA volunteers at fedayeen bases in Lebanon and has been arranging sizeable arms shipments to the Provos, members of the Provisional Irish Republican Army. Just this year a delivery was on its way to Ireland via Cyprus, but was intercepted by Belgian authorities, due in large part to intel supplied by the Collections and Research Department. Mossad is convinced that more arms shipments sponsored by Fatah have arrived in Northern Ireland or are on the way.

The intel unequivocally identifies the IRA Active Service Unit, ASU, involved in both of these activities. Their mission is to collect Soviet SA-7 shoulder-held, surface-to-air missiles from the Libyans and arms from the Palestinians. The missiles are infrared heat seekers that detonate in or near a heat source, in this case the exhaust of aircraft engines. They are difficult to detect because they do not emit signals to find the heat source, and the launch area cannot be marked either. Libya is directly responsible for this delivery, which will take place close to the sea freight port of Lisahally, north of Londonderry. The arms may already have been delivered. You can understand why the British forces are nervous.

'An ASU is usually composed of four persons who are likely to be acquainted, but who are not related, are not employed together, and are not neighbors. Since the IRA has chosen to use a decentralized framework, the ASU plans and carries out the operation. They do not follow any recognized rules of war and are in total disregard of collateral damage and civilian casualties. They blend into the setting and often are so unidentifiable that even their immediate families may not know of their involvement in terrorist activities.

'The IRA is merciless and that is why the British have requested the most merciless force on earth, Kidon, to remedy the situation.'

Rivkin called in another man who was not introduced. He unlocked a clasp on a leather folder and pulled out photographs, and a page of locations with minimal instructions, which he handed to Cam and then left the room without speaking.

'Please memorize these four faces and their locations in Northern Ireland.'

The photos showed four unremarkable men: Connor Ryan in the village of Ballycastle, Dylan Sullivan in the village of Portrush, Callum Callaghan in the village of Limavay, and Sean Kelly in Londonderry town. All locations were in an arc within easy driving distance of Lisahally, and from where these men could assemble along the coast above the port of Lisahally within an hour.

'This Sean Kelly is the contact for the ship from Libya, or will be, correct?'

'Quite correct. Would you eliminate him first?'

'No, I'd start with Ballycastle and work southeast. Since the ASU members don't know each other, the Deny boy may not think it is a problem if he can't get in touch with the others immediately. I'd want to hit all of them as soon as possible after I reach County Antrim, so I need to get in place some days before the shipment is expected. You do know when it is expected?'

'Yes we do,' replied Rivkin. 'The hit sequence you have outlined is what we have already discussed internally. We will leave the details to you.'

'I want a transporter with a four-wheel drive modified for speed. I don't want to use unknown local talent. I'll also need at least two sayanim to clean up afterwards and remove bodies for disposal. I will not communicate personally, but if I need to relay a message, I will use the sayanim.'

'You will have them. Now the bad news. MI6, British Foreign Service, is demanding one of theirs – an MI6 informer recruited by them some years ago – to go along. British military also want an SAS sergeant, a veteran of the Irish insurrection, to accompany you. We don't like it.'

'I don't like it either. And if I refuse?'

'Some noise at diplomatic level as I understand it. The informer is supposed to have become friendly with Connor Ryan in Ballycastle and has gleaned tips about the ASU.'

'Tips! I don't trust informers. They are invariably unreliable and have questionable motivations. I'll have to think hard about that one. I may take him just to see if he's legit. I can always dispose of him. If he comes along he will not be anywhere near the action. The SAS man I'll have to evaluate closely, but the regiment is trustworthy; he may be useful if it comes to a gunfight.'

'Please come again tomorrow. I will introduce you to the Kidon members you have requested, as they will want to take your measure and you theirs. You can begin planning with them. I think we are finished for today. It is a pleasure to meet you, and you will work well with Kidon.'

'Likewise, and thanks for the sandwich.'

Cam thought that it would be good to get out of the Office. Ireland – the Emerald Isle – attracted him, with Irish whisky and Guinness when they had finished up. He might take a few days extra. If Adi wasn't under orders he would fly her out.

Planning went comfortably.

Rivkin decided to take advantage of Cam's presence in Northern Ireland to solve another IRA problem for the British, and win more favors from them. The following day Rivkin was eager to put the proposal to him:

'Cam, there is a local IRA commander name of William Boyle living in Omagh, County Tyrone. The British would appreciate him being no more. Indications are that it is a sniper job, so pack your Remington 700. Your sayanim will care for it as if it was their own until you need it.'

'They had better or I'll use them to sight it in.'

Working for Kidon, every assignment began as a conundrum and ended as an enigma, impenetrable unless somebody talked, so Cam could not see or speak to Adi before he left. He enlightened Avi only to the extent that he would be away for a while and not able to communicate. Avi would tell Adi that Cam would be gone for a spell, but only that.

After dining together on the departure night, Rivkin finally informed Cam how he would travel to Northern Ireland. He would fly to Baldonnel Aerodrome, a military airfield to the southwest of Dublin, and home to the Irish Air Corps and the Garda Air Support Unit. Dublin Airport, north of the city, and Shannon Airport in County Clare were ruled out, even though Shannon was used by US military flights from time to time. Both airports had permanent IRA spotters who took photos of new faces of interest. Baldonnel was not supposed to have spotters.

There he would pick up the British contingent. Cam had other plans. He would take who he wanted, if anybody.

After arriving at Baldonnel, Cam met the MI6 snoop and straightaway disliked him. The informer launched into a lecture about recent IRA goings-on. Cam listened; he might learn something of value.

'Thanks for the sermon, chief, but that is the only thing you'll contribute to this assignment, you aren't going anywhere with me.'

'You bloody Jewish Yank, I'm in charge of this, and you are under my orders.'

'On the contrary, my dear Sherlock, I'm in charge of myself and if you call me any more names I will reduce you to a pile of the marmalade you Limeys are so fond of.'

'You've not heard the last of this, I know who your superiors are, and I will get you drummed out.'

'Fine, but you haven't the slightest idea who I work with. I don't have superiors, but I do have colleagues who will hunt you down just for the entertainment. Get out before you really embarrass yourself.'

The SAS sergeant present in the room smiled. A big muscular man, he looked Cam over. 'I'm trying to work out if you're a sandbag, an Irish reserve soldier, or a stab – a stupid territorial army bastard. At least you don't appear a total twat or, worse yet, a shiny arse. Let's get acquainted.'

'Fine by me, Tapes. Found a decent place yet?'

'One down the way; has a good ploughman's lunch and beer.'

During the meal and after the second pint, Cam decided to include the UK soldier, or Tapes, as he called him. He was the real deal. He had about the same amount of information Cam had, and hated the IRA; he had lost friends.

'I don't like including the informer on this trip, I never trust them. Do we need him for anything that we can't do ourselves?' Cam asked.

'As a good taig to the IRA, I've had some experience with informers here in Bogland and don't trust them either but have also used some to good effect. I say take him along and see what happens, we can always sort him.'

Against his better judgment, Cam agreed to find out more about the informer.

Cam would be called 'Stab' and the sergeant 'Tapes' for the rest of the journey. Humor in a dirty business.

They questioned their informer how he had come to be friendly with Ryan. He told them he had been a member of the Ulster Defense Regiment (UDR), a protestant and unionist outfit that hunted IRA. He claimed that the IRA had systematically targeted UDR servicemen when they were off duty – an on-going action of sectarian assassinations against Protestants. Eldest sons and breadwinners were favorites, and the IRA was accused of ethnically cleansing Protestants from their farms and jobs, tactics to create 'sanitized zones, a field at a time'. The informer had lost his farm, hated the IRA and volunteered to 'milk' Ryan. He had obtained the locations of the members of the ASU they were after. They decided to take him along, at least until they set up surveillance on Ryan's cottage.

Cam had arranged to meet his Mossad operatives a few kilometers from Baldonnel Aerodrome. They waited in an International Harvester Scout II – a Traveler model with a long wheel base.

'Stab, I'm happy to see you were smart enough to supply a vehicle that doesn't look like military, such as a Land Rover. Otherwise we would definitely get shot at. Safe as a baby in me mother's arms. Too bad it's from the US. You must be on an unlimited budget.'

Cam did not comment.

One transporter and two operatives with non-Semitic features had reported. One even had red hair, but many Israelis did. No introductions were made, and Cam had not expected any. Two combat shotguns were placed along the driver's and front passenger's doors of the Traveler, out of sight.

'Do you want to take the scenic route or should we get right to it?'

'Let's hump it until we get up north,' Cam replied, 'and then we can cruise around some back roads to find the targets and stay inconspicuous, which I imagine will be difficult since I'm told all Northern Irelanders are nosy, as well as being IRA informers.'

The transporter gave Cam a disgusted look as if to say he could keep a tank from attracting attention.

They headed out of Dublin to Belfast, then on to Antrim. From there it was through Ballymena until they arrived at Ballycastle, and their first chance to sight their target. The transporter had a detailed map of the tiny village, as well as maps of the rest of the target villages.

Conner Ryan lived in a small cottage on Drumavoley Road. The Ballycastle Forest was close, a good place to stash the vehicle and use as a surveillance base. Tapes and Cam meandered to within about two hundred meters of Ryan's place, which was set off from the road – an advantage. The cottage was not much, just a simple one-story, cream-washed brick building with no foundation. Smoke billowed up from a chimney and showed that Ryan was at home.

Over the next two days they watched Ryan come out and return only once a day, the second time carrying a bag of groceries with a couple of bottles of whisky poking out the top. No one else came out or approached, the man seemed solitary.

'Seen enough, Tapes, want to take him tonight?'

'Right enough. He may be well soaked.'

They headed back to the forest to inform the others what was planned. They armed themselves with hand guns and put on black camouflage fatigues and black balaclavas.

'A .357 Magnum. Nice artillery, Stab.'

'Best there is, Colt Python.'

'Get to do what you want, don't you? Where do I sign up later?'

'Sorry, special invitation only, but you may be mentioned in dispatches.'

Tapes had an old Browning high power 9mm.

They crouched close to the cottage until 23.00, when they figured Ryan might be in bed or drunk. Neither mattered much. Cam pushed their Irish stooge to the door for his debut. He knocked loudly and yelled a name and something in Gaelic, which he had been told not to do. A warning, a code maybe, thought Cam. The door opened and the Irishman went in, leaving the door off the latch. Tapes and Cam approached and stood on either side of one of the front windows where they could not be seen and took a quick look inside. Two chairs stood in the room. Ryan staggered to one of them while the Irishman kept standing and talking to him.

Tapes and Cam burst through the door and assumed combat stances. Cam was about to pull the trigger on Ryan when the Irishman put his right hand under his jacket. He wasn't looking at Ryan, he was looking at Cam. Cam was his target. That was his mistake, not looking at the decoy before pulling the piece and dropping the hammer on the intended target. Cam did not wait for it to come out. He shot him through the left temple. No hesitation. The entrance hole was round and jagged. The entire right side of his face left a silhouette, like a modern piece of sculpture.

Cam swung on to Ryan and shot him in the chest, instantaneous death from the shock, even if the brain had yet to register the lack of blood flow to it. The force pushed the body and the chair to the floor.

Two shots took under two seconds. Cam sighted on Tapes, who had the good sense to drop his weapon and hold his arms at shoulder level, palms facing him. Only discipline and training on Cam's part kept Tapes from being a dead SAS man. He kept the Python on him anyway.

'Stab… Stab, I'm good… I'm good!'

Cam motioned him to get on his knees and put his interlaced fingers on the top of his head. He covered him for a good five minutes.

'You are one lucky son of a bitch. Show me what else you're carrying.'

Tapes removed a combat knife and .35 revolver with a one inch barrel.

'Kick them over here.'

Putting the weapons in his fatigue pockets, Cam kept his eyes and the Python on Tapes as he did it.

'Turn around and walk through the door.'

Cam closed the gap between them just enough so he could shoot him if he tried to run, but not close enough for him to slam the door on a part of his body or whirl around and take a punch or try a back kick. He walked him back to the Traveler with his hands still on his head. When the sayanim saw them coming they moved out of the vehicle with their shotguns, and separated.

'Strip.'

'Stab, this is still me… your friend from the SAS. This isn't necessary.'

Tapes had nothing to conceal. Cam went over his fatigues carefully. 'Okay, I had to be satisfied you were still with us. My apologies. Put your clothes back on.' The Kidon contingent relaxed a little.

'Man, you are one rough little bastard. I'd have done the same thing. Thanks for not shooting me. Well played.'

'That Irish stooge punk had to be IRA. Any more people I don't know are not part of my outfit, ever. Bad judgment on my part.'

'I'll help you dismember him.'

After burying the bodies they moved to a pub on the outskirts of a village that they had seen earlier in the week. Despite the pub being closed for the day, the landlord served them a hearty meal, accompanied by two pints of beer and two Black Bushes.

*****

CHAPTER TWENTY FIVE

Dylan Sullivan was next.

They took the Straid Road into Portrush and soon found East Strand Beach where Sullivan's cottage was. It looked similar to Ryan's house, except it faced the beach and was on blocks for protection against high tides. A small tool shed stood at the back of the cottage. Five steps led up to the door. Tapes and Cam would have to kick the door in. Both front and back windows were too high to take a shot. A concussion grenade would have worked well, thought Cam, but they had not brought any. They parked the Traveler near to the beach and pretended to be tourists.

Over three days they observed Sullivan leave at 08.00 in a small car and return at around 19.00. He probably had a job and stopped at the pub on the way home. Once at home, he stayed in – a plus for them. They decided to take him on Friday night, on the off chance that no one would miss him until the following Monday when he failed to turn up for work. He, like Ryan, seemed to live alone.

At 22.00 the black fatigues and head gear went on. Cam and Tapes decided to both go, so one of them had to go first. Tapes insisted he would, but Cam told him it was his job and that he was the one hired for it. Tapes protested so they drew straws, as gentlemen do in such a situation. Tapes won, but Cam would be hugging his back when he kicked in the door.

At the bottom of the steps Tapes took a deep breath and cleared them in two jumps. The door flew open and they went left, right. Sullivan appeared around the corner of a hallway. He had a gun. After two hasty shots he ducked back, but there was no place for him to go, no back door. Tapes and Cam threw themselves around the corner, giving Sullivan a choice of which one to shoot at. He delayed shooting for a split second, which allowed Tapes to take aim and shoot. He drilled a neat hole midway between Sullivan's eyebrows. Sullivan looked surprised for just an instant before his face went slack. He slid down the wall, leaving a snail trail of blood and brains.

Cam's Israeli compatriots cleaned up. They carried a length of heavy stainless steel chain for dumping the body in the ocean.

Tapes and Cam checked out the tool shed. It was packed with AK-47s, RPGs, handguns, grenades, plastic Czech Semtex explosive and a large number of boxes of ammunition.

They had found one of the advertised Fatah arms shipments.

'We've got to let the proper office know; otherwise, an IRA rat will transfer it.'

'I'll get on to some of my chaps from the regiment who are scattered nearby to deal with it,' Tapes said. We'd best hang about until they get here. I'll meet them. You stay hidden while they take care of business.'

By Monday, when Sullivan should have been going to work, Cam's men were on the way to Limavady to make the acquaintance of Squire Callum Callaghan.

Leaving Portrush they traveled on Atlantic Road through Coleraine to Limavady. Callaghan lived near a fork separating Killane Road and Bolea Road. What must have been the ubiquitous Irish cottage was a whitewashed brick-building with two chimneys, and three windows in the front. A strong-looking storage shed stood at the back of the property. Beyond the shed and a fence were fields.

Callaghan came and went irregularly, but as with the first two targets, he did not seem to have any idea about a security routine. A potential problem loomed, though. A woman lived with him with no children in sight.

Once again they burst in, and Cam shot Callaghan while he was eating his evening meal. Tapes hesitated shooting the woman, who was also at the table. Cam was sorry to see such weakness, a misplaced morality about shooting unarmed women.

The woman surprised Cam as she ran out the back door and started to scale the stone fence to escape into the fields. Unfortunately, no steps led over the fence and down the other side, as was quite common in Ireland, so she had to scramble over. As she crested the top of the fence, Cam launched a projectile into her back, which propelled her over.

'Goddammit Tapes, what in the hell do you think you were doing? She was collateral damage, too bad, so sad, but so what? That was your one and only chance to hesitate when you work with me. Pull some discipline out your ass. Hesitation is a fine way to get killed. All right, let's check the shed and see if we get lucky again, and find more than an old washing machine.'

The shed was full of weaponry, just like Portrush, only more so. In addition to what they had previously found were flak jackets, night vision scopes, Metis and RPG-7 shoulder-held anti-tank missiles, and anti-personnel carrier missiles, also very effective in blowing up buildings, with a maximum range of 1000 meters.

There were also RK32 and SA-7 low altitude surface-to-air

shoulder-held missiles, maximum altitude 1500 meters and range 3.5 kilometers. The weapons and missiles were standard Russian issue, in field use for years.

'Tapes, you'd better get your people here in record time to clear this out. I can't believe the IRA would have only one man in each place guarding these caches, they're worth millions and could turn this war, call it what you like, into an IRA victory. You want to fight urban guerillas armed with all this?'

'No, by God, I don't. I'll have it cleared out. Look, sorry about back there…'

'Yeah, well, you still have some uses. If you are a good boy from now on, and don't soil the rug anymore, I'll keep you. I won't mention it. However, the SAS at least needs to start doing targeted surveillance and making raids on villages on both coasts, probably best between Larne and Belfast Lough and where we are on the west coast.'

'Quite. I'll see to it.'

Next morning after breakfast, the Traveler hummed towards Londonderry and ASU local commander Sean Kelly.

Kelly lived in an up-market bungalow, in a small residential street off Canterbury Park Road. The nicely landscaped cemetery nearby looked out over a bridge across the River Foyle to the city and, beyond, to the scenic Donegal Mountains.

The location presented difficulties. It was not isolated but surrounded by upper middle class families in close proximity to each other. If they repeated their method of surveillance of the previous homes, a neighbor was bound to notice. But Kelly's routine proved his undoing.

Most evenings he liked to walk up Rossdowney Road to the cemetery, where he stopped for a while by a grave and appeared to pray. Then he went across to Valley Park by way of Hillhampton Street and wandered around until dark before heading home. Their best chance was to catch him in the park. They would set up an ambush. If he walked out of their cone of entrapment they would try again the next evening. They were not going to chase him.

For three evenings they shadowed him as he made his rounds, after saying his prayers – rather fitting, Cam thought. Maybe someone would bury him in the same cemetery, as a martyr to the cause.

On the fourth evening Kelly walked into their cone like a lobster into a pot on the ocean floor. Easy to get in, but no way out. Cam's little suppressed Baby Browning was ideal for this liquidation.

No one could possibly hear the little pop of the shot in a park.

'Hey, Sean,' Cam said softly, as Sean walked past. As people do, he stopped, turned around and peered into the gathering gloom to see who had addressed him. Cam took three quick steps forward, pressed the suppressor to his jacket and let one go. The .25 slug, being small, did not drop him. He just seemed surprised at the bump and the pain. He looked down at his chest and Cam took the opportunity to put another into the crown of his head. The little hollow point disintegrated and whizzed around his brain for a second. He fell. Cam wondered again why these terrorists did not have even minimal survival training. Perhaps they were simply not front line men but only useful as storekeepers for the arrival of goods by ship.

*****

CHAPTER TWENTY SIX

Cam thought about the ship that was carrying the weapons, which was to arrive soon. It could not dock in a port so it would have to stand some way offshore, waiting for IRA people in small boats to take the shipment away. It could only do this between Londonderry, Lough Foyle and Portstewart if the men they had killed were supposed to pick it up. Mossad had identified the ship as a Small Handy of about 28 000 DWT that had been loaded in the port of Benghazi on the east coast of Libya. It was traveling under a Liberian flag of convenience. Liberia was one of the big three of convenience countries, the other two being Panama and the Marshall Islands.

'Tapes, I think as long as we are in the area we might as well have some real fun and board the cargo ship carrying the weapons shipment. The guys will find they have no one to offload to, and we don't want to cause them distress, do we? We must keep them entertained. I'm no sailor. Do you have the appetite and any suggestions?'

'As a matter of fact, I do, dear boy. Some of the Boat Troops are currently in North Bogland, and since we have my comrades excited about removing large amounts of Russian weapons to safe locations, I believe it would be valid to speculate that the Troops would be most eager to trash a rogue ship. I shall make some calls immediately.'

Tapes had clout with the brass, and soon the commanding officer of the Boat Troops was on his way for a briefing. The officer, a captain, commanded some one hundred and twenty officers and men. He had in tow a lieutenant and a warrant officer.

Cam pondered on how to make his presence legitimate and still keep his anonymity. He settled on his being from US Special Forces on assignment through an agreement at diplomatic level, and not able to divulge name or unit.

'Then you are the clipper, if I may use that American slang,' the captain said. 'You have been rather efficient in dealing with arms caches and those tending them. I am pleased to meet you, but find it highly irregular, although your SAS companion has convinced me to assist. Of course I must clear action with the regimental commander, but I am reasonably confident of a go-ahead.'

Permission came quickly considering the amount of paper that was pushed in the British Army and especially in the government offices to be informed to justify the boarding. They had incontrovertible evidence that arms were coming regularly into Northern Ireland from the Middle

East for use against British troops and civilians. Politicians welcomed an opportunity to take the limelight if things worked out. Cam thought they had little chance of failure; he was unwavering on Mossad intel.

Cam sat in on the planning but could contribute little other than what he had been told about the size, flag of registration, and port and date of embarkation of the cargo ship. The SAS Boat Troops knew how to board and seize the ship. They would deploy their fast rigid fiberglass Raiders to get the troops out to the vessel, and a few Klepper kayaks to allow them to board with minimal detection. Bigger boats would be used to haul the weapons back to shore. Cam insisted on being allowed along. He would not have missed it.

It took three days to assemble men and equipment and then it was a matter of waiting for the ship to appear. Spotters had been stationed along the coast. Sixteen Boat Troops had been considered sufficient. Little or no resistance was expected, but the men had hopes of some fun. There was little to do while waiting so the lads cleaned their weapons twice a day, inspected the floating transport incessantly, slept, ate, played cards and spun outrageous stories. For Cam, it was just like being in Nam again, except safer and cleaner.

Cam spent the time getting to know the Troops. All were seasoned SAS who had volunteered for the boats. They tried to pry out which Special Forces outfit he was from. He did not tell them, or even give hints, but that didn't stop them speculating, it was something to do. Tapes had been talking about Cam's conduct during the assassinations and gave the impression Cam was completely cold and somebody not to mess with. Finally, the boys thought they had his outfit figured out.

'You're not regular Army Special Forces,' one of them said. 'We've worked with Rangers and Green Berets. You don't act or talk like them, but you definitely are a combat veteran, seen action in Vietnam, and then assigned to crazy ass operations like this one, so you multi-task. Your hair is too long to be a regular. Tapes said you do what you want, don't take orders and don't check in during missions. A lone wolf. We've got some in the regiment and they go through a lot of special training and psych evaluations. If you actually are army, we pick you as Delta Force, one of those crazy guys who are prepared to do anything as long as you get heavy action. Since you don't have a name we're going to call you Delta from now on.'

'Tapes calls me Stab, which is just fine.'

'No, you're not a stupid territorial army bastard. You're Delta, get used to it.' They meant well and had accepted him.

One afternoon the officer in charge called Cam over. 'Have you ever paddled a kayak?'

'Nope.'

'Would you like to paddle a kayak?'

'Not at all, but thanks for asking.' Cam knew where this was going. The boarding plan called for two two-man kayaks to approach the stern, get on board as quietly as possible, secure the bridge and take the captain prisoner. While this activity was going on, the main force would come alongside the aft quarter in the fast Raiders, five SAS per Raider, and secure the rest of the ship, taking the crew prisoner.

'Well, Delta, take an interest. You're going with the kayaks to grab the captain. The lads have been taking bets on whether or not you'll be the first on the bridge.'

'Thanks for the opportunity, but you should know I can barely float, much less swim.'

'Not to worry, all personnel have to wear lightweight individual flotation devices, so you can bob up and down until we pick you up, or a shark eats you.'

He showed Cam a vest. It weighed almost nothing and the bladders were folded across the chest so that full movement in all directions was possible. It would keep the body warm for a short period, and if slashed, would still work. Inflated by pulling a toggle, it self-inflated in response to water pressure if the body wearing it started to sink for any reason, such as being wounded or unconscious. This feature reassured Cam.

Cam walked over to the kayaks, which had been assembled from their folded carry mode in preparation for a quick departure. The Kleppers had PVC hulls and cotton decks over a wooden frame. The seats were adjustable both horizontally and vertically, molded for comfort, and fitted with a backrest. Storage capacity was larger than he had expected, so the boarding gear and weapons could be out of the weather and sea spray. They took practice floats to teach Cam how to paddle and not capsize.

The cargo ship showed up two days later, wallowing about two or three nautical miles offshore on the southern boundary of Lough Foyle. The Liberian flag had been removed. The crew started flashing light signals every two hours. The SAS had decided to make things less complicated. The raid would take place at dawn, twelve hours after the ship had first appeared. Little resistance was anticipated, but the SAS was still heavily armed. Cam thought this was little more than a training exercise for them.

While Cam wore his black camouflage fatigues, the SAS wore a tan regulation fatigue. They were all equipped with the Bullpup L64/65 assault rifle, chambered for the 5.56x45mm round, an effective weapon, except it could not be fired from the left shoulder due to the direction of ejection of the spent casings. Cam carried only his Python in his shoulder rig.

The two kayaks paddled out on a relatively calm sea. One kayak went around the port side and the other around the starboard side. They met at the stern. The lead man touched his throat microphone to report they were in place. The hooks and ropes went up and over, and they started climbing.

On deck they assumed combat stances. The deck was flat with two small cranes for loading freight into the holds below. There was no crew at all on deck, not even a night watch making a round. Cam and an SAS ran softly up a ladder to the bridge and crouched under the windows of the entrance door. The bridge had six windows on each of its four sides with Kent screens in two of the windows. They peered into the interior. It was empty.

They went back down to the deck to wait for someone to show up. Soon the second officer arrived as the officer of the watch, accompanied by an able seaman. They marched these two up the ladder, where the officer of the watch produced a set of keys and unlocked the door. He spoke English, being the lingua franca among the mixed race crew as well. With a rifle barrel pressed to his head, he was ordered to call the captain to the bridge because of an emergency.

When the captain appeared, all three were cuffed and pushed to their knees. The lead man reported the bridge secure and to bring the main boarding party up. Ten SAS climbed aboard using ladders and took up pre-assigned stations around the deck. The commander used a bullhorn to inform the crew that they were now the property of the UK military, and they must ascend to the deck. Anyone presenting a weapon would be shot without warning.

Gradually, crew began popping out of various hatches, hands held high. The SAS started their clearing operation below deck. They found two of the crew trying to hide in one of the holds. All crew were cuffed and brought to their knees. They had twelve in all, one captain, one second officer, four able seamen, two ordinary seamen, one engineer, two oilers and a cook – a normal-sized crew for such a cargo vessel. They searched the crew quarters and confiscated the seaman's qualifications and passports. The manifest was obtained, and interrogations started as to where the missiles and any other military equipment were stored.

They knew nothing; they were just ordinary seamen who loaded what was on the dock. This could have been true, but the captain, second officer, and perhaps an able seaman or two, surely knew, Cam thought. Cam figured at least one of the able seamen, or perhaps an ordinary seaman, was a plant from the Libyan organization which had funded the smuggling business. This had to be the Abu Nidal Organization aka the Fatah Revolutionary Council. Cam suggested as much to the commander, who assigned Troops to isolate these individuals in pairs and interrogate them. The captain and second officer were kept on the bridge. After a while the SAS commander motioned Cam over with a crooked index finger.

'The captain refuses to talk to anyone but you.'

'What the hell for? You must have told him you are senior here.'

'He doesn't believe me, and wants "the man in black". The large revolver, in a shoulder rig, and the long hair have given him the impression you are the snake head.'

Cam sighed. 'Will he talk? How rough can I get with him?'

'I think he'll spill, he seems more afraid of someone else than he is of us. In this case I think coming on as good cop will work. I'll be with you, I can play bad cop when required, if it is.'

The captain, a Hong Kong Chinese, was good at drawing out a story to prove he was just an innocent tool in a larger operation, just trying to feed his extensive family and honor his ancestors properly. He had been trained in interrogation techniques, but most of them involved things like sensory deprivation, extreme cold or heat, disorienting noise, one rock and roll song played loud again and again. Working certain parts of the body with a sap could be effective, but Cam had also been trained in cajolery, so he kept asking the same three questions.

Finally, it came down to a promise, a real one, that he would be incarcerated in HM Wakefield Prison, the UK's most notorious Category A maximum security prison, where he would be locked down for twenty years to life and never see the sun again. His fellow inmates would not like an Asian except as a tanka, a low class Hong Kong prostitute. Cam guaranteed this several times. If, on the other hand, he cooperated and told them where the ordnance was stored in the holds, he would spend at most five years in a Category D prison – an open prison where he could lead a semi-normal life among non-violent prisoners. Cam had no authority to promise anything.

He caved in, and Cam let him go to the head under guard, who brought him back to the bridge to tell the Troops where the ordnance was, drawing diagrams of locations – all mixed in with legitimate cargo.

Since Cam had broken the Chinese gun runner he decided to go further and find out the identity of the Libyan crew member. The captain identified him as Mohy Zuwayya – the name of a large tribe in the Benghazi area. Cam's sayanim were ready to take the Chinese captain back to Israel for further interrogation.

Cam gave the Chinese captain water, and promised food for name of his contact in Libya. A SAS man stepped up, put the working end of his rifle in the Chinese captain's ear and informed him he could die immediately or be partially protected in prison. Decide and decide quickly. He decided. The Libyan was called Al-Abgari Al-Magharha, which would not be his real name, but if he worked in the smuggling racket it would be a name to start passing around on the docks of Benghazi, Zueitina and Derna ports.

The intel had been spot on. They found RPG-7 and Metis anti-tank missiles, anti-personnel missiles, and SA-7 and 9K32 surface-to-air missiles. They also found arms and ammo, heavy machine guns, grenades and Semtex.

The Troop commander contacted the regiment and obtained permission to pull out. Cam grabbed Zuwayya and handed him over to an SAS in one of the fast Raiders.

On shore the SAS took a few hours to pack up and move out. In a buoyant mood about a job well done, they wished Cam well.

Cam found Tapes and shook his hand. 'You were a good companion and a credit to the regiment. I do think that you should reconsider a career in assassination, though. It does take a certain type of personality.'

'Yeah, I have been comparing myself to you and realized I'm not quite as ruthless and unrelenting. You see only targets; you don't gift them with enough humanity to even hate them. And your eyes are disconcerting, if you don't mind me saying so. But it was an education serving with you. Take care.'

Only minutes after the SAS decamped the Traveler rolled up. If the sayanim were surprised to see Cam holding a handcuffed Libyan by the neck they didn't show it. Cam told them that they would have to carry him back to Tel Aviv. The Libyan lay curled up in the back of the Traveler and secured to a brace with a collar. They journeyed on to Omagh, where Cam was going to carry out the favor that Mossad owed someone in the UK. It was an easy ride on the A4 south out of Deny.

*****

CHAPTER TWENTY SEVEN

The Omagh assignment was very different from the ones Cam had done in the last few days. William Boyle was higher up in the IRA than the others Cam had taken care of, and had been trained by fedayeen at one of their bases in Lebanon, which put him on the Mossad black list. Israel was not fond of terrorist-trained threats anywhere in the world. The British evidently felt the same way.

Boyle worked in the city of Omagh proper. He would have to take him in the city. But that made it more difficult with too many ways to get cut off and caught, because the hide would inevitably be in a building or on top of one.

Cam had been told to stay in a three-star hotel on the Gortin Road, a half mile walk south to the city center, past a police station – a nice ironic touch, he thought. His cover was as a business traveler. The hotel was not pretentious but comfortable – something a businessman on expenses might stay in, and be inconspicuous. He had come equipped with smart casual attire – trousers, sport coat and tie. Shoes were soft leather, upscale but soled with rubber in case he needed to climb or run. His luggage was the triple locked case for the Remington 700, which could be easily taken for something that would hold clothes as well as brochures or samples.

Cam's information on Boyle told him he walked to an office located in the city center where James Street and John Street intersected with High Street and Market Street, just south of the river. Well-preserved Georgian townhouses, such as seen in Dublin, were mostly converted into offices and apartments for the upper middle class.

Boyle traveled on buses. Cam followed him to a stop where he got off a bus from Gortin, a village to the east with less than a thousand inhabitants. He hopped on to a circular bus for the center and got off at a stop close to James Street.

On Cam's return to his hotel room on the second day, an envelope shoved under the door contained a key to a townhouse overlooking James and John Streets. A small square of edible rice paper gave the address along with the word 'attic' written on it. He knew that the address was for a townhouse, but he had misgivings about using an enclosed, high space as a hide.

Next day Cam tried the key, which opened on to a well kept foyer. A brass plaque on one wall listed the businesses that occupied the building. He waited in the foyer for a while to observe the traffic, which was sporadic but normal for a business building. Dressed as he was, he was unlikely to attract much attention, just another work person. Access to the three floors was by stairs, not a lift, a relatively good thing for his purposes. Having to use a single lift was a fine way to get trapped. A rickety fire escape led to the rear of the building, but if he had to use that he would already be in trouble and running, not calmly descending a flight of stairs after the deed was done.

Cam walked up to the attic and opened the door with the key. It had been stocked with bottled water and snacks, a comfortable shooting stool and a professional rifle rest. The rest was fully extendable for length and elevation. A rotating elevation wheel allowed fine tuning of the reticules in the scope. The front of the rest pivoted a full 360 degrees to allow the shooter to place the fore-end literally over the target area without lifting the rifle from the rest. Cam blessed folks who knew what they were doing.

Cam had arranged to meet the Mossad sayanim at an agreed location and preselected times within a two mile radius of the hotel. He planned to take a day to track Boyle during his walk, to a point he had determined as the best for a no-miss shot. He would take him, and meet up with the Israelis.

The exercise was an anti-climax. Boyle walked under Cam right where he wanted him and received a 7.62 round which took most of his head off. The suppressor masked the shot well. Pedestrians panicked; they didn't bother to look up, they scrambled for cover. Cam packed up the Remington, adjusted his tie and jacket, locked the door to the attic room and calmly descended the stairs into a street full of chaos that neatly masked his retreat. Every hit should be so easy, thought Cam.

Cam took his final ride in the Traveler to Baldonnel Aerodrome, the military facility outside of Dublin, where he had arrived in Ireland and would be collected after a coded phone call from a public booth to a secure line somewhere in Israel. He bid the sayanim farewell.

Within an hour a sleek private jet set down and Cam took his seat. There was no one else in the cabin and he did not see the pilots, hearing only their voices when they wanted him to buckle up. He wished he had brought something to drink because no cute cabin attendant was on board to bring him a cold one. He caught up on sleep for most of the five-hour flight. The plane taxied into an empty hanger on the military side of Ben Gurion. A car with darkly tinted windows was waiting. A rear door opened. Inside was Mick Rivkin. Cam got in beside him on the rear seat. Rivkin reached out and shook his hand.

Cam spoke first. 'Hiya, Mick, how's tricks?'

'You certainly have been up to some. Well done on terminating the

ASU arms smugglers, but where did you the get the idea to turn pirate with the SAS and commandeer a cargo ship on the high seas?'

'I'd never done it before so I decided to relax a little and entertain myself. You of all people should know I can't resist a new assault situation. But seriously, would you rather I hadn't taken the initiative when a good thing presented itself? We did capture a Libyan vessel that the assholes can't use anymore, a heap of serious weapons, and fresh meat for an interrogation, plus the name, probably false, of the rag head arranging the arms shipments from Libyan ports. You can't possibly have expected me to pass that up.'

'You could have compromised Kidon if you had been identified.'

'Hey, you ordered me to take the SAS guy and the IRA snitch with me, I didn't want to do it. You do know the snitch is dead, don't you? He was going to kill me. He was obviously IRA, not Ulster Defense Force.'

'Yes, I know that. Harsh words were exchanged with MI6 through other Mossad channels.'

'Well, in future I work alone or only in conjunction with other Kidon. Please keep that in mind. We didn't trust spooks in Nam and I don't trust them now. They always have their own hidden agendas. Only intel from the Collections Department and the Research Department will be considered, and even then, I want to know that Kidon is more than convinced by it, because I will correct mistakes, if I survive them, with severe retribution. Clear?'

'More than clear, Cam. It won't happen again. My apologies.'

'Nothing for you personally to apologize for, we won't mention it again. By the way, those sayanim were exceptional. I wouldn't mind working with them again. Bunch of magicians.'

'It is unlikely you will work directly with them again; it is not usual policy to create units that work more than once together. There are security reasons, of course, but psychologically a unit develops ties that interfere with the ruthless work we do. However, I'll keep your remark in mind. They thought you were quite the magician as well. Our Libyan sailor will be ready for interrogation tomorrow and per your request you may sit in and enjoy the show. You must be ready for some refreshment, come along to headquarters.'

Once again a medium roast beef sandwich and a small salad were served. 'Good thing I like roast beef sandwiches.'

'Yes, I noticed. It may become a habit between us when you return from a mission. Kidon is well pleased with your performance, you can expect more work.'

Cam walked a few blocks, looking for a tail, and then took a taxi to the Office. He called round to Avi's place to say hello. Saray answered the door.

'Shalom uvracha, welcome home, stranger. Are you well?'

'Very well, you gorgeous creature. Is Avi in the building?'

'He has just returned and is cleaning up in his quarters. I'll call him. Would you like tea?'

'Certainly. Why don't we wait for Avi, and perhaps Amzi is free and would like to join us. I'll wash up, too, and change into fresh fatigues. I'll tuck the Python into its cage.'

'Don't trouble yourself. It has become so much a part of you that no one notices it anymore. I'll prepare the tea service.'

Cam passed Avi in the corridor. A handshake and hug were exchanged. Avi knew better than to ask where Cam how it had gone.

'Hell, you didn't get wounded. Are you hiding in the bushes now?'

'If I weren't in a good mood I'd kick your ass. We're having tea with Saray and Amzi. See you when I shower and change.'

Amzi greeted Cam like a lost patriot. He also didn't ask questions. He had introduced Cam to Rivkin and knew how Kidon worked.

After tea Cam asked Saray about Adi.

'Go ask her yourself. You are such a terrible rasheh to keep her in the dark all the time. She is on base, go and see her right now or I will make your life a misery.'

Cam did not call the base, but waited around the entrance to Adi's barracks and chatted with a couple of the soldiers on security duty. When Adi came out, on some errand or other, she didn't see Cam, she was all business.

'Adiela!'

She looked at Cam with widened eyes and walked over to him. When close enough her hand reached out to the injured side of his face and stroked it lightly, saying nothing, a ritual greeting she would perform from then on when he came home from an undertaking.

'Avi wouldn't tell me where you were or what you were doing.'

'Motek, Avi didn't know where I was or what I was doing, he really couldn't tell you.'

'I don't believe you, you and Avi are like brothers, more than brothers, you are brothers-in-arms. I insist that he tells me what you are doing when you go away.'

'He is usually with me, so both you and Saray know what we're up to, but this time I simply can't tell you anything.'

'Then I think you have got involved with a part of Mossad that is not supposed to exist. It makes me afraid for you. And for us.'

'Hush now, you know everything I do is off limits. Please, let's not talk about it now and enjoy each other. I've missed you.'

'I am calling Ahuva right now and we will have the evening meal at their apartment. We will bring all of the family together with Avi and Saray. You be ready.'

Even Cam opposed the use of electrical implements and near drowning techniques, which Kidon experts performed in the interrogation of Mohy Zuwayya. He preferred the refined, intuitive approaches, but these more subtle methods took longer. Mohy Zuwayya revealed the real identity of Al-Abgari Al-Magharha, who was immediately given the target name Nasir. They would catch up with Nasir in the near future. Zuwayya jabbered a bit more information of questionable veracity before he was terminated.

*****

CHAPTER TWENTY EIGHT

Mick Rivkin summoned Cam and said, 'You've been involved in this arms smuggling thing for a while now. Do you want to follow it up in Libya?'

'Might as well, I haven't been there before. I'm sure there are some nice tourist attractions.'

'The only attraction you are going to concentrate on is getting Sayyid Nasir back here for his singing debut, direct descendant of the Prophet that he pretends to be by assuming the title.'

'Since I can't speak the lingo there, I must be going to get some companionship.'

'You are indeed. Mossad have had a fellow from the Collections Department in place there for quite a few years. He speaks standard Arabic, Libyan vernacular Arabic, Berber, Awjilah and Domari. Luckily for you, many educated Libyans speak English so there is the possibility of making yourself understood by Nasir once you have him. The spook does not deal in physical exertion or violence, which is where you come in. You will have another man with you to help in that area.'

Rivkin called out, 'Come in now, please.'

In walked Avi.

'I damn well knew you were Kidon, you mongrel, I just knew it. Adi and Saray are really going to be pissed off about this one.'

'Yes, I'm always there before you, and you can't get rid of me. This ought to be fun. I haven't kidnapped anyone for a while.'

'Please don't kiss each other,' Rivkin said. 'Our operative in Libya, we'll just call him Collections, has determined that Nasir is operating almost routinely in Benghazi; that was the point of embarkation for the arms you captured, Cam, and most likely the port of origin for the arms you captured in Northern Ireland. He now knows what the man looks like thanks to the information that Zuwayya gave us. He has begun surveillance. The two of you need to be in Benghazi within two weeks.

'Collections will arrange maritime transport for you as it will be much easier for you to enter Libya at the port rather than risk a flight to Benina International. You must first travel to Greece by air and pick up your ship at Piraeus, which is directly north of Benghazi. You must make this detour because any ship registered in Israel, or that has ever docked in Israel, is not allowed to take a berth in a Libyan port. It is only a few days' sail.

'The captain and second officer know that you are working for

Israel but certainly not in what capacity. They have performed this service before and are adept at keeping their mouths tightly shut. They are not necessarily patriots, but they do know that once they have taken our money we will bring retribution down on them and their immediate families if they compromise the transaction. Call it an effective form of blackmail.

'As you know, some cargo carriers also take passengers and that is what you will be until you reach Benghazi. You will have a small double cabin between the captain's cabin and the second officer's. The chief engineer is also on this deck, so if you need to take control of the ship, you have the main players close to you.

'You will take your meals in your cabin and will avoid the crew as much as possible. Please do not speak to anyone, Cam. Your accent is still recognizable as either American or British, both nationalities unwelcome in Libya at the moment. Avi's Arabic will suffice if any conversation is required.

'At Piraeus you will simply walk on board and disembark at Benghazi as able seamen. You will carry valid Tunisian seaman's books which preclude the need for passports or visas. Libya presently accepts these papers as legitimate for entry. Look after them; you will need them when you leave with your hostage. You will be provided with documents for Nasir. How you get him on the ship is up to you.

'Western style apparel is very common, such as a loose cotton shirt worn outside trousers. You will be able to move around quite freely without anyone becoming suspicious of your clothing.'

'Yes, but it limits our ability to carry weapons, they definitely can't be visible,' Avi said.

'But we can carry a blade in a trouser pocket,' Cam replied. 'A clasp knife would not attract much attention even if it was found. Lots of men carry clasp knives; it looks conventional and typical for a working seaman.'

'That could work, but you definitely can't carry handguns on board your transport ship. I'll have Collections supply something you can carry in an ankle holster.'

'Neat but small,' Cam said. 'Only up to .32 caliber is possible, and with a very short barrel, but I suppose we won't be doing any work at a distance of more than a few feet.'

Rivkin nodded. Cam switched his focus.

'Mick, I've been doing some thinking about my language barrier, and I may have come up with a solution. Disguise me as a man with an injured face. The injuries prevent me from being able to speak. I saw a lot of facial injuries during my own reconstruction after Nam and, taking a cue from that, here's what we could do.

'Put a convincing fake scar from an entry wound directly under my jaw. Make it small and circular, like from a small bullet, or a bit jagged from a piece of shrapnel. Then concoct a prosthesis that I can put over my teeth on the side of my face that hasn't been reconstructed. The prosthesis should distort my face, making it look like I can't move my jaw or mouth properly. I can't form words because of the distortion. I can only make grunting sounds.'

'Brilliant, I'll get the right people working on it and have you measured for it.'

'Wait, I'm not finished. As an added touch, put a jagged exit wound on the opposite side of my face. Make it an unhealed opening with a small piece of bone just visible. Also make it slightly hollow. Contrive a semi-liquid gel streaked with red and yellow that looks like a mixture of pus and blood that will go in the hole, and that I can clean out and replace periodically. When I push the jaw prosthesis against my cheek, I'll put pressure on the exit wound and force out bodily fluids most people don't want to see. I'll carry a handkerchief and periodically wipe the exit wound. I can tell you from experience that only a doctor, or a very warped individual, will take a close look at something like that.'

Rivkin and Avi looked at Cam as though he had taken leave of his senses. Cam continued:

'Finally, make up some business cards printed in Arabic that say something like "Wounded in the glorious service of the Prophet, I cannot speak. Allah akbar." In a tight spot I can just peel off the facial makeup and spit the prosthesis out in a matter of seconds, totally different person.'

'Cam, you are one devious and sick bastard, but we'll try it. Don't overdo things with Nasir. Do not kill him unless it is unavoidable, and I'm confident you will know when that is. You can hurt him, of course, but we need his head intact, we need his thoughts, his memories, we are after much bigger game than him.'

Communications had managed to obtain photos of Nasir with a Polaroid camera. They showed a man in his late forties, pudgy, with jowls, thinning hair, a long Arab nose and fat lips. No problem to manhandle, Avi and Cam thought.

At Piraeus docks, they easily found their vessel – a bulk dry cargo carrier, and much like the one he had stormed with the SAS off Northern Ireland. A crew of twelve manned a well-maintained ship that flew the Greek flag.

The captain and second officer met them at the gangway. Cam decided to test his disfigured disguise to see how effective it was. Both sailors had trouble looking directly at him and the second officer swallowed a couple of times as if trying to keep his lunch down, so Cam thought the disguise was repulsive enough.

When they docked in Benghazi no one disembarked until port officials had examined the ship. They didn't have to present their seaman's books until customs inspection. Like every customs gate in the world, the personnel were surly and objectionable, and Cam knew this would be the best test of his disguise. With a classic customs scowl, the customs officer looked at him, looked at his book, and looked at him again. 'This is your book?' he asked. Cam had pressed his handkerchief against most of his face but now removed it like a magician pulling fake flowers from his sleeve. He wiped some pus off. The customs officer took a step back and waved him through. Avi's Arabic got him through easily.

They walked down Shari Ahmed Rafiq al Mahdawl, which fronted the ocean, and took a right on to a small street that led to the old town hall, where Communications was to meet them. It was busy and close to the Osman and Atiq mosques. Cam made a note of the locations. They could hide if need be among the amin performing salat five times a day.

A slight, inconspicuous man, who could have been taken for a clerk, approached Avi, said something in Arabic and slipped in two words of Hebrew, menaseh le'amin, 'try to believe' – words they had been instructed to use to tag Communications. They exchanged the usual Libyan greetings, salaam alaikhum, 'peace be unto you', and wa alaikhum as-salaam, 'and unto you be peace'. Cam had kept the cloth over the side of his face so as not to startle anyone, at least not until it suited.

They walked with him to Umar Al Mukhtar Street, where he stopped in front of a shabby building, a merchant seamen's hostel – their temporary stay.

'Very sorry about the surroundings,' their contact said, 'but they are typical of what a sailor just off the boat would stay in. We obviously can't deal with Nasir here so we will have to find a house to detain him once you've got him. I'll help you with that. Please now change your clothing to the more typical loose cotton shirt and trousers so that you will blend in on the street.'

Cam figured it was time for their contact to get a look at his face, so he took the cloth away. Communications let out a yelp and involuntarily backed off.

'What in the bloody hell is wrong with you? I was not informed that you were disfigured, my God, you are mutilated!'

'Don't get your boxers in a bunch, it's a disguise. You must have been informed that I don't speak Arabic so this fright mask precludes me from having to utter a word, and generates the right amount of disgust to keep most of the attention on Avi, who does speak Arabic. I've got a card, too, take a look.'

'This is most unusual. In all my years in the field I've never seen anything like it. Very clever. Can you eat and drink?'

'Yes, but I'm not very appealing when I do. I dribble on command when drinking and need to cover my mouth when I chew, but it makes a good show. Of course, I can remove it in seconds if I need to.'

Their contact dropped a briefcase he had been carrying onto one of the beds and opened it. Inside were two small handguns in light canvas ankle holsters. He handed one to each of them. Cam's was a Walther PP, often dubbed a 'mouse gun', one of the smallest semi-automatics available in a caliber larger than his .25 Baby Browning. It was only fifteen centimeters in length and shot a Browning SR/.32 ACP round, the most punch packed by so small a pistol. It would have to suffice in a short range gunfight, which he fervently hoped would not happen.

'These must be returned on your departure; it is very difficult to obtain handguns and ammunition in Libya. These are courtesy of the CIA, and come to me through the American Liaison Office which has been staffed by Americans after the U.S. embassy was closed in 1972. A delicate matter.

'Now, let us have some food and tea, after I will walk you around a bit. Then you are on your own, but you may contact me at the Atiq Mosque during the afternoon prayer, asr, or sunset prayer, maghrib. I partly keep up my cover as a Muslim by observing the fard as-salat, the daily prayers. Get yourselves a white knitted Muslim prayer cap, taqiyah, so you look as if you have been attending prayer, salat, and stand around a short distance from the mosque. When it empties out, mix in with the men leaving, like you were part of the congregation. Walk up and greet me politely, and we will have tea somewhere while you tell me what you want.'

Avi and Cam had considered learning the prayer ritual so they could actually go into mosques, but decided that performing the eight steps – the kneeling, standing, hand movements, reciting chapters of the Qur'an and mouthing Allahu akbah five times – was just too much Islamic conversion.

They wanted to leave the run-down hostel as soon as possible, but needed to be careful in choosing a house for detaining Nasir. They inspected the harbor so they could get Nasir to a ship in a reasonable period of time, and under most circumstances. The most plausible area encompassed a rough square, bordered by four streets.

After a few days of wandering around they became familiar with the winding inner streets and alleys. They looked for a typical middle class house, not an apartment. Due to a high unemployment rate more unoccupied houses were available than expected. Even though Libya had become one of the richest countries per capita in the world with its oil and gas industries, Benghazi had not benefited all that much. Most goods loaded for export were wool and wool products, hides, sheep and goats. Ras Lanuf, a few miles away, prospered much better as a major oil port.

They found a traditional house on Al Bazzar Street, just a block south of Ahmad. There were no windows on the first floor level. A few windows on the second level were barred with iron filigree. One heavy-wooded door allowed entrance, which would be a problem if they came under siege. Libyan houses typically had no other entrances but the main one. A wall enclosed a small garden, which further decreased the odds of someone peering in. A balcony, running the length of the second story, gave them a good surveillance of the street and courtyard. Overall, it provided a suitable location for concealing a kidnap victim and burying a body if they had to.

They cased the place for a few days. No one came or went, and it remained dark at night. Al Bazzar was relatively quiet with few vehicles and not much foot traffic. Fiercely protective of their private space, Libyans tended not to pry into what the neighbors did.

It was time to go in and take a look. Cam picked the lock. Later, he would install a chain lock and a dead bolt on the inside of the door.

Inside, the house was bare. An elegantly carved staircase led to the second level where the household would live, off limits to anyone but the family. A second staircase led to what Avi told him was a marabour, a room where a husband would entertain guests, none of whom would ever see the women of the abode. In contrast to the lack of furnishings elsewhere, cushions and mattresses rested on the floor of the marabour – an ideal room to isolate Nasir. On both levels rooms led off from the center of the house where Avi and Cam could make a den for themselves.

They chose to eat mainly rice and vegetables, or cracked wheat, the Libyan staple for making couscous. With no electrical power they secured two kerosene lamps, a kerosene-fired cooking ring and fuel. They decided just to squat, they wouldn't be in residence long enough to face a landlord. Neighbors would keep quiet about them.

In their duffels, various liquid sedatives had been poured into generic bottles, and sterile syringes and needles had been sewn into the fabric. Among the drugs, Cam had scopolamine if they wanted to interrogate Nasir; its antidote, physostigmine, would bring him around and morphine would combine with the scopolamine to induce a twilight sleep. A background in biochemistry served Cam well in this department.

Cam had also packed a muzzle gag made of leather that fastened around the head with buckles and straps. A flex pad fitted over the mouth, cheeks and chin, and a lockable strap went around the neck. It muffled virtually all sound. Simple but effective gear.

The following evening, after finishing his prayers at the Atiq mosque, Communications showed them photos of Nasir and the places close to the docks where he conducted business – on the street or in the workers tea houses.

Their first sighting was on Umar Ibn Al Aas Street. Nasir ambled along, deep in conversation with another man. With hands on each other's shoulders, they appeared to know each other well.

Nasir and his companion ducked into a side alley and entered a building. A small plate on the door identified, in Arabic and English, the business as a brokerage for general freight. Cam and Avi loitered in doorways nearby.

After about an hour Nasir came out and turned right into a small lane. He entered a building with a brass plaque displaying his alias: Al-Abgari Al-Magharha, Agent for Conveyance of Exceptional Cargo by Sea and Air. Bills of Lading Arranged. A grandiose title for a smuggler, Cam thought

Around 14.00 Nasir closed up and went to an eatery near the Italian Consulate. Two men joined him for a typical Libyan one-pot dish of couscous prepared in a spicy sauce of hot peppers, tomatoes, chick peas and vegetables. After the meal, they drank traditional green tea and discussed business.

After collecting papers and exchanging handshakes with his guests, Nasir went back to his office where he remained until sunset. A muezzin called the faithful to prayer.

Every other day, Nasir walked along Algeria Street which led directly to the port. He stopped frequently to mop his brow. At the Al Madinah Ar Riyadiyyah section he entered an office, presumably that of a collaborator in the smuggling racket.

After visiting the port office on three occasions, Avi and Cam were certain they had located the expediter. They discussed scoring a two-for-one by abducting the expediter as well as Nasir. They could do it, but Nasir remained the primary target.

The expediter was busy on the phone most of the time. Periodically he would go to a pier and chat with a captain or second officer. In just a few days the expediter visited ships flying flags of Liberia, Mauritius, Burma, Tonga, and, of much interest, Georgia. Georgia, Cam reasoned, was the port in the Soviet Union that transshipped the Soviet arms for Libya's trade.

One ship flew the flag of Mongolia, the largest land-locked country in the world. North Korea used this ruse because of its designation as a pariah nation. Intel for Mossad to know, and it made Cam more determined to bring the expediter back to Tel Aviv along with Nasir.

After discovering the basic routines of Nasir and the expediter, Avi and Cam decided to hang around the docks, dressed in their seamen's clothes, to see what else they could glean.

'I think Nasir is after new information about cargoes, destinations, that kind of thing,' Cam said. 'It could be he's out to recruit moles like Zuwayya; it does seem that he wants one on board when he arranges a consignment. It doesn't have to be arms either, could be anything. Let's hang out in his territory, try to get him interested.'

They continued to follow Nasir's movements, and when he headed down to the port, they made sure they arrived before him. They stood at the dock entrance of his preference or by a ship flying a flag of convenience moored to a quay. Since staring is not necessarily considered rude in Arab countries, they eyed Nasir to gain his attention. After a few more days of showing their interest in him, Cam placed his right hand on the tip of his nose which conveyed an Arabic message that generally meant 'I see it in front of me' or 'I see I must initiate this'. Nasir gestured back, holding his fingertips together, hand up at waist level and moving the hand slightly up and down, meaning 'wait a little while'. They had hooked him.

Two days later, Nasir strode over and greeted them with 'salaamu aleikum'. He shook their hands in the Arab manner, longer than in the West and less firm, and standing close at less than arm's length. He spoke in Arabic, so it was time for Cam to begin his act of not being able to talk. He wiped the pus off his 'wound' and let him see all of his face. This revelation elicited consternation and disgust, but he recovered his composure. Cam had one of his business cards ready. After he read it he peered closely into Cam's eyes, smiled slightly, and raised his right hand to pat Cam gently on his right shoulder as a gesture of conciliation and concern. Cam placed the palm of his right hand on his chest, bowed slightly and closed his eyes, meaning 'thank you in the name of Allah'. Cam went further and flipped his hand near his mouth and made a clicking sound as best as he could, which told him 'not to worry'.

Nasir spoke directly to Avi from then on. He invited them to take tea in a tea house close to the port that served mainly navies. He appeared to be well known by the proprietor, who offered miniature cakes, mamoul, common in most Arab countries and made from sweet dough filled with dates, pistachios and walnuts, and magrood, a Libyan favorite filled with dates, cinnamon and sesame seeds.

Nasir expressed interest in cultivating business with them. Cam kept up his act by refusing to eat. Avi extended Cam's apologies, explaining to Nasir that Cam felt embarrassed when eating with strangers, but the tea was welcome. While drinking, Cam dribbled a bit, using a handkerchief to wipe his chin, which exposed his face again. Nasir pretended not to notice.

Avi and Cam spent several more days observing this ritual until Nasir invited them to his business tea house next to the Italian Embassy. They expected a proposition and got one. Nasir wanted them to ship out on a vessel headed for Egypt with a sensitive cargo. Avi signaled Cam to nod slowly to indicate interest. They agreed to meet Nasir again at his office.

At the appointed hour, Nasir freely gave information. He told them the name of the ship, and that it would be flying under a flag of convenience, and where and when it would dock. They would need to meet with the second officer to confirm their identities. Only the captain and second officer would know their real reason for being on board, but they would still have to work as able seamen to keep up appearances. His expediter would give them a copy of the manifest that would indicate by a code symbol the packages of interest and the holds in which they would be stored. They were under no circumstances to disturb the packages once loaded.

In a breach of security procedure, Nasir revealed that they would unload the live cargo at the Egyptian port of El Arish on the Mediterranean coast. The suspect cargo would be carried by small boat from the ship to the city of El Arish for transport overland to its final destination. Avi and Cam were aware that the port was only about forty-five kilometers from the Israeli border and the Palestine Territories, which could be reached along the Al Kantara Shark-Al Arish Road. Communications would pass on this information to Mossad.

Nasir showed them, in a token of good faith, a wad of American currency. He peeled off a few bills as advance payment, the rest to be given by the captain when they arrived at the final port of destination. Cam touched his right fingertips to his forehead and bowed slightly to show respect.

Nasir invited them to another meal before they shipped out. He introduced them to the expediter, who was clearly disturbed by Cam's appearance. When Cam gave him his card that cast him as an affiliate of a violent side of the Muslim struggle, he began to sweat and fidget. He made the sign to ward off the evil eye, the isabat al-'ayn, where the hand of Fatima is formed by putting the middle fingers together, pointing upward, and the thumb and little finger pointing outward. He also uttered the blessings of God, tabarakallah, to ensure his defense.

Avi and Cam knew that Nasir and the expediter were superstitious, and the occasional visit to the mosque reassured them about getting into paradise.

After servings of the ubiquitous couscous green tea arrived. Avi and Cam took their time sipping their tea. The expediter offered his grateful thanks for a fine meal. He was desperate to leave. Once outside he pulled a small silver flask out of a pocket, took a quick swig and broke into a run.

Avi and Cam had decided to bundle Nasir off at the first convenient opportunity, and having the fat man enjoy the afterglow of a big meal seemed as good a time as any. They offered Nasir more tea and cakes which he accepted with eagerness.

While Avi distracted Nasir, Cam tipped a powder – rohypnol – into his tea cup. Nasir drank it down. Within a minute or two he still talked, but was clearly confused.

They stood Nasir up and supported him on both sides. He could shuffle along and still react to suggestions. Any passersby would not notice anything amiss unless they looked closely, which Arabs do not normally do, especially at night. They walked him across Naser and Al Aas Streets, into Al Bazzar, and up to the door of the house. They laid him out on cushions.

While Avi took a turn around Al Bazzar and the surrounding streets to check all had gone undetected, Cam bound Nasir at wrists and ankles with elastic cord, and removed his watch. Since the room had no windows he would not be able to tell what time of day it was, or even which day. Cam lifted an eyelid and poked him in a few sensitive places. The dosage had worked. He would come round to full awareness in about an hour. Cam fastened the muzzle gag around his face and sat back to enjoy a few pistachios and a bottle of water.

Avi returned and reported all quiet.

'Do you think we should do our own interrogation before we turn him over to the Office? We could at least score some morsels and give the boys and girls at home a head start. You inclined to waste some time on that?'

'Might as well, we've got nothing much to do until we grab the expediter. Go for it.'

Nasir awoke, and they gave him some water and more time to clear his head. He was confused and frightened. Cam decided it was time to show him he could speak.

'Welcome Sayyid Al-Magharha, welcome to the custody of Mossad. I do expect that you speak English, so in this room let that be your second language, you will hear and respond to English and Arabic interchangeably. We will not execute you and we will not hurt you if you cooperate fully. We intend to offer you a holiday in Tel Aviv, which is lovely this time of year. We will now ask you a series of questions. I must remove the gag so that you can answer. No one will be able to hear you if you make loud noises, but if you do consequences will happen. Nod your head if you understand.'

Nasir pleaded with Avi in Arabic.

'You will speak English at all times from now on. We have given you the name Nasir, and you will respond to this name. Besides, we know that Al-Magharha is not your real name, but rest assured, we will discover what it is.'

'Please, I have done nothing, why do you treat me like this? What do want of me? I am a simple businessman, please.'

'Now Mr Nasir, you are an arms smuggler, arms from the Soviet Union. Do you recall a man named Mohy Zuwayya? We captured him on the ship you recently sent to Northern Ireland. He gave you up along with other valuable information. Please let me express my regrets that Mr Zuwayya is no longer with us, but I hope he is residing in paradise, insha'allah. I have personally eliminated the Irish Republican Army men who were to receive that shipment. We found the weapons you already sent to Northern Ireland, so your efforts were for nothing. I imagine you are safer with us than with your colleagues when they find out about your failures. We know much about you but intend to discover more. Please cooperate and all will be well.'

Nasir went pale as the proverbial ghost and started trembling.

'I am not the man you claim, I am just a small businessman trying to feed his family. You are mistaken. Please let me go and I will say nothing.'

'Please do not insult our intelligence, Mr. Nasir. You are precisely who we say you are. Now, let us begin a friendly conversation, I believe you would like to unburden yourself from all this secret activity.'

Avi and Cam had planned to use the standard interrogation technique that involved no violence. They would take turns in posing questions and offering conversation at opportune moments. They had time.

'Mr. Nasir, we will take this exercise a step further.'

Cam broke out the scopolamine, a syringe and a needle.

'Please, I have cooperated fully. I have told you everything I know. Please do not kill me with poison, I beg you.'

'It is not poison, Mr. Nasir, we are not going to kill you, I have already assured you of this. This drug will help us to be certain that what you have told us is the truth.'

Under the influence of the drug, Nasir corroborated most of what he had told them while sober. Cam administered the physostigmine to bring him out of it.

They obtained a description of the smuggling network, which also dealt in drugs, and in women destined for the Soviet Union, the Philippines and Malaysia, for prostitution, mail order brides, and the slavery industries. Cam extracted names of others involved in smuggling arms in ports around Libya and other ports in the Middle East, and in Northern and Western Africa – all of value to experts at Mossad and the CIA.

Cam stayed in the house while Avi caught up with Communications at the Atiq mosque and delivered their interrogation notes for transfer by fax to Tel Aviv.

'I'm bored,' Cam said, on Avi's return. 'Let's go pick up the expediter.'

'With you, but he seems like the type to panic and run, so if we have to bop him, we'll bop him. Just slightly.'

'I've got a better idea. Let's show up at his office at the end of the working day and use the rohypnol trick again. We'll just force him to swallow half a tab, wait for it to work, and escort him back here. Blood on the streets may not turn out to be the best look.'

'Okay, but you are definitely spoiling a chance for some exercise.'

The expediter hesitated about letting them into his office. Avi immediately powered him down into his chair and applied a headlock. Cam produced the tablet and some water and forced him to swallow.

They took him to the room and bound and gagged him.

When he came round Avi explained what was expected of him if he didn't want to visit his virgins.

Avi let Communications know that their ship back to Greece would have to house two very ill men instead of one.

With two days to prepare for extraction, Cam gave a small dose of flumazenil, the antidote to benzos, to both captives. He injected .06 mg into a vein and let it work for an hour. They became more alert. They must be in a condition to walk, more or less normally, and not attract attention.

They bundled the two men into the car without incident. They eased up to their vessel where the captain and second officer were waiting. After a thorough check, Cam and Avi moved the men to the room allocated for them. An ambulance, staffed by sayanim, was waiting at Piraeus ready to transport their bipedal cargo to the Ellinikon Airbase, seven kilometers south of Athens. Their captives boarded an Evergreen International flight to Ben Gurion, arranged by the CIA and Mossad. Cam and Avi would not be involved in the interrogations.

A car took Avi and Cam to the airbase where they boarded an unmarked private jet. On board was Michael Rivkin.

Cam, in jubilant mood, spoke first. 'Hiya Mick, did you fancy a short flight on a nice airplane? Got any cold beer?'

'Shalom, Cam. Your face looks like something that's been buried in soft ground for three months. Did the girls bother you very much?'

'I was completely submerged, it was difficult to breathe. This other guy here didn't get a look in, I was so popular.'

'Yeah, Mick,' Avi chimed in. 'Cam made a much better impression than usual – more handsome.'

Rivkin popped the tops off three beers.

'Seriously, Mick, what do we owe this special privilege to? We could just as well have reported at home.'

'Yes, you could have, but I wanted to get the straight story from you first before the inevitable distortions creep in and begin to obscure the kosher details. We sent you out on a simple kidnapping, and you come back having fingered an entire intercontinental smuggling operation that's got Collections, Political Action and Research running around like whirling dervishes. It's a good thing you're Kidon so you will not be connected in any way with this operation. Otherwise, no one would see you for years due to the testimony you would have to give. Oh, by the way, well done.'

'Just doing our job. Do we get paid more for two instead of one?'

'No.'

'Come by headquarters now. Roast beef is waiting, accompanied by a tot of single malt. Mazel u'Bracha.

That night, Cam dreamt he kept hearing the words that Ralph Pines uttered, 'You will pay a price for surviving. They will try to turn you into a machine. Don't let them do that.'

Out of the darkness, a voice spoke. 'You have become a machine – a brutal one.'

Cam awoke in a sweat and screamed out, but no one answered.

*****

CHAPTER TWENTY NINE

Cam had left Adi for a long period during which she had no indication what he was doing or where he was. He had cloaked his activities in absolute secrecy. The reunion was going to be hard.

Cam knew his relationship with Adi was one between a man and a woman in the real world, an imperfect relationship that not only brought pain and uncertainty but also a tremendous desire.

As was her custom when they met, she touched her fingertips to the side of his face and beamed tenderness from her gold-flecked eyes.

'At least you are not bleeding or broken this time. I suppose that's something to be grateful for. Often what I dream for us is like silent music. Do you ever hear the silent music?'

'Neshama, listening to music is like pondering eternity.'

'You know, Cam, that someone once said that only one thing matters wherever we go, and however we go, we hear the music of life.'

'I wish I could believe that. I think to survive, and not let mysteries distract. Your beauty distracts me, though. Everything about you – the whole package.'

'So now I'm a package? Which market did you find me in? Have you done a great deal of comparing?'

'Sheket bervakasha, you know what I mean.'

'You mean that I'm a pleasurable diversion, a distraction from what you are and what you do, what you enjoy and will never give up.'

'I mean no such thing. I try very hard not to think of a life without you, I would not recover and possibly become the murderous full blown sociopath that people expect me to be. I'm not that, not at all. I simply don't understand how other people can dwell all the time on the actions they take to preserve their version of reality. There are as many versions of reality as there are fools to advocate them. Reality is nature in full force. It doesn't care a damn for humanity and, especially, not for individuals. I've chosen to fight for my version, and for people I care if you believe I can care for anyone. Do you believe I care for you?'

'Yes, as much as I can. I also believe you care for my family, and for Avi and Saray, and some others you work with. But I also believe you will never care for more than a very few people. You let people come and go.'

'If I had a different perspective on the world, perhaps, I wouldn't let them go. But at least I let some come and I keep them, living or not. I just feel bad about people who won't fight back against injustice.

Never walk meekly to the scaffold.'

'Cam, I am worried about the future of Israel. Are we all going to live like this for the rest of our lives? In fear and fighting for our survival. War affects us all. We all suffer – our wounds run too deep to treat. The price we have to pay is too dear. Instead of compassion for our neighbors we are taught to hate them. If we lose our sense of compassion, what are we as human beings?'

'Adi, Israel must show strength, not weakness; otherwise, they will walk all over you.'

'Yes, but we have alienated ourselves from the rest of the world with our policies to take over Arab homes in Israel and to establish settlements by our people in the West Bank, Gaza Strip and East Jerusalem. The Holocaust turned the world towards us. Now, we are turning away from the world. We have a home, but the home is for us, not for them. We will never have peace with these kinds of policies.'

'If they cease their terrorist activities then there may be a way to negotiate and resolve the problems you are talking about.'

'I don't know. All I know right now is that I care for you.'

'The feeling is mutual, Adi.'

'You will come back to me.' It was a statement, not a plea.

'I will.'

Cam was about to hold Adi in his arms, but the floor seemed to rise to the ceiling. His vision blurred and his legs gave way. He reached out, and with the support of Adi's shoulder, steadied himself.

'Are you all right, Cam?'

'I'll be fine. The injury in Vietnam… it sometimes affects my balance.'

'I know a good physician.'

'No, it comes and goes. There is nothing they can do. I have tried already.'

'Cam, you don't have to take part in any more ops. You have done enough already to help Israel.'

Cam remained silent for a few moments. What Adi said made sense. He could stop now and settle down in Israel with Adi and raise a family. His only family had been the kids at the Rest. What would it be like to be part of a real family? The idea started to grow on him.

'Let me think about it after the current op, Adi.'

'Promise,' Adi said, as they parted after a long embrace.

Cam could see tears welling up in her eyes. 'I promise.'

Avi and Cam had been hunting fedayeen – Arab guerillas operating against Israel – in the Palestinian Territories.

The fedayeen wanted to eliminate the Jewish state and replace it with a Palestinian Arab state. Violence took on the face of a religious jihad.

Lebanon provided a haven for the fedayeen until they started causing trouble there as well, but the Lebanese seemed reluctant or powerless to evict them. South Lebanon became the staging area for shelling Israeli towns across the border and for raids against civilians.

An atrocity occurred on 15 May 1974 that started Israel thinking hard about removing the PLO, Palestinian Liberation Organization, from Lebanon. A massacre took place in the town of Ma'alot in northern Israel, nine kilometers from the Lebanese border. Three terrorists dressed in Israel defense force uniforms stormed a school, leaving twenty-five dead, twenty-two of them students, and sixty-eight injured. The Sayeret Matkal, the classified Special Forces unit of the Israel Defense Forces were sent to annihilate the terrorists but got in each other's way and did a poor job, although the Arabs were finally killed. This perceived failure led to the creation of Yamam.

Yamam, Yehida Merkazit Meyuhedet, the elite border police counter-terrorism unit dealt with domestic operations in hostage rescue and offensive take-over, SWAT-type duties and undercover police work, but only in combat situations. Most of Yamam's duties were highly classified and often credited to other units.

Yamam was divided into teams containing operators with a particular specialization such as entry, medical emergencies, sniping, demolition, and bomb disposal. Members trained and operated together as part of the same unit. All had military and combat experience. Since it was self-dependent, Yamam had developed a rapid deployment plan, and a highly coordinated team, made up of various squads.

At the Office, Amzi let Cam know that Yamam were interested in Cam's expertise.

'How in the hell would Yamam know about us? We're supposed to be securely locked away in the bosom of mother Mossad,' replied Cam.

'You should be locked away permanently, far away. Unlike Kidon, with which no one including Yamam will ever know about, you are a member of the Special Operations Division, remember. A very few, and I do mean a very few, people know you work here. Yamam is possibly the second most classified operation in the IDF, so they have their ways of getting information. However, I will be making inquiries about how they came to know about you. They only have rumors and will never get to read your dossiers.'

'Are you trying to get rid of us? I'm not transferring to Yamam, they can stick that. I doubt they serve tea, for one thing.'

'Perish the thought. You will serve out your full sentence with Mossad, no parole. If Yamam accepts you, it will be on a case by case basis. Be good boys and try it, some good for Mossad could come of it. An entry into that enigma is most unusual.'

'We'll need to have a word with Mick Rivkin. If he's not fussed, I'm not fussed.'

It turned out that Mick was also interested in what sort of intelligence they could turn up. Internal department rivalry was alive and well.

Despite some misgiving, Cam and Avi fitted in well with the Yamam team. Cam's Remington 700 and Leupold scope created special interest, especially when he consistently made shots over 1100 meters. Avi was the archetypal spotter. Yamam signed an agreement for their services.

Om March 1, 1978, eleven militants of the PLO faction Fatah carried out an attack and hijacking against civilians traveling the coastal highway about halfway between Tel Aviv and Netanya. Fatah called it 'Operation of the Martyr Kamal Adwan', after the PLO chief of operations was killed by Sayeret commandos during Operation Wrath of God in Beirut in 1973. Time magazine characterized it as 'the worst terrorist attack in Israel's history'. Israel named it the 'Coastal Highway Massacre'.

The head of Mossad called an emergency meeting in his office. At a conference, they listened to the latest news commentary:

... No count yet on how many there are. They seem to have walked up to the highway from the beach; it is less than two kilometers.

... Reported automatic weapons fire, the targets are passing cars. They've got a white Mercedes taxi, several bodies thrown to the pavement. Now headed in the direction of Tel Aviv.

... They've abandoned the taxi and hijacked a bus. A full bus. Still headed toward Tel Aviv, shooting and throwing grenades at passing cars. One body thrown from the bus.

... A second bus is being hijacked. Passengers from the first bus are being herded onto the second bus. We now have spotters in place but not enough armed troops to engage. There appear to be eleven terrorists armed with AKs, RPGs and explosives.

... A road block has been set up by police. There are civilian police with black pants and white shirts. Also some military police with white helmets and the mem tzadeh stenciled on.

... There is a tremendous amount of gunfire now, wild shooting from our police. Bus passengers trying to escape are being shot.

Now some Magav are arriving, combat police with the silver and grey shoulder patch on their dark green combat fatigues, carrying automatic weapons and rucksacks. Also some Magav with no insignia, could be Yamam. They may be too late. Much firing inside the bus, terrorists maybe committing suicide, and killing as many hostages as possible before dying.

...Oi Va'avoi Li. Nishtu Gedacht! A grenade or an exploding fuel tank has set the bus on fire.

The news commentary went on for some time until finally word revealed that thirty-eight Israeli civilians had been killed and seventy wounded. The eleven terrorists, one of them a woman, were dead.

The mood in the room was decidedly somber. Everyone knew that Israel could not let this one go after the numerous PLO incursions and shelling, and the Ma'alot massacre in 1974. It had been four years since the victory of the Yom Kippur War. It was time for another.

A telephone – the blue one – chirped on the head's desk.

'Hofi here. Yes, Mr. Begin, we have all the details that are available at this time. Yes, Mr. Prime Minister, it cannot be tolerated any longer. I understand sir... immediate mobilization.'

No turning back. 'Yes sir... of course Mossad is prepared. Political Action is already in contact with our major allies, and the Research Department will have hourly situation reports prepared. Forces in the field will have access to all situation reports as required.'

'What about Special Operations Division? Are we using them?'

'Yes, Prime Minister, the Special Operations Division is at the disposal of the military and border police.'

A brief explanation followed concerning the Special Operations Division and the involvement of Mossad.

'Those two gentlemen are with me now. I will explain the request. Cabinet meeting tonight at 17.00 hours. Thank you for inviting me. I will liaise with Major General Gazit when I arrive.'

The head of Mossad broke the news:

'We are at war with the PLO. Our goal is to establish a protection belt between the Israeli border and the Litani River, pushing out the PLO and other Palestinian militant groups, until they are north of the river. Israel also wants to bolster our ally, for the moment at least, the Maronite Christian Philangist South Lebanon Army which is also fighting the PLO and Muslims in general. Get busy.

'Avi, Cam, stay a moment. Major General Ben-Gal, officer-in-charge of the Northern Command, has been pestering the PM about assigning you to the Palsar Sayeret Company of the Golani Brigade.

The request actually came from Brigadier General Reuveni who will lead Golani into this action, which is now coded Operation Litani. However, the Magav also want you to serve with the Yamam, which in turn will be reinforced by Yamas and Yamag. A compromise has been reached. You will serve directly with Yamam, which will send two teams, platoon strength, to support the Golani Brigade. Cam, you will report immediately to Golani Brigade, on the border with Lebanon. Present yourself to the deputy battalion commander. Behatzlacha, Hayalim Kedoshim.'

'Yihyeh beseder.'

Avi said goodbye to Saray in the foyer of the head's office. Cam had no time to find Adi so he tried calling her at Kyria, but no luck. His last resort was her sister Ahuva who was so busy in Research that she had exactly one minute for him. She told him to fight like a lion of Judah. Adi would expect no less.

Cam and Avi hooked up with Yamam on the way to the border. Since their involvement was not secret this time, they were given the Yamam patch to wear on the left sleeve of their fatigues and the badge to wear on their green berets. Cam still wore his Mossad dog tags to remove any confusion as to which organization he ultimately reported to.

The deputy battalion commander laid it out for them. The infantry, supported by armor, was going to first take the village of al-Hiyam, seven kilometers north of the Israeli border. Being so close to the Galilee panhandle, al-Hiyam had been occupied for years by the Fatah faction of the PLO, launching missiles and artillery into northern Israeli villages. It had to go. One of the two Yamam platoons would assume sniping duties during the infantry advance and would remain in place after the capture.

Golani would then move to capture Marjayoun, fifteen kilometers further north, and then push on to Rashaiya el-Foukhar, ten kilometers east of Marjayoun, almost on the southern bank of the Litani River. The job of the second Yamam platoon was to advance in front of the infantry and armor, and pick off any Muslims they came across. Then they were to set up hides in Marja to do as much physical and psychological damage as they could while the infantry secured the place. They were to repeat the sequence on the way to Rasha.

Cam was put in command of the second platoon, because of his seek-and-destroy experience. Avi became co-commander, because that was the way Cam wanted it to work. They were nominal captains, but were not going to wear any badges of rank.

Cam set up the platoon differently than was usual for a

reconnaissance unit connected to a regular mechanized battalion. He reasoned their first job was sniping and they would move swiftly to have maximum effect. Following them would be a cut-down version of a company. After the snipers were placed in the villages the rest of the unit would begin to soften up resistance before the full battalion pulled up.

Their follow-up would be equipped with two M3 or M5 half-tracks carrying a 20mm cannon and two MG 34 machine guns in the rear corners, ideal for close infantry support. One M1 13A1 Zelda armored car would be equipped with an M2 HB .50 caliber machine gun and two Belgian MAG 7.62 machine guns on either side of the crew compartment door. Finishing the complement would be 52mm and 60mm mortar crews, RPGs and rifle grenades, three fire teams of three men each, and medic and stretcher bearers.

The Golani Battalion backed up with self-propelled artillery with a 155mm gun and Soltam 160mm mortars mounted on a Sherman tank chassis. Centurion tanks, called a 'whip' or a 'shot' by their crews, had L7 105mm guns. Rifle companies, consisting of one hundred and twenty troops and a heavy weapons platoon of forty troops, had three 81mm mortars.

With no time to perform the reconnaissance that Cam would have done to become familiar with the landscape, the army had to move fast.

Topographic maps detailed the planned Israeli routes of advance. With a hearty God speed they were on their way. Cam supposed they really must have believed that he knew what he was doing. The Yamam platoons began operation two days before the regular army started their push.

The rugged, mountainous country leading up to the Litani River provided adequate concealment – perfect for snipers, but could play havoc with heavy mechanized infantry.

Since Cam's platoon did not have the time to scout, they set up ambushes along the planned Israeli lines of interdiction, and shot any Arabs that offered resistance. Avi and Cam established an ambush strategy that the platoon quickly named the Star of David. Ambush positions roughly followed the outline of the six-pointed star. Two teams would set up at each point, and a single team would plant themselves along each arm leading to the points. This created overlapping fields of fire which prevented the enemy from running to another position.

Cam set the teams up between 700 and 800 meters from point of contact – the longest range from which they could hit targets. They were not after stealth killings; they wanted the enemy to know they were being picked off from locations they could not identify, a very effective way to instill fear. Watching the man next to you go down and not knowing if you were next, played havoc with your nerves. No one to see, no one to fight.

Normal small arms did not have the range to reach them, and the only alternative was artillery or mortars, which did not worry them much. If the Arabs fired this ordnance they would leave and set up again down the trail. When they had done all the damage they could do at one location, they would move briskly to stay ahead of the rapidly advancing army.

The Golani Brigade quickly captured al-Hiyam and moved towards Marjayoun, which they occupied days later. Scattered resistance remained so Cam left one squad of snipers there to help the regulars. The rest of the platoon continued to set up the Star of David on the way to Rashaiya el Foukhar, which they reached a day and a half before the main force, the 12th Battalion of the Golani. They backtracked to support them.

About midway between Marjayoun and Rasha, Cam observed some of the best tactics he had seen terrorists perform; he could hardly believe them capable of it. From their hides they watched as an M5 halftrack and an M1 13A1 Zelda, ahead of two rifle platoons, were attacked. Two Arabs armed with an RPG scurried from cover and fired on the M5. The Arabs turned and fled. Israeli armor turned to chase, followed by one of the rifle platoons. In this way, they lured the Israelis into a cul-de-sac between two hillocks. A large contingent of Arabs then opened up with combined arms, machine guns, RPGs and AKs. Interlocking fields of fire supported each other.

The enemy boxed in the Israelis with machine gun and RPG fire. They did not attempt to penetrate the armor itself but rather fired volleys of RPGs at the front ends of the vehicles, disabling them and starting fires. As the armor crews bailed out they came under intense fire.

By this time the other rifle platoon had come up to engage, trying to outflank the Arabs. Facing RPGs and small arms, the Arabs began an ordered retreat up the hills that comprised the ambush site. The Israelis found it impossible to make a frontal attack. The enemy continued to fire from one position and then moved to another. The Arabs feigned an opening through which the rifle platoons came, but they were engaged from machine gun positions, again with interlocking fire. Eventually the Arabs simply faded away. Amazingly, the Israeli soldiers received only wounds, none severe.

The complexity of the attack pointed to at least a platoon or even a company level of command structure. Cam kept glassing the region surrounding the ambush to see if he could locate the Arabs responsible for setting up the attack. He finally found them. Avi gave him the numbers and they went down, one shot apiece. Cam felt good.

Cam radioed the 12th Deputy Commander and recounted what we had seen. It was not really part of his brief but Cam went ahead and suggested tactics to counter more of these coordinated attacks. The rifle platoons had fired wildly, with little accuracy and too much ammunition expended for too little result. The troops had to conserve rounds because there was no way to resupply them and, in any case, the attack had been carried out with lightning speed. Applying the fundamentals of marksmanship would increase the ratio of kills to shots fired.

It became obvious that the Arabs were learning more about armor vulnerabilities and how to use their limited weapons systems to exploit them. Cam had no advice for countering this but was certain the armor experts would.

Cam suggested the use of more scouts to prevent Israeli forces from being trapped in situations where movement was restricted. Unrestricted movement was vital.

Cam learned later that the 12th Deputy Commander had taken notes and briefings. The advice was passed on to other units and eventually became standard practice although infantry and armor experts would add refinements over time.

The deputy commander complimented the Yamam platoons on good sniping. His advancing troops were continually coming across bodies. The count so far was in excess of 125.

When the 12th occupied Rasha, Cam left a squad with them to keep harassing Arab stragglers. The remaining two squads went with the 12th as it advanced west along the Utani, capturing a number of villages along the way and finally stopping at Aabbassiye, about fifteen kilometers east of Tyre. Israel had cleared a protection belt and now stood on the south bank of the river. The PLO had retreated beyond the north bank.

The Yamam squads ranged back and forth along the river, scoring kills. On one occasion, Cam was called to communications. It was the deputy battalion commander.

'Captain, you have an advanced degree in biochemistry, correct?'

'Yes sir, I do, but I haven't cracked a book on the subject for years.'

'No matter, you're the closest thing we have to an expert in the vicinity. A recon patrol has found a warehouse or a laboratory, we're not sure what it is, and it's full of specialized equipment we can't identify. It is some kind of technology we would not expect to see here. I want you to inspect it and tell me if it is potentially dangerous to Israel.'

'Very good, sir, we are just mopping up a bit so I can be there as soon as possible. What are your coordinates?'

The commander gave him the coordinates and said, 'We can send transportation for you.'

'Actually, sir, I can make it faster on foot, it's only five kilometers. Please give your men my description so they don't shoot me. I'll be carrying a Remington sniper rifle. The Arabs don't have anything like it.'

'Don't worry, we won't perforate you. ETA?'

'About an hour, I'll still have to keep an eye out for enemy patrols.'

'Avi, I've got to take a little sightseeing trip, should be back by the end of the day. Keep our delinquents occupied so they don't fight among themselves.'

Cam borrowed a 1M1 Galil SAR in case he needed automatic firepower.

Along the way a PLO tossed a grenade, which went wide of Cam, while a second PLO offered badly-aimed AK fire.

Cam stood and returned fire. He thought he clipped at least one. He hid for about an hour until he judged it safe to continue.

When he encountered Israeli sentries, one of them took a look at him and started hollering for a medic.

'What the hell are you doing?'

'Sir, you're bleeding, your shoulder.'

Cam looked down and blood had spread from the top of his left shoulder into his tunic – there was no pain, though.

The medic arrived at high speed, followed shortly by the 12th deputy commander. 'I was warned you can't keep out of trouble. What happened?'

Cam related his skirmish. The medic dug out a jagged bit of metal, a grenade fragment, from a muscle bundle that connected the top of the shoulder with the neck.

'Could have been worse, Captain. The fragment was red hot and made something like a cyst in your muscle so it didn't travel anywhere else. Lots of nerves around there. That notch will just have to fill itself in, I can't stitch it.'

Great, Adi was going to beat him up and Avi was going to laugh himself stupid.

'Right, Colonel, let's see what sort of treasure you've got.'

*****

CHAPTER THIRTY

Moments after they entered the building Cam knew something substantial had been found. He could tell that the equipment was for some sort of fermentation plant, and not a brewery. He undertook a careful tour.

'Colonel, I think I know what this is for. Could I please have some writing material and I will make a list of the equipment and what it is used for.'

The list included …

High efficiency particulate air filters to remove 99.9% of particles 0.3 microns in diameter or larger, meaning all bio agents especially bacteria and viruses.

Two highly polished 700 liter stainless steel fermenters.

Glass vessels up to five liters for inoculation and culture preparation.

Sterilizing apparatus.

A small centrifuge, mixing tank and spray dryer.

Heating, ventilation, and air conditioning equipment with separate local control.

Laboratory fume hoods. Purified water system and filters.

The makings of negative pressure chambers and airlocks, air flow fans and sensors to regulate them, and perforated ceilings for the pressure chambers.

Two minus twenty degree freezers.

'Colonel, what you have here is most of a bio-weapons factory, probably for bacteria, as I don't see any appliances for tissue culture which are necessary to grow viruses.'

Cam realized the danger they were facing.

'Get your people out of here now,' he said. 'Anyone, who has been inside, needs to take a shower and scrub themselves with Lysol, or something similar. And that includes you and me. Put a heavy guard on, and instruct them by no means to enter the building. I suggest you alert some microbiology specialists from Tel Aviv University, or wherever else you can find them, to take a look once we get the bits back to Israel. They will need biohazard gear and clothing. I don't know what is in those freezers, I hope nothing, but only a real expert should find out. Good job locating this, you have deterred a possible national disaster if any Arabs in the vicinity had put it together.'

'We stumbled on it. Where could it have come from?'

'Most of that kind of kit is only available from the US, Japan or Germany, but I did see some Mid-Eastern writing on some of the crates. Did you recognize it?'

'Of course, that stuff was shipped from Iraq.'

'That would make sense. Iraq is chummy with the PLO at the moment. Saddam enjoys the occasional threatening gesture toward the West and bio agents are as scary as anything else.'

'How would a bio agent be used against Israel?'

'Easy. Some bio agents are so virulent it would take less than a kilo of dried culture to poison entire water systems. Any punk could simply carry the powder across the border. Or you could use some delivery systems developed in the States during the cold war, for example, the bomblet, a small metal ball holding a small amount of liquid. Then there is a cluster munition – a cardboard box on a parachute which carries powder and can be dropped piecemeal from the air. It delivers around 540 bomblets at a time. Drop one on Tel Aviv or Jerusalem and, well, you can guess.'

'Elokei!'

'Oh yes. Since I am the only high ranking Mossad agent in the immediate vicinity I am declaring this a top secret location and a top secret operation. I'm sure you agree.'

'Yes.'

'Put me on communications, and I can get a secure line through to Tel Aviv to give and receive instructions. The Golani Brigade now has a very important infant to babysit. I'll assist. The sooner we get this cleared, cleaned up and moved the better. Zeh mesukan.'

Cam let Avi know that he had to stay at his current location for at least a few days. Since they were on the regular communications and not a secure line, he just told him the 12th had come across something unexpected and dangerous.

'Don't waste 'em all until I get back.'

'There are always plenty to choose from. I expect a good story when we can talk in private.'

'I've essentially taken over here on behalf of Mossad; it's that kind of operation. No one is shooting, yet. It's a sort of hold'em'till we fold'em thing. I expect some bad boys from Special Ops and Magav to arrive shortly to lock the place down. If some flies come snooping around I'll ask for help to SWAT them. Good joke, eh?'

'You are a joke, a bad one. Check in once a day at least.'

As it turned out, the next day brought something completely unexpected to the troops and Israel in general. The offensive was halted, not just scaled down, but halted. In response to Israeli retaliation against constant terrorism from the PLO and Muslim Lebanese, the UN Security Council, in its infinite wisdom, had passed Resolution 425 and Resolution 426, calling for Israel to withdraw from Lebanon. The UN Interim Force in Lebanon (UNIFIL) was created to enforce the mandate. UNIFIL forces arrived in Lebanon to set up headquarters in Naqoura. This was an exceptionally fast response, indicating to Cam that plans to humiliate Israel must have been in the works for some time before the resolutions were passed.

Punishing the Muslims and putting a stop to rampant terrorism was bad form, according to Cam. Even under siege throughout Operation Litani, terror groups had rained down heavy artillery fire on Israeli communities adjacent to the northern Lebanese border. Civilians, not the army, were the targets, as they had been for years, but that seemed to be overlooked by the UN.

Defense Minister Ezer Weizman ordered the IDF to pull its forces out of Lebanon, an embarrassment to the Begin government. Twenty Israeli soldiers had been killed. Estimates of enemy dead ranged from 1,100 to 2,000 and perhaps 250,000 refugees had fled the fighting.

This stunning reversal of victory halted the neutralizing of the bio-weapons factory.

'Amzi, we have to get the factory components out of here now. We can't allow the PLO to have it back, and I sure as hell want to keep it out of the hands of the UN. Can't Israel use bio-weapons as some sort of leverage to justify pushing out the terrorists? Or is it also just good clean fun to let them continue to develop one of the most terrifying weapons imaginable? I mean, come on, what are those fat assed digits in New York thinking? Terrorists are just misguided and need a warm bowl of soup and a hug before they get tucked in at night?'

'It's done, Cam, everybody here is devastated. But I agree with you, that factory must be brought here and destroyed. What are you proposing we do?'

'Once it's in Israel, and before it's destroyed, it has to be studied. I have no idea how the components got here or why they were sold to a hostile government or governments, but Iraq seems deeply involved. Collections and Research are going to need to put some time in answering those questions. I suggest the supplier companies be given a hard look. I think they believed they were selling to legitimate clients who are fronts for, or dupes of, the actual end users. Of course there could be employees who are not above taking money for record falsification and the like. This will take years of study. How many of these things may be dotted around the Arab world? No one seems to have had a clue, it is very frightening.'

'I would think a dedicated task force will be set up within Mossad and Aman Military Intelligence, Cam. Not really your problem now. It was a good thing you were there to identify what the factory is for.'

'Fine. Anyway, I need three semi-trailers here yesterday to move the equipment. A squad should be sufficient manpower. I suggest you ask for volunteers, it is unusual duty. They will need to be gowned like surgeons. No one, I repeat, no one is to open the freezers. That has to be done under sterile containment by experts. I suppose we can make this look like part of the general withdrawal.'

'Yes, we are moving at our own pace, we are not going to rush just because the damned UN is underfoot. I'll have things moving within two hours, expect the trucks tonight.'

'Just so you know, I'm moving Avi in with a sniper squad to set up a Star of David. He'll drop the hammer on any observers or would-be infiltrators with towel heads. Golani is supplying some troops as well, if any dimwits try to take the factory back. I'll keep the firepower in place for a few days after the move is completed.'

There were no glitches during the removal. After four days Cam resumed duty with the Yamam platoons. A slower withdrawal gave them time for a little more activity, only in self-defense.

During the withdrawal, Israeli positions in Lebanon were gradually turned over to the South Lebanon Army. Fighting continued. The SLA, frustrated with the kid glove treatment of the PLO and Lebanese Muslim forces, shelled UNIFIL headquarters, killing eight UN soldiers. Syria, unfriendly towards Lebanon at the time, pounded Christian towns in the southern part of the country. Hostilities went on and on with no end in sight. Since the UN has never been effective in quelling armed factions, the PLO resumed terrorizing Israel. The Lebanese civil war also intensified.

Back in Tel Aviv, the mood around the Office was not buoyant and reflected the whole of Israel. Victory had been snatched away from them.

*****

CHAPTER THIRTY ONE

'Gents, I have received word from on high that due to meritorious service over the last years, you are to be awarded medals,' Amzi said to Cam and Avi, during a tea ceremony.

'Medals? We don't need medals. Amzi, we're not in it for the glory, you know that. I could refuse to accept. What if I refuse?'

'Completely out of the question. You would dishonor Mossad, your close colleagues, your distant colleagues, the men you fought for and with, need I go on? You will accept and put a big grin on your faces while you do it.'

'No, really, there are thousands of people who deserve medals more than we do. It's extremely embarrassing, too much.'

'Sheket. Enough! In any case, since you are in a clandestine organization, the ceremony will be held behind closed doors. You won't be allowed to wear the medals anyway; you barely exist, remember. It is enough that Israel knows you have contributed to her survival.

'You both will receive the Medal of Courage, the HaOz, for acts of gallantry at risk of your lives during combat duty, as well as the Medal of Distinguished Service for exemplary bravery in the line of duty. If that isn't enough to explode your already swelled heads, you will accept the Israeli Police Service Medal for outstanding contributions to the goals of the police. The Medals of Courage and Distinguished Service will be presented to you by the Army Chief of General Staff, the only active officer with the rank of Lieutenant General. The Chief Commissioner of Police will present the police medal. You have been requested to wear battle dress. Since Mossad does not have a uniform or a beret, you will wear the Golani brown beret for the military awards and the green beret of the Yamam for the police award. An intimate luncheon will follow the ceremony, a rare honor. Is this finally getting through to your pea brains?'

'Can I pin on my wings and tuck my trousers into my boots to show I'm stupid enough to jump out of airplanes?'

'I suppose so,' Amzi sighed deeply.

'If he does, I get to wear my wings too.'

'How about my ribbons for the Bronze and Silver Stars?'

'Rachmana litzlon, I should stop you. Finished?'

'Who do we get to invite? I definitely want witnesses when I burst into tears of joy.'

'Nobody.'

'Not fair, you will be there, right?'

'Yes, along with the Head and the Deputy Head.'

'If you get to come, I think Ahuva should attend.'

'She'd like that, she's so proud of you already.'

'Good, arrange it. And while you're at it, I want Adi there.'

'Saray comes if Adi does.'

'I give up. I'll try to get agreement but say nothing to the women until I do. Right now they don't even know you are getting medals.'

So it was done. There was much huddling and running around by the women, mostly about what to wear and how to act. Avi and Cam stayed out of it. It was more dangerous than combat, thought Cam.

Adi decided to wear her uniform. She had been promoted to rabat, corporal, and joined the training for the Research Department of the IDF Directory of Military Intelligence, AgafHaModi 'inlit, Aman. This entitled her to wear the bottle green beret and the Aman shoulder patch. Cam was bemused by the design of the patch, it was green and white, and had a stylized figure that looked either like a modern art rendering of a sword with wings, or a rocket.

As a member of Aman, Adi would immerse herself in analysis of information gathered by Aman's collection units and from the larger intelligence community. Intelligence would be used to evaluate security policy and military planning, tactics, strategies and assessment of operations. She could end up reporting to military and political decision makers, including the Prime Minister. It suited her. Her clever brain would be put to good use and best of all, for Cam, she would not be in the field. She would have the opportunity to work closely with Mossad and keep the profession in the family with her sister and brother-in-law.

The ceremony was held at the Knesset. Cars flew the Israeli flag above the headlights.

Upon arrival they were taken in hand by a young captain. They skipped security, but Avi and Cam took a close look at procedures. They may not have been directly responsible for security any longer but they had a vested interest. Some of the Knesset Guard and Shin Bet bodyguards recognized them and saluted as they passed.

Their escort opened the door and came to attention as they filed in. Waiting for them were the chief of staff, the chief commissioner of police, and to their surprise, the commander of the Golani Brigade and his deputy commander.

'Shalom, ladies and gentlemen. We are pleased to welcome you to this solemn but pleasurable occasion. Would you care for coffee or tea?'

An orderly in a crisp white jacket, black trousers and tie, linen cloth draped on his left arm, deftly fulfilled requests. A few minutes passed in small talk, the high officials putting their party at ease.

Ahuva and Saray looked stunning, and charmed every male in the room. Adiela looked every bit the professional soldier. When introduced to the dignitaries she came smartly to attention and saluted crisply. The senior officers did their best to make her feel comfortable.

As Cam looked at her he became aware of another person that he had not seen before. She could never be replaced. He wanted to take care of her but not in the way he had previously looked after his colleagues in combat. She looked a beautiful woman, but she had been trained in the elements of war; she was as fierce as a sabra could be. Cam felt he was plunging into the unknown.

The medals were presented in polished olive wood boxes. They were not pinned on them, but would find a home in a safe at the Office. That they had been awarded would be noted in their dossiers.

The lunch was a full formal affair with more white-coated orderlies serving. The china and silver cutlery bore the crest of Israel, a menorah flanked by olive branches, and the acronym for the Israeli Defense Forces, Tsva Haganah le-Yisra'el.

After they had dined, the chief of staff said in his address concerning Cam that he would be known in the annals of Israel's history as the "Jericho Man" – the man who interceded with the President of the United States for Israel. A murmur of agreement signaled everyone's approval, knowing that Israel had avoided the nuclear option, on the resupply of arms by the US.

The chief of staff then directed his attention to Cam:

'We all have difficulty finding the correct term with which to address you. You have held various military ranks as suited the situation and no rank at all when carrying out your more covert activities. We feel that 'operative' or 'agent' is not appropriate for the level at which you work. Any suggestions?'

'Please call me Cam, everyone does. Rank doesn't mean much to me personally, it's mainly a way for me to know with whom I'm dealing and how they should be dealt with.'

'Yes, it's been noted several times that you have, how may I say this politely, a rather cavalier attitude toward authority.'

'Yes, sir, I suppose that's true. In a gunfight I'll take a conscript private over a general if he knows what he's doing and keeps me alive. Performance and grace under pressure are what count with me.'

'The Infantry was interested in your Star of David approach to setting up sniper positions. It was very effective and has been passed on to other units, as have your observations concerning tactics, techniques and procedures for fighting with armor and ground troops in hilly and mountainous terrain.

'It could not have been foreseen that our forces would find a bio-weapons lab in the middle of nowhere and that you could deal with its identification and disposition. Any advice?'

'Not really, sir. The only thing to be done is to track the sources of equipment and how it makes its way to the terrorists. Finding factories and destroying them will now have to be a routine undertaking by the Intelligence services. It is a nightmare. In fact, sir, I believe a small but complete bio-weapons factory could be mounted in stages on the back of two or three semi-trailers. You could just drive it from place to place, it would be virtually undetectable.'

The officials looked at each other in bewilderment, and Cam knew that another assignment was in the offing.

'Yitzhak, see to it that Cam liaises with chemical engineers who are under the highest security clearance. How quickly can you come up with the plans?'

'Soon.'

'Cam, you were described to me once as a ruthless individual. Are you?'

'A very pointed question, sir. I don't think "ruthless" is quite the right word. I think "without conscience" would be a better description.'

'Then we are all relieved you are engaging in the Israeli struggle. Why have you embraced our cause so closely?'

'Sir, Israel reminds me of who I am. I am determined to survive the odds by any means necessary. For the first time in my life I also feel as if I have a family. I still have to work on that connection. It has been quite unknown to me until recently.'

Cam exchanged brief smiles with his Mossad family and a longer one with Adi, who glowed radiantly.

'On behalf of all of us, we welcome you as an Israeli citizen. We need you.'

'Thank you, sir. It means a lot to me.'

That night Avi and Cam sat drinking in the Office club. Being Jewish, the Mossad gang had hosted yet another meal after the awards, as if lunch had not been enough.

'You ever think about getting out of this racket and into civilian life?'

'Let's see, I've been stabbed, shot at, hit by grenade fragments, and my face extensively fixed twice…'

'Which must still have been an improvement over the original.'

'Go take a flying jump. As I was saying, what's not to like about this job? Where else will we get a chance to waste bad guys and perform other feats of skill and daring without the least bit of supervision?'

'We're not getting younger. I'm already starting to feel some light physical distress in places I've never noticed before.'

'Me, too. All that means is that we need to be less impulsive and more cunning. We could get other people crazier than us, if they exist, to do some of the work. We can make godlike pronouncements that will be obeyed.'

'You've had too much to drink. Really, have you thought about letting things go? You do have Adi to think about.'

'And you have Saray. I just can't picture us sitting behind a desk like Amzi, God bless him for the good friend and professional that he is. Maybe we need to cut down on the combat a little, but I don't see us anywhere but in the field. I'm fine there. I can't wait to see what comes next.' Cam raised his glass. 'L'chaim, Achi.'

Cam rose from his seat and the next moment was looking up at Avi's face. His legs had crumpled and the room wobbled like a top coming to rest. Everything went blank.

He awoke to see Adi looking into his face. She was holding his right arm, caressing it gently. 'Hello, Mr Warrior. You have returned.'

'Where am I?' Cam asked.

'You are in the Hertzliya Medical Center, getting medical care.'

'How long have I been here?'

'About thirty-six hours.'

'When can I go…'

'Soon.'

Cam fell asleep. Avi, Amzi and neurosurgeon professor Ian Weinberg joined Adi at Cam's bedside.

After introductions, Professor Weinberg said, 'We believe that Mr. Campbell has a progressive degenerative disease of the brain which is normally associated with boxing and other close contact sports. It is casually known as 'punch drunk' syndrome. In Mr. Campbell's case, though, it seems to tie in with a violent blow to his head he received in the Vietnam War. The brain degeneration is associated with loss of balance, aggression, paranoia and dementia. Currently there is no cure for the disease. The disease can only be positively diagnosed after a person dies by carrying out an autopsy of the brain. We think that in Mr. Campbell's case the degenerative condition has reached an advanced stage and could lead to a deep coma. The best we can do is to keep him as comfortable as possible. I regret to have to tell you this.'

'Thank you Professor,' Amzi said, after a lengthy silence. We appreciate your candor. We will do what we can for our friend.'

Cam was still sleeping after an hour. Amzi and Avi had left. Adi remained at Cam's bedside. Not long after, Cam stirred, and Adi said, 'Cam, I have some news for you, from your friend Ralph Pines.'

'I can hear you, Adi. Please tell me.' Adi read the letter:

Dear Cam,
You will be pleased to hear that I have made progress about your family background. Your grandfather emigrated from Scotland during the Great Depression and your father, William Campbell, served in the American forces during World War II. He helped in the repatriation of refugees after the war had ended. He met and married your mother, Malka Hillel, a Jewish refugee from Kyustendil, a town in the west of Bulgaria and famous for its hot springs. Your father suffered from post war depression and had violent episodes. Your mother could not cope and unfortunately took her life. I am sorry to bring you this sad news, but I am sure you understand that the effects of war are far reaching in many lives.
The fishing season will begin soon. Join me if you can.
Your friend, Ralph

Adi's eyes lit up. 'You have a Jewish mother, Cam. You know what that means. You are Jewish. That means Israel is your home. You have come home, Cam.'

'I feel at home … I am home. But what have I become, Adi?'

'War weaves its own spell, Cam. We get caught in its web and cannot escape.'

'Too late to…'

'You can start again. I know a quiet kibbutz where we can stay.'

'I'd like that. I'd teach the children about life. Real life, the chemistry of life.'

'You must rest now, yakiri.'

'I suppose I'm a walking example of why not to have a war, but damn it, I did enjoy defending Israel.'

'Shh…'

Cam closed his eyes and fell into a deep sleep. A peace he could not imagine overwhelmed him. Someone was calling him from across the Jordan River where it entered the Sea of Kinneret. The water was too deep, and he could not swim. A fisherman nearby rowed over and took him across to the other side where his mother was waiting with open arms.

*****

38539109R00110

Made in the USA
Lexington, KY
14 January 2015